A WARTIME WELCOME FROM THE FOYLES BOOKSHOP GIRLS

ELAINE ROBERTS

Boldwood

First published in Great Britain in 2024 by Boldwood Books Ltd.

Cover Design by Colin Thomas

Cover Photography: Colin Thomas

A CIP catalogue record for this book is available from the British Library.

Paperback ISBN 978-1-80549-703-5

Large Print ISBN 978-1-80549-699-1

Hardback ISBN 978-1-80549-698-4

Ebook ISBN 978-1-80549-696-0

Kindle ISBN 978-1-80549-697-7

Audio CD ISBN 978-1-80549-704-2

MP3 CD ISBN 978-1-80549-701-1

Digital audio download ISBN 978-1-80549-695-3

Boldwood Books Ltd
23 Bowerdean Street
London SW6 3TN
www.boldwoodbooks.com

To my family and friends who have supported me through a difficult year

PROLOGUE
JUNE 1914

Ellen Beckford and her sister Mary leant over the black iron railings of Westminster Bridge, waving at the boats as they passed underneath. Squealing, Mary ran out into the road to see the boats from the other side of the bridge.

'Mary,' her mother Ada shouted out, and Phyllis, Ellen and Mary's grandmother, turned round from the bridge railings and gasped.

Mary stood rooted to the spot. The driver of a Ford Model T swerved to miss her. The car brakes screeched as it came to a halt.

Ada ran to grab her daughter's arm. Her lips tightened as she looked towards the car driver, his face red with anger. 'I'm so sorry.' She pulled Mary's arm to get her back on to the pavement. 'What were you thinking? You could have got yourself killed.'

'I'm sorry, Ma.' Mary became tearful. She brushed her hands over her eyes. 'I didn't think, I just wanted to see the boats from the other side of the bridge.'

Ada frowned. 'You're eleven now – old enough to know better.' She pulled her daughter into her arms. 'You could have been seriously injured, or worse. It doesn't bear thinking about.'

Mary pulled back. 'I'm sorry, Ma, it won't happen again, I promise.'

Ellen eyed her younger sister before shaking her head. She watched her walk back to the railings and peer over them. Glancing across at her mother, she forced a smile to her lips. 'When you were a child, did you used to come and wave at the boats?'

Ada smiled. 'I did. My father used to bring me on Sundays and Ma brought me along in the week. It was one of my favourite things to do, and still is. I waved at them just like you are now, and many other children have done before us.' She shook her head. Her father would have loved bringing the girls to wave at the boats, reliving memories with them. Sadness washed over her as she remembered how the laughter-filled trips had stopped when he became ill. He had long since been taken from them, and, like others, her family had been too poor to find the money to pay for doctors.

Phyllis smiled. 'You also liked running around Hyde Park, and in the summer, you used to paddle your feet in the Serpentine, and watch others swimming in it.'

Ada grinned at her mother. 'I remember, I was never brave enough to get in. People even swim there in the middle of winter.'

Ellen and Mary laughed at their mother's incredulous expression.

The sun glinted off the River Thames. Ada fanned her face with her hand and lifted her head slightly to enjoy the breeze that rippled along the river, breaking up the heat of the early morning June sunshine. Pulling out a handkerchief, she dabbed at her forehead and cheeks. The summer of 1914 was going to be a hot one.

Ellen smiled as she waved frantically at the men on the boats before squinting up at her mother again. 'I love being on the bridge watching the boats and the people rushing about. Do you ever wonder where they're all going?'

'Sometimes,' Ada said with a chuckle.

Phyllis nodded. 'You could write stories about them, Ellen; they could be going on an adventure somewhere.'

Ellen shook her head. 'I'm not that clever.'

Ada placed her fingers under her daughter's chin and lifted it slightly. 'I'll not have any of that; with hard work you can achieve anything you want. Yes, you might need help and then maybe it's about pulling together with friends or family, but anything can be done with determination, you don't have to rely on a man to look after you. If you get married it should be for love and no other reason.'

Phyllis frowned at her daughter. 'Of course, you are right, Ada, but it's not always easy for a young woman to get work and it's even harder when you have children.'

Ada tilted her head. 'I know, Ma, women have always done the best they can but that's why it's important we prepare our girls for the future, to hopefully get a say in how this country is run and not have men holding all the cards.'

The bells of Big Ben rang out. Startled, Ada jerked round to stare at the tall clock that towered above the Houses of Parliament and the river.

Mary looked up from watching the boats to smile at the horses pulling their carts, leaving piles of dung in their wake. The everyday pungent stench went unnoticed by everyone. Ada turned and smiled at her eldest. At fourteen, Ellen was growing into a fine woman, and Mary copied everything she did.

Ellen looked thoughtful as she gazed up at her mother. 'Is that what you and Pa did?'

Ada frowned. 'What?'

Ellen shrugged. 'You know, pulled together and worked hard.'

Ada nodded. 'Your father has always worked hard to give us the best life he can and he has a good job as port foreman on the docks, which is a big responsibility for him to carry.'

Phyllis smiled at Ada. 'I remember the first time your father brought him home for dinner.'

Ada grinned at her mother before looking back at her daughters. 'Your father was an apprentice in the boot factory where my pa worked, and he had no family of his own so Pa brought him home for dinner a couple of times a week.'

Mary tilted her head slightly. 'Did you marry him straight away then?'

Phyllis laughed. 'Definitely not, but he gave up the place he was renting to live with us, and the money did help us out. He has always been a kind and considerate man, who only wants the best for his family.'

Ellen frowned. 'Why did he leave the factory to work at the docks?'

Ada laughed. 'So many questions.' She took a breath. 'He left to earn more money so I wouldn't have to go out to work.' She paused. 'So I could stay at home and have fun with my two lovely daughters.'

Mary screwed up her nose. 'Do you miss going to work?'

'Sometimes, but your father is a traditionalist.' Ada took a breath. 'It takes him a while to embrace change; even though there have been times when the extra money would've come in handy, he stuck to his guns.' She shook her head and smiled at her girls. 'But look at the fun I would have missed. Come on, less chatter, shall we go to Foyles Bookshop before Gran takes you home so I can go shopping?'

'Oh yes, this is turning into a perfect day.' Ellen giggled. 'I don't mind helping with the shopping, so you don't have to do it on your own.'

Ada rested her hand on her daughter's shoulder. 'Thank you, but I quite like shopping by myself, and sometimes I meet people I know along the way, and we have a catch up.' The small heels on her black shoes clipped the pavement as they all strolled across Westminster Bridge towards Big Ben.

Crowds had gathered outside the Houses of Parliament. Ada glanced over, intrigued by what they were all looking at. Shrill voices chanting 'Votes for women,' carried through the air. Clutching her daughters' hands, she took a step towards the crowds that were gathering.

Phyllis nudged her. 'I think we should go. Harold wouldn't like us listening to all this, let alone standing here with them.'

'Ma, my husband may not like it but he's not a woman living without a say in what happens to her.' Ada stood on tiptoes, stretching her neck to see above everyone, but all she could see were the placards held high. She wrinkled her nose as the strong smell of tobacco wafted around her. The crowds were spilling onto the pavement now.

Men frowned and shook their heads as they were made to step into the road.

A deep voice shouted out, causing the spectators to look around, 'Get back to your kitchens!'

'It shouldn't be allowed. God help us all if women get the vote,' another yelled as he walked by.

Phyllis shook her head. 'This isn't going to end well.'

Ellen stared at her gran. 'I don't understand it all, Grandma, but do you think the ladies are wrong to want the vote?'

Phyllis frowned for a moment. 'No, I don't, and I pray there's a better life to come for you girls, I'm just not sure if this is the best way to go about it. Let's face it, the men don't like it.'

Some women jeered in response at the men as they walked by,

while others mumbled to each other. People stopped and stared. They all wanted to see what the commotion was about, but not wanting to get involved, they moved on quickly.

Ada wanted to push through the crowd to hear what was being said but she knew her mother was right: Harold wouldn't like his daughters being there; they had argued about it on so many occasions. He would be furious if he knew she was standing there with them, never mind her filling their heads with what he called 'that nonsense'.

A stout, grey-haired woman walked through the crowd, wearing a tall, black, wide-brimmed hat. She was carrying a long white cotton bag with 'Votes for Women' emblazoned on the front of it. The bag rested against her long black skirt, while her white blouse rippled underneath the strap. She stood in front of Ada, thrusting a handful of leaflets at her. 'Take one, miss; this is all about your future, and your two daughters'.'

Ada looked down at the white paper with 'Votes for Women' printed across the top in large, thick black letters.

The old lady moved her white-gloved hand nearer. 'Go on, you know it's important we all stand together.'

Ellen stared down at the leaflet. 'What's it about, Ma?'

Ada reached out and did as she was bid. 'It's about you having a say in your futures, in all women's futures. That's what these ladies are fighting for.'

Ellen shook her head. 'I've heard you and Pa arguing about that, and he doesn't think it's right.'

Ada smiled. 'I know, but he'll come round. Your father doesn't like change so it will take him a while to realise it's not the bad thing they all think it is.'

The woman smiled at them. 'Your ma's right, it's going to take time, but it will happen, we must keep trying to get people to listen and join our cause. Remember it's not for me or your ma, it's for you young 'uns.' She nodded before moving on into the crowd.

Ellen frowned. 'What would we be voting for?'

Ada gently ran her hand down her daughter's cheek. 'I will explain it all to you later.' She glanced down at her wristwatch as they continued. 'Come on then, let's go, otherwise we won't be having any dinner tonight.'

Ellen's eyes pleaded with her mother. 'We can still go to the bookshop, can't we?'

Ada laughed. 'Would I be brave enough to say no?'

Ellen and Mary giggled.

Phyllis watched the delight on the girls' faces. 'I can stay in Foyles with them and take them home afterwards.' She laughed. 'The time they like to spend in that shop you'll probably get home before us.'

'That's a good idea.' Ada thrust the leaflet into her small handbag and they turned right onto Whitehall. The tall buildings, with all their architectural details of pillars and scrolls, stood proudly on either side of the road as they headed towards Charing Cross Road and the W & G Foyles Bookstore.

'Read all about it,' a newspaper boy yelled, pulling at his flat cap to keep the sun off his face. His brown jacket looked worn and threadbare. His black trousers sat an inch above his scuffed shoes. 'The heir to the Austrian throne and his wife shot dead in Sarajevo.' Men in suits swarmed towards the boy from all directions, while searching in their trouser pockets for the halfpenny needed to buy the newspapers that were under the lad's arm. 'Your change, sir.'

'Keep it.' One man stepped away, staring at the front page. 'Come on, lad, I'm already late for work.'

The boy handed over the paper and quickly pocketed the money.

Ada could hear snippets of the conversations between men as they discussed the newspaper headlines.

'What do you think then, about the Austrian being shot?' one smaller man asked his companion, tucking a newspaper under his arm.

'I can't see why the shooting in Sarajevo should affect this country.' The man lifted his arm slightly to thrust his own daily paper under it.

'No, let's hope not; we have enough problems with the constant threat of strikes. The unions are getting stronger and if the miners, transport workers and dockers all stop work, it will bring the country to a standstill...' He paused to listen to the women's voices as they carried through the air. 'Those women are causing havoc one way or another, filling heads with nonsense.'

The two men lit their cigarettes. Ada wrinkled her nose when the slight breeze caught the smoke and it wafted in her face. Their black trousers held sharp creases, which had been ironed in, front and back, matching their long sack coats. Bowler hats were perched precariously on their heads. She had a strong urge to defend women to both these men but knew it wouldn't be right with her girls there. They heard enough of it at home. Ada was always trying to show her husband that women were more than domestic help, but he thought the same as the two men: that women should either be in the bedroom or the kitchen and definitely not voting on important issues like who ran the country. She sighed, wondering if she would ever see that day. Anxiety threatened to engulf Ada; she didn't want her girls to suffer the hardship of going hungry or not having enough money to buy food. Having no desire to overhear any more of the men's conversation, she ushered the girls behind her and stepped out into the wide road.

Ada quickened her step. Her hand tightened round the small

hand of her youngest daughter. Mary swung their clasped hands by her side, brushing against her mother's black ankle-length skirt. Ada stepped back onto the pavement as a red tram trundled past, the breeze blowing a stray strand of her long brown hair across her face. Her slender fingers pulled it away and pushed it behind her ear, under her narrow-brimmed hat, before checking the small gold earrings nestling in her earlobes that had been a present from her father before he died.

They crossed Trafalgar Square, where the tall column was sited, with the famous admiral looking down on Londoners going about their business. The National Gallery stood tall and vast on her left as she made her way along Charing Cross Road. Drivers of the horse-drawn carriages were careful to avoid the motorcars as they drove past. The dull thud of the hooves clip-clopping on the tarmac provided the usual melodic background for the engines coughing and spluttering above them. Horse dung lay in a line along the road, the earthy smell mingling with the overpowering fumes from the cars. Shopkeepers said good morning to everyone they saw as they pulled down awnings to protect their produce from the early morning sunshine.

Ada watched their practised hands wipe down the windows with rags, reminding her of the many hours she had spent with her mother removing buttons from shirts and cutting up old sheets to make them into rags for cleaning. She had been brought up to make her money stretch and not waste anything. Her lips tightened. That had stood her in good stead in her married life.

Mary beamed up at her mother as the bookshop came into view.

The Foyles Bookshop frontage was unmissable. The message was clear. They were the largest booksellers in London, with six floors. If a book was purchased and returned after it was read, there would be a refund of two-thirds of the price for each book.

They had created quite a name since William and Gilbert Foyle had started selling their own unwanted books in 1903. Ada had heard that everyone who started working there was told about their vision of having a bookshop for the people. She smiled; her daughters had picked up her love of spending time riffling through the many books they sold.

The shutters had long since been lifted and bookstands were already placed by the entrance and to the side of the store.

'Morning, Mrs Beckford.' A slim man towered above her. His black jacket was open, showing his matching waistcoat with the gold chain hanging from his fob watch, which was tucked inside a pocket. He nodded. 'Mrs Burton, it's lovely to see you and your granddaughters here again today.' He smiled.

Ada looked up at Mr Leadbetter's friendly face. His grey hair was greased back as always. 'Good morning, sir. I don't think I can leave the house without bringing my daughters here.' She laughed as colour filled her cheeks.

Mr Leadbetter stooped down to address the girls. 'If you need any help at all you can come and find me or speak to Alice at the counter near the payment booth.'

Ellen's eyes twinkled. 'We won't get lost; we've been here hundreds of times.'

Mary giggled. 'Thousands of times.'

Ada shook her head. 'I think we get the picture, girls.'

Phyllis glanced at her daughter. 'Go on, say your goodbyes and we'll see you at home.'

Ada wrapped an arm around each of her daughters and held them tight. 'Be good for Grandma. I'll see you back home.' She let go of the girls and peered at her mother. 'Thank you, I shouldn't be long.'

Phyllis nodded. 'Stop worrying, you're only going to the shops.'

Ada smiled at her daughters. 'Go on then, find a book each because you don't have very long.' She watched as both girls strode off into the shop. 'Sorry, but this is like a second home to them.'

Mr Leadbetter shook his head as he watched them go. 'Don't be sorry; to give a child a love of books is a wonderful gift that will last them all their lives.'

Ada nodded. 'Thank you. I'll see you back home, Ma.' She turned and left the shop.

Mr Leadbetter grinned at Mrs Burton. 'It's always lovely to see you here but if you need any help, please come and find me.'

'I will do, thank you.' Phyllis nodded and followed the girls into the shop. She wandered up and down the aisles, scanning the spines of the many books. Beaming, she pulled a Louisa M. Alcott book off the shelf. She stared down at the green cover. *Little Women*, that was it; that was the book she had bought for her own daughter many years ago. She hugged the coming-of-age novel tight, remembering how much Ada had loved the story and how her daughter had passed that love on to Ellen. Phyllis felt tears pricking at her eyes as she was overcome with pride at the strong woman she had raised, and now Ada was making sure her daughters were going to be the same. She instinctively knew they would fight for what they believed to be right, and she and Ada would support them in that fight.

'Grandma?' Mary's voice rang out.

Startled, Phyllis stepped towards the end of the aisle looking for Mary.

Mary rushed towards her. 'Grandma, I've found this book, *Alice's Adventures in Wonderland*. It's about a girl who falls through a rabbit hole.' Her voice got higher as her excitement grew. 'The rabbit is wearing a waistcoat and carrying a pocket watch like Pa does sometimes.'

Phyllis laughed. 'Well, it's certainly got you excited.' She paused. 'I've not read it, but I don't want you buying a book that will frighten you.'

Mary giggled. 'No, Grandma, I've already read a few pages and I can't wait to get home and read the rest.'

Phyllis smiled and shook her head. 'Have you seen your sister?'

Mary laughed. 'The last time I saw her she was engrossed in something; I think it was *Anne of Green Gables*.' Mary shrugged. 'I don't know what that's about, but Ellen only grunted at me when I spoke to her.'

Phyllis nodded. 'Let's go and find her, pay for these books and get ourselves home.'

An hour later they were pushing open the front door to their home, each girl laughing as they hugged their books close. The three of them stopped dead at the sight of a policeman standing in the hallway.

Phyllis pushed past her granddaughters, taking in her son-in-law's ashen features. 'What's going on, Harold?'

Harold didn't answer. He fell backwards on to the second step of the stairs.

The policeman tightened his lips before turning to Phyllis. 'I'm sorry, are you family?'

Phyllis nodded, pulling the girls close. 'I'm Mr Beckford's mother-in-law. What's happened?'

The policeman sucked in his breath. 'I'm sorry to be the bearer of bad news but I'm afraid there's been an accident and Ada Beckford has died.'

Phyllis gasped; she clutched her chest as she tried to breathe.

Harold jumped up and gently placed his arm around Phyllis before lowering her down on the stair he had vacated. 'Take some breaths, slowly in and out.' He looked up at the policeman. 'Are you sure it's Ada?'

The policeman nodded. 'The butcher, Mr Preston, identified her and told me where she lived.'

The hall was silent until Mary's sobs filled the air.

1

SILVERTOWN, LONDON

January 1918

Ellen Beckford pulled at the collar of her coat. The January wind blew hard along the River Thames, cutting through her as she pushed against it while striding along the footpath at the docks. Her gloved hands gripped her shopping bag close, while the river crashed against its banks.

She jerked at the sound of metal rattling against metal, echoing in the darkness. Flags flapped as the wind found a way under it. She could barely hear the sound of the men working. Ellen shivered. It reminded her of some of the books she had picked up in Foyles Bookshop and when she'd seen their dark scary covers, had quickly returned them to the shelf. Was someone going to jump out at her at any moment? She sucked in the cold air, realising she should have brought Mary with her if only to stop her imagination from running away with itself, but it was important someone stay at home with Grandma. Ellen would never forgive herself if she had a fall or something and was on her own. Looking up, but seeing nothing but blackness, she hoped the fog would keep the Zeppelins and the Gothas away. With no lighting around the docks, the dense fog made it difficult to see what was ahead of her.

Suddenly, something barged into her, causing her to stagger backwards. There was a clattering noise, quickly followed by a thud as something hit the ground, catching her leg as it fell. 'Who's there?' Fear ran down her spine. The whiff of smoke and carbolic soap caught in her throat. Her hands were clammy as she squeezed her elbows in tight to her body. She tried to concentrate, her eyes scanning the darkness. Ellen shrilled, 'I don't have anything worth stealing.'

A man's nervous laugh came from behind her. 'I'm sorry, I shouldn't laugh but I would never steal something from you. It was an accident; I didn't see you. It's so dark here you can't see the hand in front of your face.'

Ellen turned and squinted at the shadowy figure of the man as she bent down to pick up the bag that had hit her leg. The clasp sprung free, and the bag opened up. What was inside clattered together. 'I'm so sorry, I didn't mean to break it.'

The man glanced at the bag before taking it from her. 'You didn't, it happens all the time.'

'Thank goodness. It sounds like you have a bag full of crockery.'

The man stood upright and laughed before touching the brim of his trilby hat. 'Once again I'm sorry, I didn't mean to scare you.'

Ellen tried to focus on him and noticed he was a good few inches taller than her, then her head jerked round at the sound of her father shouting at someone nearby.

'What? That's not possible. I tell you, I only popped out for five minutes. That wasn't long enough for someone to break in, besides I locked the door.'

Ellen could hear the frustration in her father's voice. She

concentrated hard on the muffled reply but couldn't catch what was being said. She turned back to speak to the man she had collided with, but he was gone.

Forgetting her fear, Ellen raced towards her father's voice.

The voices were silent for a moment. 'I can tell you, sir, a lot of damage can be done in five minutes and has been. As an officer of the Port of London Authority Police, this matter needs to be taken very seriously.'

'I'm telling you, I locked the door.'

'That's just the point; you didn't. To be honest I think our voices probably disturbed him because we came to talk to you about tightening security on the gate and around the docks as theft is on the increase. I can only assume he heard us and scarpered before we got here,' a third calmer voice replied. He paused before sighing. 'Look, Harold, you've worked here for as long as I can remember, and I know you've been having a rough time since your wife—'

'Don't bring my wife into it, I'm fine.'

'Look, I shouldn't have to explain to you there's a war going on and we must be extra careful we don't leave things lying around. You may not be on the frontline, but our work here is important, and we don't want information getting into the wrong hands. I know you read the papers every day and must have seen the posters about being mindful about what you say and do.'

Harold shook his head. 'Of course, and if I'd seen someone, I would have chased them, and what's more, I'd have caught them.'

The officer's clipped tones cut in. 'All right, all right, so where are the keys to the office and the filing cabinet? Show me.'

Ellen caught up with the voices just as they were walking towards the cabin that was her father's office. A stream of light flooded the pathway when the door was opened. She watched her father slump down onto a chair, and noticed papers were everywhere. Ellen stood outside, unsure what to do as her father ran his hands over his face. Was the man who bumped into her the same one who broke into her father's office?

'How has this happened? I know I locked it. How has my office been ransacked, and what were they looking for?'

The police officer shook his head. 'Come on, Harold, you're the port foreman, it's not hard to work it out.' For a moment the silence was deafening. 'You are the one person who knows everything that's coming into this port and what it's carrying, whether that's food, soldiers or government-sensitive things that are being shipped along our coastline to London. It's obvious your office, and you, would end up being a target. It's why we spend so much of our time here.'

'It doesn't look good for you, Harold.' One of the men, who was wearing a grey suit, bent down and grabbed some papers as a breeze blew through the cabin; they rustled as he straightened them up. He noticed a shoe print had been left on one of them. He handed it over to the policeman. 'I don't know if this might help.'

A large open window banged against its frame as the wind caught it. Harold sighed as he stood and reached across and shut it.

The police officer took the paper, turning it this way and that. 'It might, but the trouble is, it could be anybody's.'

The man in the suit nodded. 'Thankfully these seem to be old papers. Let's hope whoever it was didn't find anything that could change the course of the war for us.'

Harold screwed up his face, as he stared at his manager. 'This is nothing to do with me. I don't even believe in this damned war.'

The officer sighed. 'Be careful what you say, you don't want to make things any worse for yourself, after all we only have your word the office door was locked.'

Harold slammed his fist down on his desk. 'Don't tell me to be careful. Do you know how many men I've seen crying on this dock when they think no one is looking? I can tell you, too many, because they've had the telegram saying their sons have died as heroes. Lives, families, are being changed forever and for what?'

The man in the suit tightened his lips. 'I know it's heart-breaking but we all have a part to play and it's not for us to decide what's right or wrong.'

The officer stepped towards the office door. 'That aside, we're going to have to interview everyone who works on the docks, and I don't just mean the ones that are here tonight.'

The policeman pushed the office door; it snapped shut, so Ellen could no longer hear them. She hesitated. Should she wait for the two men to leave or should she knock and go in?

Before she could make a decision, the office door opened slightly. 'I won't be able to protect you if you don't follow the rules, so just make sure those keys are with you at all times and this door is kept locked.' The man in uniform came out following the man in the suit. They both nodded at Ellen. 'This may not be a good time, Ellen; your father has a lot to think about right now.'

Ellen frowned. 'I won't stop, I've just brought his sandwiches.'

Both men nodded again and marched away into the darkness.

Ellen's gaze followed them before she turned to watch her father scanning the mess around him. His eyes narrowed as he rubbed his chin. He glanced at a bunch of keys lying on the desk. They jingled together as he picked them up and opened a drawer, then thudded as he dropped them inside. He stopped and stared at his daughter. 'Ellen, what are you doing here?'

Ellen frowned, wondering if those were the keys the man had asked her father if they were kept on him at all times. 'You forgot your sandwiches again; I can't have you going hungry.'

Harold shook his head. 'Good job they know you on the gate, as security will be stepped up now. I think they may even be calling in the police, so it could be outside the Port of London authority, but I expect that depends on what they find out. It's lucky old Sam was on security to let you in tonight.'

'Pa, what's going on?' Ellen stiffened as the silence dragged on. 'Come on, Pa, they've known me since I was knee high, it's not as if I'm a spy or something.' Watching her father pick up a framed photograph of the sun shining on the river just outside his office, Ellen remembered her mother had loved it; she had been so proud when he had taken it.

Harold stared at it for a moment before sighing and standing it back on his desk. 'That's true, but as we're always being told: there's a war on and we shouldn't trust anyone.' He studied her. 'And just for the record, I don't want you out and about, either day or night. You know it's not safe; bombs could drop at any time, never mind what happened to your mother.'

Ellen tightened her lips. 'Ma wouldn't want me to let you starve.'

Harold scowled. 'Yeah well, your ma's not here, and it's my job to look after you, your sister, and your grandmother.'

2

'I can't believe it's 1918 and the war is still raging on.' Molly Greenwood sighed as she tightened the woollen scarf around her neck. Cars trundled along London's Charing Cross Road, coughing and spluttering as they drove in and out of the sludge of melting snow, careful to not let it spray on the pavements and the people walking by. 'It feels strange coming to work without Alice; it won't be the same in Foyles without her. Do you think she'll come back when the baby is a little older?'

Victoria frowned as she glanced at her friend while stepping over a small pile of dirty grey snow that had been gathered together. 'I know what you mean but her priority is David; he's only a few weeks old and Arthur is not even three yet. We need to make sure we visit her regularly, especially as her family had us all around at Christmas.'

Molly nodded. 'I always have good intentions, but the time just seems to fly by, and it doesn't help having to queue for ages for food.' She beamed. 'It was certainly a Christmas to remember. I can't believe you asked Ted to marry you; you are braver than I am.'

Victoria giggled as her cheeks filled with colour. 'To be honest I didn't think about it for too long – otherwise I wouldn't have done it. I just couldn't stand by and let him leave my life again without speaking out. I know I was only sixteen, but he broke my heart when he just left without a word.' Her mind suddenly took her back to that day. She had always thought Ted would help her through the shock of losing her parents in a train crash and the huge responsibility of having her younger brother and sister foisted upon her, but he had just left and not come back. They hadn't had any discussion about it. She sighed. 'Still, a lot has happened since then. I'm twenty-four now and like to think I'm older and wiser and let's face it, we were both young back then, with no experience of life. He told me he regretted it but wasn't brave enough to come back so he enlisted into the army.' She paused for a moment; a smile crept across her face. 'You're right though, it was a Christmas to remember. It was lovely to have Stephen home from the front; when he walked into the basement at Foyles, it's a wonder I didn't pass out. To get to spend Christmas with my newfound family from Brighton and my friends is not something I will ever forget. Alice and her family were so kind to invite us all round to their house.'

'Your brother was obviously happy to be home.' Molly smiled. 'Although, thanks to Alice, I don't think her family had much of a say in it.' She laughed. 'It was certainly wonderful to not think about the blasted war for a few hours.'

Victoria nodded. 'Yes, but we are back to reality now.'

The Foyles Bookshop frontage came into view. The message was clear with its large white lettering, which stood out in the greyness of the day. 'W & G Foyles. The Largest Education Bookseller in London, Novels 3d and 2d Given on All Returns.' Everyone who started working there was told about their vision of having a bookshop for the people, making it easier for everyone to buy books and return them. They offered a much-needed distraction to many. Some customers stayed in the shop for hours escaping inside the pages of a book.

'Good morning, Miss Cooper. Sorry, that should be Mrs Greenwood.' Mr Leadbetter smiled at Molly, breathing in her floral fragrance. 'I'm hoping now you are married you won't get up to so much mischief.'

Molly chuckled as she looked at the grey-haired man. 'I will try, Mr Leadbetter, but I'm not making any promises I can't keep.'

Mr Leadbetter grinned as he pulled out a fob watch from his black waistcoat pocket and automatically pressed open the lid. He glanced down at the time. 'I haven't had a chance to say before, but you and your husband did well at Christmas; all the children were very happy with him dressing up as Father Christmas and the books they went away with. It was a good idea of yours. I must admit I wasn't sure about it at first, but you were right. If the smiles and laughter were anything to go by, the children will have good memories of sitting on Father Christmas's knee and will want to come here again. Considering it was all organised with very little notice, the owners are very happy with how it all went.'

Molly beamed. 'Thank you. As you say, it was all organised quite late so I don't think we could have asked for more.'

Mr Leadbetter turned to Victoria. 'Morning, Miss Appleton, I'm sure you enjoyed your Christmas; have you set a date to get married yet?'

Victoria blushed and suddenly felt the need to remove her scarf. 'No, sir, not yet. Ted is still in Endell Street Hospital. His head injury is healing, thank goodness; what's more, the bandages have been permanently removed from his head and eyes. The doctors say his eyesight is improving, which is good because they didn't know if he was going to be blind. They have medically discharged him from the army because his eyesight will never be as good as it was.' She raised her eyebrows. 'I'm just so relieved he can't go back to the front. From what I hear at the hospital, Ted's lucky to be alive; the shelling in France has injured and killed so many of his battalion and others, I'm sure.' She took a breath. 'I'm hoping he will be out of hospital soon.'

Mr Leadbetter nodded. 'Does he have somewhere to go?'

'I have a spare room so he can stay with me.'

Mr Leadbetter studied Victoria for a moment. 'Is that wise? I mean, you know what gossips can be like, I'd hate for you to be a subject of that.' He paused. 'If you change your mind, I have a spare room he can use, and to be honest I'd be glad of the company.'

Molly gave him a cheeky smile. 'That's very kind of you Mr Leadbetter. If Ted doesn't take you up on your offer, would you consider letting another injured soldier use it?'

Mr Leadbetter fidgeted for a moment before glancing at the young girl he had always felt a fondness towards; she was like the daughter he never had. 'Well, I suppose so. To be honest, I have never thought about doing that, but it would be good to help out where I can.'

Molly nodded. 'Excellent, sir, but please make sure you don't overdo things; we don't want you scaring us by collapsing in the shop again. We never did get to the bottom of why you passed out.' She glanced across at Victoria. 'Make sure you use Victoria, so you don't have to work so hard. None of us want you to faint again. It's a good job Alice was here because her ambulance training helped; I was of no use whatsoever.'

'I only fainted. It was probably just the heat. After all, it was in July, and I do wear a three-piece suit and tie.' Mr Leadbetter gave a wry smile. 'You can't get rid of me that easily, but I get your point: I'm not getting any younger and need to start handing over the reins of management.' He stared at their sombre faces. 'I promise to take care.' He glanced back down at his watch and snapped the lid shut. 'It's nearly time we were opening. With Mrs Leybourne not here we need to think about getting a replacement.'

Victoria nodded. 'Has Alice said she's not coming back?'

Mr Leadbetter placed his fob watch back into his waistcoat pocket. 'No, but I would imagine she will be missing for at least a couple of months, and she may decide not to return to work at all.'

Molly frowned. 'I'm sure she will want to work; she loves her books too much to not return.'

'You could be right.' Mr Leadbetter glanced at Victoria. 'Can you make sure someone is helping Albert, in the basement, to check all the books for damage? We'll probably have a few returns over the next few days, and I don't want damaged stock going on sale.'

Victoria nodded. 'Of course, but Albert does take pride in his work, so I know he checks them thoroughly.'

'I know he is a valuable member of staff, but he will need help over the next few days if the returns come in as I expect. It's the same every Christmas; customers think they are doing the right thing buying loved ones books, and indeed they are, but sometimes they choose the wrong ones. Hopefully when they are returned, they will buy another one and we must encourage that by offering to help them choose another title.' Mr Leadbetter stepped aside. 'You had better go and clock in otherwise you won't be getting paid.'

The girls nodded and headed towards the back of the shop. They heard the chatter and laughter before they reached the staff area.

Victoria stepped through the open doorway first. 'Good morning, ladies.'

A chorus of mornings greeted them.

Molly was searching out her name on the clocking-in cards when a woman's voice shouted, 'Don't bother; I've already clocked you both in.'

Molly turned round and smiled at the grandmother of the ladies in front of her. 'Thank you, Vera, but you're going to end up getting into trouble if you're not careful.'

Vera cackled. 'Yeah, all they can do is sack me and, thanks to this war, there's more jobs than people to fill 'em at the moment.'

A chime sounded from the clocking-in machine; it was coming up to nine o'clock. Victoria raised her hands and gave a couple of quick claps. 'Thank you, Vera. It's time we all went to our counters otherwise we'll all end up in trouble.' She waited for Vera as the ladies filed through the doorway and into the shop. 'Vera, I would like you to give Albert a hand today, Mr Leadbetter thinks there will be a rush on returns. I don't want anything with the slightest damage coming up for resale.'

Vera nodded. 'Yes, Miss Appleton.' She turned to head towards the door to the basement before glancing over her shoulder with a smile. 'Of course, it means I get the first pick of the books.'

Victoria returned her smile. 'Just make sure they are checked thoroughly.' She scanned the room, looking for Rosie Burrows. 'Ah, Rosie, as one of the youngest here would you mind running the returns from the counters down to Albert and Vera please, but do be careful with the stairs and don't try and carry too many at a time. If it gets too much, I'll find someone to help.'

Rosie beamed. 'Of course, Miss Appleton.'

Without another word, Molly and Victoria quickly removed their coats and slung them over a chair, nearly brushing a folded newspaper off the table, before rushing out to the shop.

Molly smoothed down her black calf-length skirt and checked the buttons on the white blouse she was wearing. 'I'd better get upstairs to the children's department before I get into trouble for not being at my counter.' She giggled as she patted down her blonde hair. 'And you just know I will be the first person Mr Leadbetter checks on.'

Victoria nodded. 'I've got to get the book stands outside under the awning. I should have got here earlier and been ahead rather than chasing my tail. Perhaps we'll have lunch together?'

Molly nodded, then spied Mr Leadbetter talking to two young women. 'Definitely. Right, I've got to go because he's coming this way and you know what that means...'

Victoria followed her gaze to where Mr Leadbetter was. 'Those girls come in most days, although I don't think they buy books like their mother used to.' She paused. 'From what I hear they used to come in with her and spend ages looking, and she would find a corner to sit in and read to them. It's sad she died when they were so young.'

'If they have fond memories of being here with her, maybe it makes them feel close to her again, you know, reliving those memories.' Molly's eyes became watery as she watched Mr Leadbetter smile at them before she sniffed and cleared her throat. 'Anyway, I must get going, I'll see you at lunch.'

* * *

Alan Hutchins' gloved fingers tugged at the collar of his brown calf-length coat, pulling it closer to his navy-blue woollen scarf. The cold wintry wind whistled around him. His breath was visible like grey swirls of smoke before disappearing into the smog. His heart pounded as he raced under the arch of London's Victoria station and stepped inside.

The station was bustling with women and children waving and crying as the whistles blew and steam billowed into the air as the trains pulled away from the platforms. Others were patiently waiting for trains to come into the station, hoping their men would be coming home. Injured men were being stretchered off, and some walking wounded were leaning on more able soldiers. So many broken young men, some more lucid than others, their faces weather-beaten and hardened from their experiences. Their boots and uniforms were caked in dried mud from the trenches they had escaped from. Alan shook his head as he thought about how the despair of war was seen there, and many other stations, every day. Something needed to happen to bring it to an end; they had to find a way to win this war.

Glancing over at the tea table, he watched the women setting out the many cups for the tea and soup needed for those returning home.

Alan walked past soldiers who were sitting propped up against a wall; all had various bandages on them, each splattered with blood and dirt as others had been before.

A lady handed out packets of cigarettes and matches to the men, helping some to light them. The smell of tobacco mingled with the men's body odour. Spirals of grey smoke joined the steam from the trains waiting patiently at the platforms before slowly disappearing into the roof. There were murmurs of thanks. Then there was silence amongst them. Some hung their heads with exhaustion while others leant back against the fencing and closed their eyes. Like time ticking away, their cigarettes gradually burnt down to their fingers.

Alan marched past them, keeping his gaze focused ahead of him.

A grey-haired man stepped out in front of Alan. 'You're late.'

Alan tightened his lips. 'Sorry.'

The man shook his head. 'My train will be leaving soon so I don't have time for a cuppa and a chat now.'

They both stepped aside to let someone pass.

The older man eyed Alan. 'So, how have you got on?'

Alan thrust his hand into the inside pocket of his coat. He pursed his lips before handing him a thin white envelope. 'You tell me. It's harder than you think but I've managed to get by.'

'Well, I can't keep supporting you, so you'll have to get a job. I'm sure they would take on a strong lad like yourself at the docks.' The man pushed his hand inside his coat pocket and pulled out his own thicker envelope. 'This might help.'

Alan took the envelope and peered inside; his fingers moved aside some of the folded paper. 'At last. I was beginning to think you were never going to come through for me.' He unclipped his bag and poked the envelope inside before shutting it again.

The man shook his head. 'I know you are new but things take time. Now you need to do your bit and get on with it. As I said, get yourself a job.'

Alan gave a small smile. 'I have – at the local paper. I'm the official photographer.' He collected his camera from his back to show him. 'I might take some photographs before I leave the station.'

'Don't draw too much attention to yourself.' The grey-haired man nodded. 'There could be many opportunities, especially if you get some big stories; make the most of it and make it work.'

A child screamed out. Alan spun round to scan where the sound had come from. A young mother had wrapped a protective arm around her crying child, hugging her close to her legs as they stepped aside as one. It was only then that he noticed two men in suits standing nose to nose. One snatched something from the other's hand before pushing him to the ground. The man still standing pointed at the one on the ground before marching away.

The grey-haired man pulled on his gloves. 'It's time to go, I don't want to miss my train.'

Alan nodded. 'Of course not. Will you leave me the address of where you'll be staying?'

The grey-haired man gave a cynical smile. 'Don't worry. I'll be in touch when I'm settled.' He marched towards the platforms without a backward glance.

Alan looked back at the man who had been pushed over, wondering what had happened between the two men.

An elderly woman rushed towards the fallen man, who was just getting up from the ground. 'Are you all right?'

Forgetting why he was there, Alan stepped nearer in the hope of finding out what was going on.

The man noticed everyone was staring at him. 'Yes, yes, it was just a misunderstanding.'

A policeman came running over. 'Are you hurt, sir?'

The man shook his head. 'No, I'm fine, thank you.'

The constable pulled out his notepad and pen. 'Do you want to tell me what happened, sir?'

The man stayed silent as he ran his hands through his dark hair before bending down to pick up his trilby hat and placing it on his head.

The constable nodded as he scribbled something in his pad. He suddenly looked up. 'Can I take your name, sir?'

The man shifted from one foot to the other, accidentally knocking his black leather briefcase over. 'I don't think that's necessary; I have no desire to take it any further thank you, Constable; the poor soul obviously needed the money.'

The constable raised his eyebrows. 'That may well be the case, but we can't have people scaring women and children, let alone breaking the law.'

The man swung down and collected his bag. 'Look, I have to go.'

The police constable stared at him before nodding. 'But if you change your mind about taking it further then come to the station and ask for PC Albright.'

'I won't; it's only money.' The man brushed his hand down his suit trousers before turning on his heels and marching out of the train station.

Alan's gaze followed him. He lifted his camera and adjusted the viewfinder to take a photograph of the man, but nothing happened. He frowned, remembering he hadn't changed the used spool of film. With practised fingers, he opened the back of the camera and removed the used film, and dropped it into his bag before loading the new spool. He hadn't noticed the grey-haired lady bent over a walking stick just to the side of him and was startled when she spoke.

'Somefink ain't right there. Who would let some bloke get away with robbing yer? Na, trust me, yer can't be too careful these days. Yer certainly can't trust no one.' The old lady cackled. 'Ain't yer seen the posters? He's probably a spy.'

Alan stared ahead but the man was lost in the throng of people.

3

Christmas had come and gone without notice in the Beckford house. Ellen thought about her younger sister; at just fifteen years old, Mary's memories of her mother decorating a tree, singing carols and wrapping presents before carefully placing them around the tree would soon fade. It was something they hadn't done since her mother had died four years ago. It was getting much harder to find the money to do those extra things. Was that it? Was her father worrying about money and that was why last week he hadn't locked his door at the docks, although he was insistent he had? She shook her head; he had become increasingly forgetful; she had lost count how many times she had taken his sandwiches to the docks because he had forgotten them.

Ellen could feel the tears pricking at her eyes as she remembered how the house used to be filled with laughter; even the chores had been fun, but that was no more. Her father no longer smiled; he had become a man she no longer recognised, he isolated himself from his family, not allowing them out of the house unless to buy food. His grief at losing his wife was locked inside him. Her gran had tried to talk to him about what his wife, her daughter, would have wanted for his girls but he hadn't listened, and Ellen suspected he never would. She had started to write down her memories of her mother and things she had said and done with them so Mary would always have that to hold on to. Finding the time had made it difficult to complete but she had to stop with the excuses and get on with it before she also forgot them.

Gripping the old, stained dust rag, she scanned the bedroom several times to make sure it would pass inspection. She stopped to admire the oil lamp her mother had never used; Ellen could hear her laughing about how she didn't want flame marks ruining such a beautiful thing. The base wasn't the usual brass, it was patterned with colour. She stared at it and couldn't resist touching it. Sighing, she mimicked her father's actions by moving to run her fingers along the edge of the chest of drawers, which sat next to the large window. She lifted her hand to examine it; there was no dust, but she ran the rag over it again just to be sure. She stepped back to make sure the wash bowl and jug were centred on top of it. The windows rattled and the heavy brown curtains fluttered as the wind blew through them, bringing with it the familiar sweet malty smell from the Horseshoe Brewery on Tottenham Court Road. Wrinkling her nose, she wondered if she would ever get used to the stench of the spent grain that had been left fermenting in the storage bins. All she could do was hope the wind would change direction and take the smell with it.

Ellen straightened the curtains and peered outside, but the lace pattern of ice on the glass blurred her view. She ran her fingers across the inside of the windowpane; the cold scorched her fingertips and the ice clung steadfastly to the glass. Her gaze watched the distorted figure of her father marching briskly along Great St Andrew Street. He stopped walking to let out several hacking coughs. Ellen frowned as she watched him. Had the cold air caught in his throat or was he becoming ill? Was something taking root in his lungs? She couldn't help feeling his cough was getting worse but there was no money to pay for a doctor and he was too proud to let his daughters go out to work. Her gaze didn't leave him as he strode nearer to the house.

Ellen turned and noticed the chamber pot was visible from where she was standing. She quickly pushed it further under the bed with her foot. She had made her father's bed, the blankets tucked in tight, just how he liked it. Dusting his room, to the exacting standards he had rammed home to them after his wife had died, she thought about how there was no sign her mother had ever lived there, despite being there for many years.

Wiping her hand across her eyes, Ellen remembered the day their world had fallen apart, a day she'd never forget. Aged just fourteen, she had reminded herself of the promise made many years earlier to her mother to look after Mary and her father if something should happen to her. Shaking her head, she walked towards the open doorway. A stack of folded newspapers was sitting on top of a slatted wooden chair. Impulsively, she grabbed the top one. The paper rustled as she opened it. An article immediately caught her eye about how approximately eighty-six bombs had been dropped by the Germans around London just before Christmas. She glanced down to find the name of the writer at the bottom of it, but it wasn't there. Furtively, she peered over her shoulder for a moment, was that the sound of creaking floorboards? She hadn't heard the front door slam. Ellen listened for a moment before shaking her head; she must be imagining things. She briskly folded the newspaper in to its original creases and placed it back on the pile. Her heart was racing. Her father wouldn't want her reading the newspapers and knowing what was going on in the world; that was why they were in his room. Ellen sighed; she told herself he was just trying to protect them.

She pushed the rag into her apron pocket and took a last look around the room before running out and down the stairs. She frowned as each step creaked underfoot, announcing her impending arrival downstairs. She was thankful she had lit the fire earlier, but she still needed to boil some water for her father's bath.

'Where's the fire?'

Startled, Ellen turned on her heels. The narrow hall closed in on her. She took a deep breath; the smell of beeswax hit the back of her throat, causing her to cough. 'Mary, you startled me. There's no fire, I just have a lot to do today. Pa will be here in a minute, and I haven't prepared his bath yet. I don't want to put him in a bad mood.'

'Isn't he always in a bad mood?' Mary frowned. 'Look, let me help. Why don't I quickly dust the front room while you boil some water and then I'll come and see what else needs doing.'

Ellen's lips tightened. The last time Mary had helped her she'd shouldered the blame when their father had laid into her because it wasn't done right.

Mary tilted her head to one side. 'Come on, let me help; it's not fair that you must do everything. I'm old enough. Pa said now I'm fifteen he needs to find me a husband.'

Ellen stiffened. 'Did he? You never said.'

Mary flicked her long chestnut brown hair over her shoulder. 'I suppose I just forgot.' She smiled. 'I don't think he meant it; you know what he's like when he gets started. I was probably getting on his nerves, or his bath water wasn't done to the right temperature. Anyway, you're the eldest so he needs to find you a husband first.'

Ellen stared at Mary, forcing a smile to her lips while alarm bells were ringing in her head alongside her mother's voice shouting, trying to make itself heard. *You have to marry for love, and not because you're a burden.* She needed to do something before it was too late, but she didn't know what.

Mary smiled. 'I think he just wants us to be well looked after.' She paused. 'But let's face it, who is going to want to marry a dock worker's daughter, except maybe another dock worker?'

Ellen's eyes narrowed as she forced herself to smile. 'Maybe.' She pulled the rag from her apron pocket and held it out for Mary to take. 'Go on then, dust the front room and then maybe you could start cleaning the spare bedroom; that tends to get forgotten because we don't use it. I think the gas light in there needs cleaning – maybe we can do that together later.'

Taking the rag, Mary beamed. 'I promise I'll do a good job.' She turned and bounced towards the front room. 'If we're quick we could go to the shops; we might even be able to buy some more books from Foyles, especially if we return some.'

'Maybe; we'll see how far we get with the jobs.'

Mary turned round to face her sister. 'He explained yesterday that he didn't want us going out by ourselves because he was afraid of losing us, especially since he lost Ma. I think he really misses her, and we remind him of her, so in his own way he's clinging on to her through us.'

Ellen arched her eyebrows. 'Is that what he said?'

'Pretty much.' Mary smiled. 'The last bit was my thoughts.' She turned to go into the front room and stopped short before glancing over her shoulder. 'I think we may have misunderstood him and perhaps he's still grieving for Ma. Maybe we should feel sorry for him.' She paused. 'It's a shame he's clinging on to us because I'd like to do something to help with the war, you know, like other women do, but I know I'm probably too young.'

'You could be right about Pa.' Ellen hesitated before giving her sister a small smile. 'I'm sure there will be something you could do; I'll give it some thought.' She tilted her head to one side. 'As

I'm putting the kettle on, ask Grandma if she'd like a cuppa.' Frowning, Ellen watched her sister disappear into the front room while holding her hand up.

'I'm sure it will be a yes.' Mary chuckled as she went. 'I've never known her to say no to a cuppa.'

Shaking her head, Ellen paced into the kitchen and turned on the tap, not noticing the cold water splattering against the sink and splashing her apron. She thrust the kettle under the tap; the water rattled against the metal, but her thoughts were still with her mother. Would she ever be able to provide for them all like their mother had done? Her mother had done everything with a smile and always showed kindness to everyone she met, giving them her last shilling if it was needed. Ellen shook her head as she thought about what money she had every day to provide for them all. How had their mother managed on so little and yet made them so happy? They were certainly big shoes to fill.

A cold breeze sped through the hall and into the kitchen just before the front door slammed shut. Heavy footsteps got louder as they approached Ellen.

'Is my bath ready?'

Ellen looked up at her father as he walked in. 'It won't be long.' She paused for a moment. 'Was everything all right at work?' She eyed her father and decided to persist, hoping he would talk to her. 'You seemed angry when I dropped your sandwiches off.'

Harold frowned before snapping at her. 'That's nothing for you to worry about. I just want to have a bath and go to bed.'

Ellen breathed a sigh of relief when he marched out of the kitchen, but she wished she'd found the courage to talk to him about getting work.

* * *

Alice carefully pushed the pram through the open door of Foyles Bookshop. She loosened the soft woollen scarf around her neck, undoing the top few buttons of her black winter coat before breathing in the woody scent of the many books stacked high on the shelves. She turned to her husband, Freddie, and beamed. 'Oh my, I love coming to this shop. I had almost forgotten how much I adore being surrounded by so many books.'

Freddie chuckled as he shook his head. 'I hope you're not thinking of buying any more; we are already overrun with them.'

Alice stood on tiptoe and kissed her husband's rosy, but cold, cheek. 'Don't be a grouch; you've always known books were my first love.'

Freddie's eyes shone as he gazed at her. 'Don't I just, but it's a wonder customers can find anything because there are so many.'

Mr Leadbetter ambled over to Alice. 'Good afternoon, Mrs Leybourne, it's lovely to see you. You haven't by any chance come to save us, have you?'

Alice frowned. 'Save you?'

Mr Leadbetter laughed. 'Yes, you are sorely missed by everyone. I don't need to tell you that you are a valuable member of staff. But, also, we are short staffed at the moment.'

Alice could feel the heat creeping up her neck.

Freddie chuckled. 'You're not trying to entice my wife back to work, are you?'

'Of course I am.' Mr Leadbetter looked sheepishly at the young man in front of him. 'You can't blame me for trying.'

Freddie smiled as he shook his head. 'Hmm, that explains a lot.'

Alice looked from one to the other. 'Wouldn't you want to work surrounded by books instead of being stuck in that stuffy police station all day?'

Freddie feigned astonishment. 'I'll have you know I like being a policeman, especially as some days a beautiful young woman pops in to give me my lunch.'

Alice smiled. 'Really, I'd better keep an eye on you.'

Mr Leadbetter cleared his throat and peered into the pram. 'How is your little boy doing?'

Colour flooded Alice's face. For a moment she forgot about the bookshop and Mr Leadbetter. 'He's lovely, we're quite fortunate that he is a very contented baby.' She gave her husband a sideways look. 'We had the best Christmas we could have, what with the war going on.'

Freddie grinned. 'Yes, and to think it all started here on Christmas Eve.'

Mr Leadbetter nodded. 'It was certainly an interesting time on Christmas Eve, with all the staff and customers in the basement trying to protect ourselves from the German bombs. Still, I think it was one of the best Christmas Eves I've ever had; everyone was in good spirits sharing their food and drinks and we certainly had plenty of books to read.' He chuckled. 'And, I understand you had quite a houseful on Christmas Day.'

Alice giggled. 'It was wonderful to have so many friends and family under one roof. I'm sure my mother would tell you it was hard work, but she loved every minute of it.'

Mr Leadbetter grinned. 'There's nothing like family, and especially at this current time; we should all look after each other.' He peered over his shoulder before turning round. 'Have you come for anything in particular, or are you wanting to have a chat with your friends?'

Alice frowned, trying to suppress the smile that was threatening to break free. 'As if I would, Mr Leadbetter. I know how busy it gets in here. Actually, I've come to buy a couple of children's books. Arthur's nearly three now, so I thought I'd try and teach him to read. He does have some books that we all read to him but it would be nice for him to have a change so I thought I'd come and have a look and see what else I could get him.'

Mr Leadbetter eyed her suspiciously. 'Well then, you'll have to go and see Mrs Greenwood. As you know, she is quite an expert on the children's section.'

Alice wanted to laugh because it wasn't lost on either of them that she would probably stay upstairs chatting to Molly before buying any books for Arthur.

'Enjoy looking at them, and please remember we will always welcome you back whenever you are ready.' Mr Leadbetter smiled and turned to walk away when he stopped short as he eyed Molly bounding towards them with an armful of books. 'It looks like someone has already been told you are here.'

Alice followed Mr Leadbetter's gaze. Her face lit up. 'Molly, how wonderful, I was just on my way to see if you had any recommendations for Arthur.'

Mr Leadbetter threw back his head with laughter, which caused Freddie to join him. 'Mr Leybourne come with me and I'll make you a cup of tea; they are going to be chatting for a while.'

Freddie rested his hands on the handle of the pram before glancing at Alice. 'Go on, I'll take David; you two can chat in peace then, but don't take too long because I'm sure Mr Leadbetter would rather Molly got on with her work.'

Alice let go of the pram. 'Thank you. I promise I won't be long.'

Freddie and Mr Leadbetter grinned at each other as they walked away.

Alice watched them manoeuvre the pram around customers and bookshelves until they disappeared from view.

Molly adjusted the books in her arms. 'I must just get rid of these returns; someone left them at the children's counter. I'll have a chat with Albert downstairs because it keeps happening lately. I don't think it's him but whoever it is needs to be told.'

Alice laughed. 'Look at you taking your job seriously; who would have thought that day would ever come?'

Molly smiled. 'You know what they say. "You don't know what you've got until it's taken away." I might have earned more money at the munitions factory, and obviously that's where I met Andrew, but I was grateful when Mr Leadbetter gave me my job back after the explosion.'

Alice nodded. 'Yes, he's been good to all of us. I think he's a softie really.' She tilted her head, trying to read the titles on the spines of the books in Molly's arms. 'Have you got anything interesting there?'

Molly glanced down at the books. 'They are mainly for studies, although one of them is *Little Women*; have you read that one?'

Alice beamed. 'No, I've been meaning to for years, but I've never got round to it.'

'Well, now's your chance.'

Behind them, a woman put down her bulging shopping bag before she spoke. 'I'm sorry but I couldn't help overhearing what you were saying,' she said. 'If you are unsure, I can definitely recommend it; it was one of my mother's favourite books and I've read it many times.'

'Thank you, it's always good to have a recommendation.' Alice glanced back at Molly and giggled. 'Freddie will kill me!' She pulled it away from the other books. 'As it's a return, has it been checked for damage?'

Molly nodded. 'Yes, they've all been checked; it's just been left upstairs by mistake.'

Alice flicked through the pages before looking up with a huge grin. 'I'll take it. I'm obviously meant to read it because it has been brought to me and it's been recommended as well; it doesn't get any better than that.'

Molly giggled. 'I'm sure Freddie will agree.'

The young woman glanced down at the bag of books she was returning. She sighed, picked it up and stepped away. Alice called out to her. 'Thanks again for recommending it.'

The woman peered over her shoulder and smiled at their reasoning.

* * *

Ellen's flat black ankle boots crunched on the fresh snow, which had fallen overnight, leaving their mark as she avoided where others had stepped on the pavement. The cold January wind hadn't calmed down and snow flurries chilled her cheeks, while also resting on every available surface as far as the eye could see. Shivering, she pulled her scarf close and up over her mouth. Dampness hung in the air. Ellen no longer noticed the many war posters that had invaded every available space. Lord Kitchener pointing to everyone who walked past telling them 'Your country needs you', which mingled in with the 'What did you do in the war, Daddy?'

Ellen stopped at the small parade of shops and peered in one of the windows at the bundles of wool and material in glorious bright colours. She noticed a small white sign on the inside of the glass reading 'Help Wanted'. Ellen fought the temptation to go inside and enquire about it, but she knew from the many times she'd asked her father about getting a job that by doing so she would only make him angry. There was no point in thinking about it; the answer was always the same.

'Get yer morning newspaper here,' a young lad shouted out. 'Come on now, give me a penny and I'll give you a paper.'

Ellen looked round at the boy.

He moved from one foot to the other. 'Come on now, get yer paper, read how we're winning the war.' He turned to look at Ellen. 'I've got to say something to get rid of these papers.'

Ellen chuckled.

A lady approached the boy and handed over a penny.

The boy passed her a newspaper. 'Thank you, ma'am.'

The lady smiled as she stepped away from him. She quickly opened the paper, scanning each page in turn until she got to page four. Her face lit up. She turned round to face a middle-aged man in a black suit. 'Look, I made it, there's my article.' The paper rustled as she waved it around and she beamed as her gaze moved from the newspaper to the gentleman with her. 'Look, Frank, I made the cut.'

'You mean *we* made the cut.' The well-dressed man grabbed the paper and eyed it. 'You should be aiming for the front page, Irene.'

'Of course.' The lady smiled and gave him a loving look. 'But don't be grumpy, darling; it's exciting.'

Intrigued, Ellen stepped forward and opened her handbag. Pulling out her purse, she undid the clasp and reached inside for a penny. 'I'll take a paper please.'

The lad grinned at her. He took her money and slipped it into his pocket.

Ellen watched the couple walk away. The woman appeared deflated as she moved to throw the paper into the bin they were walking by. At the last minute she pulled her arm back and hugged the paper close. Ellen turned to page four. It was all war news with no names attached to any of the articles, so she had no idea which item Irene had written.

She sighed, closing and folding the paper again, and walked towards the butcher's. It was only eight o'clock in the morning and already the queue for some meat snaked around the road. Women and children stood patiently waiting.

A woman clutching a child's hand turned to the woman behind her. 'I wonder how long this is going to go on for? It's too cold to be standing outside, especially with a young child. The last thing I need is for her to get sick.'

The grey-haired lady pulled on her headscarf and rubbed her gloved hands together. 'I agree. It's ridiculous but at least we have things better than our boys on the front line.'

The young woman lowered her eyes and nodded. 'That's true.'

Ellen shook her head, wondering if there would be any meat left by the time she got to the front of the queue.

'Morning, Ellen,' the rotund butcher shouted out over the heads of his customers.

Ellen stopped, pulled down her scarf, and smiled. 'Morning, Mr Preston, it looks like you have a busy day ahead of you.'

The butcher frowned. 'Unfortunately there's not enough to go round...' He paused before adding, 'That reminds me, thank yer father for doing me that favour before Christmas.'

'Favour?'

Mr Preston looked sheepish. 'He'll know what I'm talking about.' He smiled. 'How's he getting on at the docks?'

Ellen frowned, wandering what he was talking about but decided not to pursue it. 'He will never admit it but I think he finds it hard going these days.'

Mr Preston nodded. 'I expect he misses your ma; she was a good woman. Why don't you pop back later for a cuppa? Mrs Preston will be pleased to see you.'

Ellen smiled. 'I'll try but I have to find something for dinner first.'

Mr Preston chuckled. 'You come and get yer meat from 'ere; at least you know you won't be short changed.'

'Will do.' Ellen waved as she pulled her scarf back over her mouth before carrying on towards the market in Great White Lion Street. She gingerly upped her pace as the barrows came into view. The smell of hot coffee and soup was tempting but she didn't have money for that. Breathing a sigh of relief, she noticed her usual market trader, Peter, had only a few ladies queuing at his fruit and vegetable barrow.

A grey-haired lady beamed. 'Thank you, Peter, you are a true gentleman.'

Ellen noticed he had Harry, his nephew, helping him and wondered when he would have to go off to war. She watched him as he quietly worked and assumed he must be around seventeen years old, so it probably wouldn't be long before he was off to the front to fight. She thought about the young, injured soldiers she had served tea and cake at Victoria train station, some too badly injured to make it to the table. Sadness gripped her; she knew none of them would ever be the same again.

Peter grinned back at the old lady. 'Well, if I can't give an extra couple of potatoes to my favourite customer, what can I do? Do you want me to deliver them to you later? I don't want you slipping on this snow now.'

The lady tilted her head slightly. 'I shall be fine. I'm stronger than I look.'

'I don't doubt that, just take care.' Peter picked up a couple of apples and placed them in her bag. 'You know what they say, "an apple a day keeps the doctor away".' He handed over the bag. 'Now please be careful.'

'Thank you, you're very kind.' The lady chuckled as she waved him goodbye.

Blowing on his fingers, Peter fidgeted from one foot to the other as he looked over. 'Morning, Ellen, and what can I get you today?'

Ellen opened her purse and peered inside. Frowning, she pulled out several silver coins. 'I have two shillings and ten pence so can I have maybe a couple of pounds of potatoes and whatever vegetables I can get, as well as a small loaf of bread. That's if my money will run to that.'

Peter smiled. 'Don't look so worried; I'm sure the coins will stretch to what you need. My friend, Joyce, baked the bread this morning so it's nice and fresh. Now let's see what I can give you.' He reached out for her shopping bag and began weighing potatoes before tipping them into the bag. He casually threw in some carrots, parsnips and Brussel sprouts.

Ellen frowned. 'Don't forget I have less than three shillings.'

Peter smiled and walked round with the bag. 'Let's call it one and six and you can go and see the butcher. You might be lucky enough to get some sausages.'

Ellen felt guilty as she bent down to look inside the bag before grabbing the handles. 'Are you sure?' She handed over one silver coin and six pennies. 'It must be more than that.'

'Of course I'm sure.' Peter nodded. 'Be careful, it's heavy.'

Ellen twisted as she glanced over her shoulder. 'Can I be really cheeky and ask you to keep my bag until I've finished my shopping?'

Peter threw his head back and laughed. 'Of course.' He took the bag back and leant it against the barrow's leg.

'Thank you.' Ellen turned and walked away, but before she turned the corner, she peered over her shoulder to see Peter wrapping his arms around a young woman. She smiled. Annie was a lucky girl – such a good man was always going to be spoken for.

Ellen carried on weaving her way through the market stalls.

4

Victoria beamed as a tall dark-haired man with a slight limp approached her. 'It's good to see you, Mr Williams. I hope the world of news is treating you and your father well.'

'Yes, it's not too bad, thank you, although we're struggling to get staff, but I expect most businesses are the same unless you're paying higher wages like the munitions factories.'

Victoria nodded. 'They do seem to pay well but it's dangerous work.' She sighed. 'I can't believe we're nearly at the end of January already; time goes so quickly, but it's good to see that despite the snow you're managing without your walking stick today.'

Mr Williams frowned. 'Some days are better than others, although it's slippery out there so I should have brought it for support. I suppose I should be grateful I'm alive, even though it doesn't always feel that way.'

'Here, let me get it for you.'

John Williams glanced over his shoulder and watched a young brunette reach up for a book for an older lady.

Victoria followed his gaze, watching the smile creep across his face. 'Miss Beckford also loves her books. She's in here most days.' Victoria began to write out the bill payment slip ready for the payment kiosk. 'Your father must be so relieved to have you back home safe and sound.'

John watched the brunette for a moment before turning back to Victoria. 'My father is pleased to have me back from the front; this war has a lot to answer for.' He forced a smile. 'Still, I'm being kept busy; he's got me learning the trade, which helps to stop me from brooding about things.' He watched as Victoria wrote out the bill payment. 'Although the way I keep buying books and not returning any I'm going to need a bigger home.'

Victoria laughed. 'That problem puts you in good company.' She tore off the slip and handed it to him before picking up the four books and placing them on the counter behind her.

John laughed. 'I shall be back in a moment.' Clutching the bill payment slip, he turned back to watch the brunette. He took a couple of steps towards her before stopping. He looked around him and caught Victoria watching him. She nodded her encouragement. He turned back to the girl just as two books fell from her arms. Wincing, he rushed forward. 'Allow me.' He bent down to pick them up.

The young lady blushed as he passed them to her. 'Thank you, that's very kind of you.'

John grinned. 'Trust me when I say it's my pleasure.'

They stared at each other for a moment.

'I... I had better go. I'm meant to be buying some food, not books.'

John nodded and let her walk away, wishing he'd remembered to ask her name. He watched her disappear before turning towards the payment booth.

Victoria waved at Vera to take over from her so she could have her lunch, and take the weight off her throbbing feet. A couple of minutes later, Victoria slumped down on the wooden chair in the break room. 'I didn't think I was going to make lunch today, it's so busy out there.'

Molly glanced up from her sandwich. 'Yes, I noticed we seem busier in the children's section. Maybe people need to escape the war news and the best way to do that is to read a book.'

Victoria nodded. 'Well, there's certainly not much food to spend your money on, although what there is has shot up in price.' She peered at Molly's sandwich. 'What have you got in that?'

Molly wrinkled her nose. 'It's not the best thing I've ever eaten but I had some left-over potatoes from dinner last night, so I thought I'd put them in a sandwich for lunch today. As the poster says, eat it and don't waste it.'

Shaking her head, Victoria laughed. 'I suppose that's a different filling.' She began to unwrap the paper around her own sandwich. 'You know Mr Leadbetter's right, we do need more staff; I've spent the morning behind Alice's old counter, which as you know is one of the busiest in the shop, but we have no one else we can use. I might ask him about it later,' she said, then smiled as she changed the subject. 'I think I've just witnessed the start of a budding romance.'

'You're such a romantic since Ted's been back in your life.' Molly smiled as she nibbled on her sandwich. 'I don't get the impression Alice will be back any time soon. Maybe when Ted's eyesight has fully recovered he could get a job here. I mean, I assume he will never go back to the front again.'

Victoria peered at Molly. 'That's quite a good idea, except he's not really interested in books, so he won't know what anyone is talking about.' She grinned at her friend. 'I think Ted might be coming out of hospital tomorrow, all being well that is.'

Molly cheered. 'That's wonderful and we should be at Monico's having tea and cake for such momentous news.'

'That's true, we haven't been there for ages.' Victoria paused, her eyes twinkling. 'Maybe I should leave my other bit of news until we can get there with Alice.'

Molly's eyes widened. 'No, you can't do that now. What is it?'

Victoria giggled. 'Ted and I have decided to get married sooner rather than later so there'll be no big fancy do—'

'But you do want us to be bridesmaids though, don't you?'

Victoria eyed her friend for a moment, until she was unable to keep a straight face any longer. 'Of course, but we'll sort all that out when we finally set a date and that won't be until he comes home from hospital. I want to see how he copes with his new life first.'

Molly looked sombre as she glanced at her friend. 'If he's unable to cope, does that mean you won't marry him?'

Victoria arched her eyebrows. 'No, definitely not, but I want him to feel confident about us. In his mind he thinks he can't provide for me, and I want to make him see he can. Not that I need him to, but he needs to think he can.'

Molly nodded. 'Don't forget though, you've both been through a lot so you're not the same people you were when your parents died. None of us are.'

Victoria stared down at her sandwich, momentarily remembering when she couldn't afford to bring any lunch to work, and she was pawning all her parents' things. She glanced at Molly. 'That's true. I now have a family in Brighton, which I am very grateful for and a brother I didn't know I had. I have been truly blessed, especially with finding Ted again. Thankfully he seems to think the same.'

Molly finished chewing her mouthful of sandwich. 'It was

obviously meant to be when you chose to volunteer at Endell Hospital instead of one of the other ones in London.'

The chime of the clock-in machine caught Victoria's attention. 'I'd better get back to work, I don't want Mr Leadbetter regretting promoting me from the payment booth.'

The door marked private was pushed open, its hinges squeaking louder the further it opened. 'Mornin', ladies.' Albert, with his arm full of books, almost fell through the doorway.

Victoria jumped up. 'Albert, let me help you before you do yourself some damage.'

Albert gave an almost toothless smile. 'I'm all right, girl, don't yer go worrying about me now.' He stepped away from the door, which slammed shut behind him.

Molly stood up. 'You might as well leave those books with me, and I'll make sure they get put back on the right shelves.'

Albert chuckled, clutching the books tight. 'Are yer trying to do me out of a job?'

Victoria laughed. 'Of course not, this place wouldn't be the same without you. Now careful on those apple and pears, I don't want you hurting yourself.'

Albert threw back his head and roared with laughter. 'Well done, yer remembered some of the cockney rhyming slang I taught yer.'

'Of course, now let me take the books from you.' Victoria reached out for them.

'Yer 'ave made my day.' Still laughing, Albert passed them to Victoria. 'Be careful. Some of the books we're getting are so 'eavy, yer could use 'em as doorstops.' He chuckled as he turned to get back to the many books he still had to check.

Victoria shook her head. 'You should let someone else bring them up, someone with legs younger than yours.'

Albert chuckled. 'Then I wouldn't get to see you beautiful

ladies.' He closed the door behind him as he descended the stairs to the basement.

Victoria was smiling when she turned back to Molly. She opened each book in turn to find out who the publishers were. 'I'll take these because I expect you'll be needed back on the children's section.'

Molly nodded. 'I don't mind working on Alice's counter if you'd rather, I know that's the busiest and nearest to the payment booth.'

'Thank you.' Victoria nodded. 'I'll speak to Mr Leadbetter. I want to speak to him anyway, about the staff shortages and the way the books are on the shelves by publisher. He knows we're short staffed but I'm not sure he's done anything about it. To be honest he thinks you do a wonderful job with the children, so he'll probably want you to stay there.'

Molly picked up a newspaper that was on the table and grimaced at the war news.

Victoria peered down at the paper. 'I wonder how many lives have been lost on both sides. It strikes me nobody ever wins a war.'

Molly turned to look at Victoria. 'Look at you getting all political; you never used to express an opinion on any of it.'

Victoria gave a faint smile. 'I suppose that's having Ted back in my life. To think he nearly died on the front line. I'm very lucky to have him home.'

'What, really home?'

Victoria giggled. 'Yes, really home.'

Molly laughed. 'I suspect the gossips will have a field day, you having a man living in your house and you not married. Scandalous, I tell you. It's scandalous.' She could barely keep a straight face when she patted Victoria's arm.

Victoria laughed. 'I don't know what got into me when I

proposed to him at Christmas, never mind me saying he could live under my roof. If anyone had said I would do such a thing I would've laughed and vigorously denied it, so it just goes to show none of us know what we would do until it comes to the crunch.'

'That's so true. I'm glad it all worked out for you, Victoria. I know he has always been the love of your life.' Molly beamed. 'We should arrange to pop in to see Alice and the two boys. I expect Freddie's glad he was home for the birth of the second one.'

Victoria nodded. 'Yes, he missed quite a lot when Arthur was born. Hopefully, now he's back being a police sergeant again he's making the most of being a father.' She sighed. 'It's criminal when you see all the injured men in hospital, let alone the ones that are never coming back to their families. We can only hope this war is over soon.' She turned to walk away, but added, 'Come on, you're meant to be in the children's department, and I should be telling you off because you're here reading the newspaper. We're lucky Mr Leadbetter hasn't caught us.'

Molly frowned. 'Nothing really changes, does it?'

'No, we still have to earn our crust.'

The paper rustled as Molly folded it shut. She gazed over her shoulder in case Mr Leadbetter was on his way. A smile crept across her face as she thought about how she always seemed to get caught when she was in the wrong place and doing the wrong thing. 'We are all very blessed to have our family and friends around us, but you have got a wedding to plan and none of us saw that coming.'

* * *

Alan Hutchins put his bag containing his Kodak Folding Brownie camera and film down by his feet, as he stood up on tiptoes and stretched his neck to see what was going on. The freezing fog was gradually lifting but the once wet and muddy ground underfoot was now rock hard. The queue of men to get on to the docks had come to a standstill. With a sigh, he lifted his arm and squinted at his wristwatch. He rubbed the back of his neck as he looked around him. He tried to focus on the people behind him, but they were just shapes in the darkness, which wrapped itself around them all as they stood in line to get past the security. Some were chatting and raucous laughter could be heard further down the queue. Peeling off his gloves, he brushed his clammy hands down the sides of his trousers. Closing his eyes for a moment, he took a calming breath before thrusting a hand in his coat pocket to pull out a box of cigarettes and matches. Alan prodded the man in front. 'Would you like one?'

The thickset man turned round. 'No thanks, I gave up smoking. I can't afford it.'

'Do you mind if I do?' He held a cigarette between his fingers.

The man chuckled. 'Of course not. I'll enjoy breathing in the smoke.'

Alan forced a smile as he glanced at the man standing in front of him. 'I'm not used to queuing like this. I'd heard they were tightening security but at this rate it will be time to go home before we get to the gate.'

'There was a break-in, wasn't there. By all accounts, they made a right old mess of Mr Beckford's office.' The man turned back around and stood on his toes to see what was going on. 'It looks like they're letting his daughter on though; she's probably got his sandwiches. Apparently he forgets them more often than not.'

Alan craned his neck again but couldn't see her. 'If things are being tightened, you'd think she would be made to leave them at the security hut.' He placed the cigarette between his lips and struck a match, breathing in and tasting the sulphur, sucking hard on the cigarette until the end glowed red. He shook the match to kill the flame as he blew out the grey smoke. 'Checking everyone's papers is all very well but there's work to be done. Let alone it's bloody freezing standing here.'

The man fanned his hand in front of him as the smoke came his way. 'Hopefully it will start moving again soon.'

Peering ahead again, Alan saw a Port of London officer pull someone from the queue. 'They're checking everyone's papers thoroughly and I think they've just pulled someone out of the line.' Then he saw a policeman coming their way, his heavy foot-steps crunching on the ground as he approached. 'Is everything all right?'

Startled, the policeman's eyes snapped wide open. 'Of course.'

Alan watched him disappear into the darkness before turning back to crane his neck to see what was going on. He frowned as he moved from one foot to the other. 'Do you think they're looking for someone in particular?'

The man in front of him was silent for a moment before clearing his throat. 'I don't know, but there's a lot of talk about who could have done it and what they were after.' He paused. 'Maybe something has happened, or they're trying to prevent something, like the munitions factory explosion. After all, that wasn't that far from here; it was amazing that only seventy people died, although hundreds were injured. And to think we can't even blame the Germans for that one; the factory caught fire and with all that TNT it was never going to end well.'

Alan rubbed his smooth chin as he remembered reading about it in the newspapers. His gaze travelled past the man and focused on an officer nearby. 'Yes, it was a huge explosion. Silvertown will need rebuilding. From what I read, there wasn't a house left standing for miles.'

The man nodded as he glanced back at him. 'I'm sorry, I should have said, I'm Fred.' He held out his hand.

Alan hesitated for a moment, taking in his weather-beaten features before forcing a smile. 'Alan, my name's Alan.' He took Fred's hand and shook it. 'What do you do here on the docks?'

Fred chuckled. 'Anything that needs doing, but mainly loading and unloading. At sixty-two I'm just grateful for a job.' He eyed Alan up and down. 'How come you ain't away fighting like other men your age?'

'I tried but it seems I have a dodgy ticker, so they don't want me.' Alan smiled. 'I'm doing my bit for the war. I'm a photographer; my editor sent me to get some photos of the break-in, although I don't suppose the Port of London Police will want it splashed all over the papers.'

Several explosions sounded and light could be seen momentarily filling the sky at various points along the Thames. Everyone dropped on to the rock-hard cold ground.

A man's voice shouted out, 'The German's are bombing us. Run for your lives. Take cover.'

The Port of London police officer blew his whistle several times before yelling out, trying to be heard above the rockets and the men shouting at each other, 'They're the maroon rockets; they've been launched to let us know the Germans are coming. They're the new night-time air raid warning. Please stay calm; we have time to find shelter.'

Alan watched everybody run in different directions, looking for a shelter that could protect them. His heart started pounding as he snatched up the bag by his feet. No one was listening to the officer; panic had set in.

Fred yelled at him, 'Come on, we can't afford to wait here like sitting ducks.' He yanked at Alan's arm. 'We've got to find shelter.' Explosions could be heard from further along the river. 'The bombs are getting nearer. We've got to find cover before they get to us.' They followed the men running towards the main road, heading towards the grain warehouses. Alan felt his foot slip on the uneven ground. He scowled; he was going to get himself killed if he didn't hurry up. He reached out to try and protect himself and his camera from the fall but failed.

Fred grabbed his arm to pull him upright. 'Come on, we've got to get out of here.'

Alan reached up and gripped Fred's arm, pulling himself up. He ran his tongue over his lips and the iron taste of blood filled his mouth. He wiped the back of his hand across his face, trying to ignore the dampness he now felt.

'It looks like you've bloodied your nose.' Fred pulled a handkerchief from his trouser pocket. 'You might need this.'

Alan nodded. 'Thank you.' He took the handkerchief and rubbed it across his mouth and cheeks before holding it over his nose.

An explosion ripped through the air. The ground shook beneath their feet. Both men automatically fell to the floor, trying to save themselves. Alan's body covered his bag. Dust and debris showered down on them.

Alan's ears were ringing and the sound of men's voices became distorted. He lifted his head slightly, coughing as he breathed in the dust that was drifting around them. Bright yellow flames in the distance lit up the sky, mingling with the grey and black clouds of smoke. Men around him were beginning to move. They had been lucky the hit had missed them. His gaze travelled back to the flames licking at the black sky and he wondered how many people were injured or had died. Pulling his bag closer, he got up on to his knees. Using the handkerchief, he wiped the dust from his face before looking across at Fred, who was still face down in the dirt. 'Fred, Fred, are you all right?' There was no movement or sound from him. Alan reached out and prodded him; was this what a dead person looked like? 'Fred, come on, man, we've got to get out of here.'

Fred groaned.

Alan breathed a sigh of relief.

* * *

Ellen lay in her bed wondering how Mary and her grandma had slept after the explosions and the shouting, along with the screams that inevitably followed. Through the small basement window, she had been able to see the night sky lit up with the fires across London long after the last bombs had dropped. Explosions tended to shake the old house to its foundations, and she feared it would collapse in on them one of these days. Pressing her lips together, she realised how lucky she was to have found shelter in her father's office the previous night. She had huddled under his desk to escape the bombs when she was at the docks, all because he'd forgotten his sandwiches again. Tears pricked at her eyes as she remembered Mary sobbing in her arms when she had finally got home. Shaking her head, she didn't want to live her life in fear like her father and sister did, but it made her realise her father was right about staying indoors. If she and her father had died, Mary would have been left on her own looking after their grandma. Her father had never spoken of it, but she'd guessed the docks would be a target for the Germans. Once again, she prayed everyone was safe. Ellen stifled a yawn that was threatening to escape. What she wouldn't give for a good night's sleep.

Ellen ran her fingers through her tangled curls before glancing up at the rickety wooden stairs. She was overcome with the need to escape the cold, stuffy, damp and airless room. Her father insisted they slept in the basement every night while he was at work, so they didn't have to listen out for the policeman shouting, 'The German's are coming.' Every day she hoped the London smog would stop them dropping their bombs.

Sighing, she pulled her pink nightdress over her knees before pushing her diaries under her pillow. Reading them made her long for the happier, innocent days spent with her mother and sister, before the war started.

Ellen shook her head and told herself to get a grip. At eighteen she was the eldest and had to be strong for her sister; it was what her mother would have wanted.

Mary, sitting at the makeshift dressing table they had created in the dark basement, pulled her red knitted bed jacket around her before she peered over her shoulder at Ellen. 'Do you remember Ma taking us to the Houses of Parliament to listen to the suffragettes talking? I was only eleven, but I will always remember her being fired up about it and stuffing the leaflet in her pocket to read later. She said the future was bright for us because one day we would have a say, we would have a vote, and to make sure we used it. At the time I never understood what it all meant.' She sighed. 'I wonder what she'd make of it now. Life hasn't turned out the way she thought it would.'

Ellen looked at her sister, as she elegantly brushed her long brown hair, remembering how her mother used to rag roll it for her. Perhaps Ellen should offer to do it.

Phyllis Burton pulled herself up and adjusted her pillows. 'This so-called Great War put an end to the suffragettes calling for the vote. It was more important to support the men who were fighting for our king and country. Hopefully they will continue when it's over.'

Ellen smiled. 'Good morning, Grandma. I hope our chatter didn't wake you up?'

Phyllis flopped back down. 'Of course not. I've been awake for a while.'

Ellen stood up and walked to the small, sealed window, which provided the only natural light. Sighing, she looked up, knowing she wouldn't be able to see anything except the grey, murky sky.

The wind made a haunting noise as it whistled around outside. The clatter of dustbin lids hitting the ground was quickly followed by cats meowing, which then provoked next door's dog to start barking.

Ellen turned to look at her sister. 'I've been thinking about you wanting to do war work and your age making it more difficult.'

Mary stared at Ellen. 'What about it?'

'I think the ladies that work at the tea table at Victoria station would welcome you with open arms.' Ellen tilted her head. 'They don't get paid but the soldiers that are returning home welcome their kindness.'

Mary nodded. 'Ma would approve.'

Phyllis looked over at her youngest granddaughter. 'She definitely would; it's something she would have done. No doubt she would have been doing a lot more to help.'

Mary ran her fingers over the soft bristles of her hairbrush. 'I can't believe it's been four years since Ma passed away. I miss her so much. I used to love her brushing my hair.'

Ellen gave her a lopsided smile. 'I know, she would do it for hours.'

Mary smiled at the memory. 'You're right. It was so comforting. I never wanted her to stop. That's why I used to have my hair rag rolled, not because I wanted it curly, but because I loved her playing with my hair.' She gazed into the distance for a moment before putting down the brush. 'I love it when you and Grandma tell me stories about Ma. I struggle to remember her like you do.'

Ellen blinked quickly. 'That's understandable, you were very young.'

Mary nodded. 'Do you think this war will ever end? It's getting harder to remember life before it started.'

Ellen sighed. 'It has certainly been hard since Ma passed away, but the war has to end sometime.' She turned and glanced down at her crumpled copy of *Little Women* on the chair next to where she had been sitting last night and forced a smile. 'Maybe when this war is over, we'll get work and make a room full of books. They'll be floor to ceiling; we will have so many you will need a ladder to reach the top shelf.'

Phyllis chuckled as she listened to the girls' chatter.

Mary giggled. 'It will be like living in our own bookshop. Wouldn't that be wonderful.' She gazed into the distance. 'It would be like having our very own Foyles in our front room. They must have thousands of books in that shop.'

Ellen grinned. 'I would love to work there. Mind you, I would probably spend more time reading than working.' She walked back to the chair and picked up the worn copy of *Little Women* and opened the cover. Her mother's beautiful handwriting was scrawled across the page. There was no need to read the words of the dedication; it was scorched into her memory.

Ellen, your life will have times of strife but remember you are stronger than you think. Have faith, be courageous and strong, the future is yours to build. Your beloved ma xx

She snapped the book shut. 'Come on, read some of my favourite book; that will lift our spirits.' She reached out to give it to her sister. 'Then we'll go up and have breakfast. Although, before that, I need to light the fire in the front room so it's warm for when Pa gets home and has his bath.'

Mary's eyes shone as she took the book from her sister. 'You must know this book inside out the number of times you've read

it.' She grinned. 'But I will read it because I know you love it.'
Mary opened the book at the page with a piece of paper sticking
out of the top of it. 'We're at chapter fifteen now.' She took a deep
breath as she glanced down the page.

Ellen nodded as she lowered herself onto a hard wooden
chair. She closed her eyes, waiting for the words to wash over her.

'"*I can't sleep, I'm so anxious,*" said Meg. "*Think about something
pleasant, and you'll soon drop off.*"'

Mary's voice continued, acting out the words on the page.

Ellen opened her eyes, watching the concentration on her
sister's face before matching her soft voice with hers.

'*The clocks were striking midnight and the rooms were very still as
a figure glided quietly from bed to bed, smoothing a coverlet here,
settling a pillow there, and pausing to look long and tenderly at each
unconscious face, to kiss each with lips that mutely blessed, and to pray
the fervent prayers which only mothers utter. As she lifted the curtain to
look out into the dreary night, the moon broke suddenly from behind the
clouds and shone upon her like a bright, benignant face, which seemed
to whisper in the silence, "Be comforted, dear soul! There is always light
behind the clouds."*'

Mary looked up and smiled as she came to the end of the
passage she was reading. 'You've read this book so many times it
sounds like you know it word for word.'

Ellen clasped her hands together and frowned. 'It's those
words *"Be comforted, dear soul! There is always light behind the
clouds."* I like to remind myself things will get better.'

Phyllis raised her eyebrows. 'You must remember your ma
didn't want you to have a life of servitude, cleaning up after other
people and taking in their washing. She wanted you to be strong
and to marry for love, not for money, which she might have done
before she met your father.'

Mary studied her grandma. 'Pa's always saying money is important.'

Phyllis nodded. 'Money is important because you need it to live, even if you do marry for love. Your ma always had a dream that you would both be free to have your opinions heard, not like people my age when it was a struggle to survive without a man to look after you.'

Mary snapped the book shut. 'Do you think there will be any young men left after the war?'

Phyllis laughed. 'I think we all need to feel loved and be able to keep a roof over our heads, regardless of our age.'

Ellen sighed as she stood up and smiled at Mary. 'Come on, it's time to get on with our chores.'

5

The docks were fairly quiet, the only noise the wind catching on chains and flag poles. Harold was thankful it had been a quiet week since the evening the bombs had dropped. His throat tightened as he thought about how he had wanted to keep Ellen safe and didn't want her walking home by herself, but he hadn't had any choice. Harold stopped and looked out over the river. The water was as black as night. His face felt almost frozen against the cold air of the February evening. He closed his eyes and let the sound of the river lapping on the banks wash over him for a minute. A chilling gust of wind blew down the river, cutting through him and anything that stood in its way. He shivered as he remembered how he had stood with his wife on Westminster Bridge listening to the same river.

He lowered his head. Life was never going to be the same; she had been snatched away from him. His eyes snapped open, and he gazed out across the water and into the blackness once more. He missed his wife's laughter and her ability to take control and yet show such kindness. She knew how to talk to his daughters.

He sighed. This wasn't going to bring her back; he had to think about her mother and his daughters now. Harold pulled at the collar of his thick black jacket. He slid his hands inside his trouser pockets as he marched, with the snow crunching underfoot, along the dark path towards his office. The office keys jangled against the coins. He wrapped his fingers around them. He had checked and double-checked the door was locked, making sure he wasn't going to get caught out again. His job, as Port Master, was too important to him to get the sack. His throat tightened. After all, how else would he be able to provide for and protect his daughters now their mother was dead?

When he got nearer to his office, he saw a light flashing from inside. The hair on the back of his neck stood on end. Not again. He quickened his pace, shouting out, 'Who's in there?'

He stopped and stood still, his body tense as he listened hard but there was no noise. He crept around to the window and peered inside. There was no light now. Everything was shadowy shapes. Had he imagined it? Was this job worrying him so much he was seeing things? He stood outside his office for a moment, his breath coming in short bursts, visible against the darkness. He wondered whether to call for help or to just go inside, but apart from the light he hadn't seen anything, and wasn't even sure about that. If he called for help and there was no one inside, he would look a fool. Frowning, he bit down on his lip before taking a deep breath; there was no option but to go in.

There was a flash of light again from inside the office. His heart lurched. He hadn't imagined it. 'Hello, who's in there?' Taking a step forward, Harold reached out and put his sweaty palm on the handle. Despite the cold weather, he felt the perspiration roll down the side of his forehead. He brushed it away with the back of his hand. He took a deep breath and pulled the door open. 'Who's in there?'

A man suddenly threw himself at him as he barged through

the doorway, using a bag to knock him over. Harold was stunned for a moment, before he jumped up and chased after the intruder. The man running in front looked over his shoulder then disappeared between several rattling chains attached to posts. Harold followed him, shouting, 'You'll not get away with this.' A searing pain grabbed at his chest, and he struggled to catch his breath as he chased him.

The man suddenly stopped and turned to face him.

Harold wanted to bend over and catch his breath, but he stood firm and hoped the intruder wouldn't notice his laboured breathing. He tried to guess the man's height and what he was wearing but it was too dark for him to see him properly.

The man took a step nearer before swinging the bag he was carrying. The clasp came undone just before it hit Harold.

Harold's head swung to one side as he fell backwards, his leg getting caught in a coil of ropes and chains. His head hit something hard, and pain seared through him. His vision was blurry as he tried to push himself up.

The man mumbled, 'This bloody darkness; I can't see the hand in front of my face.' He fumbled with his bag before he punched Harold in the face and kicked his body several times. 'Stay down, you fool. Don't make me hurt you any more than I need to.'

Harold reached out; his hand floundered around him until it landed on a cold metal pipe. He grabbed it and swung it, lashing out in all directions. Harold heard the man scream several times but then he was gone.

Loud, high-pitched whistles and men's voices filled Harold's ears as he stayed lying on the cold, hard ground. His whole body ached.

'Harold, where are you?'

'Harold, make a noise if you're hurt.'

Was that his manager's voice? Harold tried to pull himself up, but he screamed out in agony as pained travelled from his legs.

'Thank goodness we've found you, what happened? Can you get up?'

Harold groaned. 'No, it's my leg.' His lips tightened. 'He swung a bag at me, and I fell backwards but my foot got caught in something.'

His manager crouched down next to him. 'Who did?'

The police officer looked over his shoulder. 'I want you all to search the area, he might still be here.' He tapped Harold's shoulder while indicating with his other hand to another officer. 'Don't worry we'll get an ambulance and they can look at your leg.'

The other officer nodded before running into the darkness.

Harold's face screwed up as the pain gripped him. 'There was someone in my office.'

'Please don't tell me you left your office unlocked?'

'No, the keys are in my pocket.' Harold grimaced. 'Check the lock, I definitely locked it and I checked it three times.' He gasped for breath. 'Someone was in there. I saw a light go on and off a couple of times.'

'What sort of light?'

Harold screwed his face up as he winced. 'I don't know, I just ran after him.' He stopped to take a breath. 'I think my leg is broken.'

'Hopefully the ambulance will be here soon.'

A police officer came over. 'I've found this.' He passed over the paper he was holding. 'We need to search this area when it's light. It's a good job we upped the security and patrols of the docks after the last attempt, at least we were in the proximity this time.'

Harold squinted. 'What have you found?'

'Don't you worry, sir, just concentrate on lying still until the ambulance arrives.'

* * *

Ellen stared at her father's leg covered in plaster. 'You're going to have to keep your leg up for a while.'

Phyllis shook her head. 'I don't know why you chased after him; you could have been killed.'

Harold shrugged. 'Well, I wasn't. I'm going to try and get to work tomorrow.'

Ellen raised her voice. 'You can't. The hospital said you'll be off for at least six weeks, but it could be as long as three months if you don't do as you're told.' She paused. 'Tomorrow I will go out and get work, because no matter what you say, we can't manage without money for six weeks.'

Harold closed his eyes. 'It's my job to look after my family.'

Ellen shook her head and spoke in a low whisper. 'You know there's not a day that goes by when I don't wonder what Ma would say or do; she was strong and kind, and I know she, in this situation, wouldn't take any of your nonsense. You do look after us. Ma would be proud of how you've managed, but it's time to allow yourself to have some help.'

Phyllis nodded but said nothing.

Harold opened his watery eyes. 'You know every time you leave the house, I worry about you coming back. Your mother only went out for some shopping and next thing I know, a policeman is knocking on the door to tell me she had died because someone had lost control of their car.' He squeezed his eyes shut.

'I know, Pa, but you must understand those sorts of accidents don't happen every day.'

Harold's eyes snapped open again. 'No, that's true, but now we have bombs to worry about.'

Ellen nodded. 'I miss Ma every day, as I'm sure we all do. She's never out of my thoughts for long and Mary was quite young when it happened so she's clinging on to what memories she does have.' She paused. 'But let me ask you, what do you think Ma would say if she was here?'

Harold shrugged.

Ellen smiled. 'You can shrug but you know she would say life is for living and when your time is up your time is up, just enjoy the time you have.'

Phyllis's gaze travelled from Ellen to her son-in-law. 'Ellen's right, Harold.'

Harold sighed. 'I know, but it's hard. You girls are all I have.'

'And you are all we have.'

There was silence between them for a moment, as each were lost in their own thoughts.

Ellen sighed. 'Pa, the rent man came for his money yesterday.'

Harold grunted at his daughter as he put a Woodbine cigarette between his lips. 'I'll talk to him next time he comes.'

Ellen glanced down at her flat slippers. 'Look, Pa, you could have been killed by whoever broke into your office.' She sighed. 'Imagine if you had – how do you think Mary and I would survive without you keeping the roof over our heads?' She paused before taking a deep breath. 'I should be working, contributing to the household bills. Remember, I do the shopping, so I know things have gone up. This isn't just about the rent, there's food and other things we need every day. It's time you let me get a job. Everyone I know is working; some earn very good money in the factories.'

Harold blew spirals of grey smoke into the room. 'I'm not going to keep repeating myself; no daughter of mine is going out to work. Next thing you know you'll be wanting to go into the public houses and swill back pints of beer.'

Ellen closed her eyes and silently counted to ten. 'Of course. Isn't that what all working women do?'

Harold screwed his eyes together. 'Don't you take that tone with me; you're never too old for me to take my belt off to you.'

Ellen took a deep breath, filling her lungs with smoke from her father's cigarette. 'I'm sorry, Pa, I didn't mean to speak out of turn, I just want to help.' She took a step away from him. 'Apart from your broken leg, you have a lot going on at work. You obviously have a lot to think about because you forget your sandwiches most days. I just—'

'You just what? Want to get on with your life and leave us to fend for ourselves?' Harold took another drag on his cigarette, puffing out more grey smoke in his daughter's direction.

Ellen coughed before shaking her head. 'No, Pa, I just want to help. Mary's old enough to do more around the house and fill the tin bath every morning, not that you'll need that for a while. You must accept they won't let you go back to the docks until your leg has healed properly.'

Harold glared at her. 'I said no.' He threw his arm out wide. 'You can stop lighting this fire every day; not buying coal will save us some money.'

'Pa, it's so cold we can't manage without the fire. You'll get ill and so will Grandma.'

Harold turned his face away from Ellen and stared at the grey ash of the dying fire. 'It's about time dinner was ready.'

Ellen lowered her head. 'It is ready but I'm afraid it's mainly vegetables.'

Harold spun round and scowled. 'How am I meant to work all night on just vegetables? Have you been wasting my money on rubbish?'

'No, Pa, I keep telling you, everything has got really expensive, and the butchers are short on meat. I managed to get a couple of sausages from Mr Preston and I've cooked them and put them in your sandwiches for later, but that was before I knew you wouldn't be going to work.'

Phyllis leant forward and rested her wrinkled hand on Howard's arm. 'Ellen is a good girl; you and Ada did a good job raising your daughters so don't let your fear stop them from being independent like you and Ada wanted.'

'That was Ada's wish, not mine.'

Phyllis nodded. 'Do you really think she would stand by and say nothing about them not working and helping the war effort in some way?'

When Harold finally spoke his voice was flat and he sounded beaten. 'Mary wouldn't be able to do all the things Ellen does.'

Ellen stepped nearer to her father and rested her hand on his shoulder. 'I'll teach her. She can come shopping with me so everyone will know she's Harold Beckford's daughter.'

Phyllis smiled. 'I'm also here to help and guide her.'

Harold hesitated for a moment before staring up at his daughter. 'I've always said my daughters will not work, and nothing has changed. The bills of this house are not your concern, and I will not tolerate your interference with it.'

Ellen shook her head. 'And what happens when we're homeless? Whose concern is it then?'

Harold had the familiar tell-tale red blotches on his cheeks. Ellen knew she had gone too far and fled the room before he had a chance to raise his hand to her. In her haste she bumped into Mary in the hall.

Mary flung her arm out and caught one of the railings on the staircase. 'What's going on? You look like the devil himself is after you.'

Ellen frowned as she glanced over her shoulder. 'Sorry, I should be more careful. I'm just in a hurry to dish up dinner. You can come and give me a hand if you'd like. It's time you learnt to run this house because there could be a time when I'm not here and you will have to step up.' She heard Mary's sharp intake of breath but continued. 'I was thinking you can start by coming shopping with me, so everyone gets to know you. I use the same shops and stalls all the time; some know Pa so they're kinder and can be more generous with the food allowances, but I never ask for more than I'm allowed. These new ration books tell us what we can have so that helps.'

Colour had drained from Mary's face as she screwed up her eyes. 'Has something happened? Is there something I need to know about?'

Ellen forced a smile. 'Pa has broken his leg so he can't go to work, and I will probably have to find a job so we can eat, but I think Pa is praying for a miracle. I know this is going to hurt but we should go through our books again and see what else we can take back to Foyles.'

Mary gasped. 'I don't want to part with any more of my books.'

Ellen shook her head. 'I knew you would say that because I feel the same, but for every book we return that's tuppence towards food.' She turned and stroked Mary's arm. 'We have to do our bit to help. Pa's not getting any wages while his leg is broken so we have to raise some money from somewhere and let's face it, we still have enough books to open our own bookshop so to part with some more of them won't hurt us.'

Mary shrugged. 'I suppose not but I want to keep the ones Ma bought us.'

Ellen smiled. 'Of course. I'll want to do the same, but we're grown-ups now and we can't let Gran starve, can we?'

Mary smiled. 'Of course not.'

Ellen squeezed her sister's arm. 'I'm very proud of you. We've had some tough times, but we'll get through them and then you can buy all the books you want.'

Mary's laughter burst from her. 'I shall look forward to that day.'

Ellen chuckled. 'Me too. Come on, let's sort out dinner.' She stepped forward before peering over her shoulder at Mary. 'Also, you are at an age when you should be preparing to run your own home. I can remember helping Ma when I was younger than you, so I just think it's time.' It wasn't lost on Ellen that she was doing the same to Mary as her father had done to her, but she didn't want to share her worries about how the family were going to make ends meet and cause her to worry. It occurred to her that maybe that was her father's thinking as well.

Mary followed Ellen along the hallway to the kitchen, their footsteps silent on the black and white tiled floor.

Ellen pushed open the creaking kitchen door, reminding her that she needed to find something to grease the hinges. 'Mary, if you set the table, I'll bring the vegetable casserole from the oven. Pa will have to have his plate on a tray in the front room.'

* * *

Ellen dropped one of the bags she was carrying and tugged the collar of her coat up against the biting wind. She bit her bottom lip as she stood outside Foyles Bookshop. The weight of the bags she had been carrying from home made her arms ache. The walk to Foyles had taken twice as long because she'd kept stopping to rest; the books were heavy and it broke her heart to part with them, but she had to show Mary it was the right thing to do. She had been inside the shop almost daily for as long as she could remember and yet as she looked up at the front door to Foyles fear ran down her spine. While she was returning the books, she was determined to ask about getting work there. Perhaps it was a mistake to try and get a job in her favourite shop. Perhaps she should wait and see how much money they could make by selling their frugal items. Ellen shivered. The money wouldn't last long no matter what her father said. Could she pluck up the courage to defy her pa?

She took a deep breath. She had come this far so it was now or never. She picked up the bag and stepped inside the shop. The woody smell of the books on the bookshelves was comforting. Memories of her mother rushed in and she knew she would approve. Ellen watched the familiar tall grey-haired man in his immaculate black three-piece suit walking towards her.

'Good morning, Miss Beckford. Are you all right? You look a little pale; would you like to sit down for a moment? I can find someone to assist you, maybe get you a drink.' Mr Leadbetter frowned as he scanned the area around him. 'You weren't out last night when those bombs were dropping were you? I understand they only just missed Blackfriars Bridge, St Pancras and King's Cross train stations; mind you, I think South London came off worse. Sorry, I'm rambling on, but I do worry people can easily get caught outside.'

Ellen took a deep breath. 'No sir, I'm all right, thank you. I did get caught in the bombing raids two weeks ago; I was at the docks because my father had forgotten his sandwiches. Being so close to it really frightened me so I'm thankful I was indoors last night. Although I did hear the warning rockets and the bombs; it doesn't seem to get any easier, does it? Every time they fall, I worry the house will get bombed and we will be stuck in the basement and never be found.'

Mr Leadbetter nodded. 'I can understand that. It will be a good thing when the war is over, and everyone is back home safely.' He ran a critical eye over the young girl. 'Well, I'm glad you didn't get caught in it all and I know I've said it before, but you do look very pale. Let me help you with those bags.'

Ellen gave a jittery laugh. 'They are books I'm hoping to return, you know, to collect the tuppence for each one.' She bit her bottom lip. 'I'm just a little nervous.'

Mr Leadbetter studied her for a moment. 'Why are you nervous? I've seen you in here before; in fact, I believe you are here most days.' He smiled. 'I remember your mother bringing you and your sister in as well. Now there's a woman who loved a book and we always have room for more.' He chuckled. 'Despite how it looks.'

Ellen nodded. 'That's right, I have good memories of being in this shop. I think that's why I keep coming back here. Well, that and my love of books. I love the woody smell of the pages when you open them.' She gave an embarrassed laugh. 'That probably makes me sound a bit strange.'

Mr Leadbetter laughed. 'Oh no, not at all, I think you'll find most of us feel the same.' He eyed the young girl in front of him for a moment before clearing his throat. 'Still, if you need any help please just ask. I'll get these returns sorted for you.'

Ellen gave a small smile. 'I will, thank you.'

Mr Leadbetter picked up the bags before stepping away to approach another customer.

Panic ran through Ellen's body and her clammy hands clenched together in front of her. *Now, come on ask him*, a voice yelled in her head. 'Actually, if you have a moment.'

Mr Leadbetter peered over his shoulder at her.

Ellen could feel the heat rising up her neck.

Mr Leadbetter gave her a lopsided grin. 'How can I help you?'

Ellen took a deep breath. 'I would like to talk to someone about getting a job here. I must admit I have no experience of any work outside of the home but I'm happy to learn if you'll take a chance on me?'

Mr Leadbetter stepped nearer to Ellen. 'Well, we do have a vacancy. As you're probably aware, this store is busy all the time, which we are obviously very pleased about. However, since the war started it's been hard to fill vacancies because there's more money to be earned in the factories these days. The staff have been complaining about how shorthanded we are, so you have just saved me the job of trying to find someone. One of my best assistants has just had a baby and it has left us short.' He paused before arching his eyebrows. 'However, I can only offer a couple of days a week to begin with and I can't promise the job will be a permanent one. I'm afraid it must be on a trial basis because of your lack of experience but I'm happy to do that and see how you get on.'

Ellen beamed at the elderly gentleman in front of her. 'I don't know what to say. I was so nervous about asking and I didn't think I stood a chance. Working here would be a dream job for me, and I'm sure most of my wages will be spent on books.'

Mr Leadbetter chuckled. 'Well, you won't be on your own there.' He looked around him to see if he could see Victoria. 'Come with me, we'll find Miss Appleton; she is a floor manager here. She'll see you settled in and tell you what's what.' He beckoned her to follow him as he marched between the racks of shelving. He stopped short and turned to look at Ellen. 'My goodness, I've just realised I didn't introduce myself or ask you your first name, how rude is that? I'm so sorry, I'm Mr Leadbetter and I manage the shop for the owners.' He held out his hand to shake hers.

Ellen took his bony hand in hers. 'My name is Ellen. Thank you again for the opportunity you're giving me; you have no idea how much it means to me.'

Mr Leadbetter nodded. 'As I said, I can only offer you a couple of days a week even though I'm quite desperate for staff, so I'll probably accept whatever hours you wish to do on those days.'

Ellen immediately thought about the money she could earn, but it was quickly chased away by the thought of her father's anger when he found out she was working. 'Ideally, I'd like to work as many hours as I can get.'

Mr Leadbetter smiled and collected the bags again. 'That's fine. Now let's see if we can find Miss Appleton.' He turned and took a couple of steps before thrusting his hand in the air and waving at someone.

Ellen recognised Miss Appleton from her many visits to the shop.

'Did you want me, Mr Leadbetter?'

'Yes, Miss Appleton, I have a young lady here who would like to start working in this magnificent shop.' Mr Leadbetter's smile travelled between Victoria and Ellen. 'Would you please let her know what working at Foyles means and how we are the best bookshop in the world.' He chuckled. 'Oh, and can you please sort out these returns for her as well?'

Victoria stifled a giggle. 'Of course, sir.'

6

Ellen strained as she waited to hear the front door key banging against the door as her father's boss and the two police officers left the house, or to feel the cold night air swirl around the hall and into the rooms off of it once the door was opened. She had wanted to stay and listen to what was going on and had waited for as long as she dared. They had been talking about the bombs that had gone off two nights ago near Euston Road, just missing two main train stations and two of the bridges that crossed the Thames. They confirmed what Mr Leadbetter had said about South London being hit badly. Ellen had made them all a cuppa, then she had been dismissed.

Ellen sipped her hot tea; her white knuckles were trying to break through her skin as she gripped the cup. Taking a couple of deep breaths to calm her nerves, she sat at the scrubbed kitchen table. She had slept fitfully, tossing and turning, mulling over telling her father about her job, spending all night rehearsing what she was going to say. The happiness she felt when she left Foyles the previous day had soon faded away. Ellen had hugged her secret close, not even telling Mary. She shook her head, knowing she should have told him yesterday but she had wanted to hold the excitement of working in Foyles close. She knew the moment her father knew, all the excitement would be taken from her. Her lips tightened. It was going to be hard on Mary; she would have to learn to cook, although their grandma could manage to do some things while she sat at the kitchen table. Her face lit up as she allowed her thoughts to wander back to Victoria taking her around and introducing her to everyone.

Mary raised her eyebrows. 'What are you smiling at?'

Startled, Ellen nearly spilt her tea. 'Mary, you made me jump. I didn't hear you come down the stairs.'

Mary chuckled while her slender fingers pushed her brown hair behind her ears. 'My goodness, the way those stairs creak you must have been in a world of your own. I always think the neighbours at the end of the road must be able to hear them.' The chair scraped across the kitchen floor as she pulled it out to sit down. 'What were you thinking about?'

Gazing into her cup, Ellen sucked in her lips. 'I'm afraid I can't tell you until I've spoken to Pa.'

'That doesn't sound good.' Mary frowned. 'I thought we told each other everything.'

Ellen leant across the table and covered Mary's hand with her own and squeezed it tight. 'Trust me, you'll know soon enough.'

Mary frowned. 'You look tired and pale. Is everything all right?'

The thud of the front door shutting made Ellen sit upright. She grabbed a cup and added a splash of milk before pouring the dark brown liquid through the stainless-steel tea strainer she was holding. She watched intently as the tea leaves gathered in it. Taking a breath, she placed the strainer on its stand. Ellen hoped her father was in a good mood. She pushed back her chair; the wooden legs screeched as they scraped across the tiled floor.

Standing up, she smoothed down her bib top apron over her plain grey blouse and black calf-length skirt and cleared her throat. 'I'll just take this cup of tea to Pa and then we'll make breakfast.'

Mary nodded. 'I'll have a cuppa while I wait.'

Ellen's footsteps were quiet as she walked into the hall, just stopping short of the front room door. She took a deep breath before pushing the door wide. 'I heard the front door shut so I thought it would be safe to bring you another cup of tea.' She studied her pa, trying to work out whether he was in a good mood or not. Ellen forced herself to smile as she passed him the cup. 'How did your meeting go?'

Harold stared at his daughter, before squinting at her. 'I told them I could still go to work but they've laid me off until my leg has healed.' He thumped the arm of the chair.

Nausea swirled around Ellen's stomach. She folded her arms around her midriff. 'Pa, you need to take care and accept help.'

Harold stared at his plastered leg; the silence was palpable.

Ellen sucked in her breath. Her words tripped over each other in their rush to escape. 'Pa, I've been offered a job at Foyles Bookshop. It's only part time and I will probably have to find something else as well but it's a start. If we talk to the rent man—'

'And what?'

'Pa, please don't be angry, I'm only trying to help.'

Harold scowled as he spat out his words. 'So, despite everything I said you went against my wishes? Is that why you didn't tell me before?'

Ellen gasped. 'I'm sorry, but I only asked about the work yesterday when I was returning some books.'

Harold's face was crimson when he retorted. 'You might well be, young lady; I didn't know you had it in you to be so devious.'

Ellen tried to play it down. 'I'm not devious, Pa. I wasn't sure when would be the right time to discuss things with you.'

'Is that right? Is that by any chance because you knew I wouldn't be happy with what you've done as we'd already discussed it?'

Ellen watched him place the cup he was holding on the side table next to the armchair. 'Don't let your tea get cold; we don't have much milk.'

Harold's hands clenched into tight fists. 'Is that your justification for getting a job? That we don't have much milk?'

Ellen shook her head. 'You know that's not the reason; we've talked about it already.'

Harold slammed his hand down on the arm of his chair, making Ellen jump. 'And yet you've deliberately defied me. You've deliberately ignored my wishes. You've deliberately gone out and found yourself a job.'

Ellen put on a brave face, determined not to show her fear and flinch at her father's actions. 'Pa, you might call it defying you and deliberately going out of my way to do what I want, but I see it as just trying to keep a roof over our heads and food on the table. I don't know how many times you have to be told you can't earn any money for at least six weeks, so it's imperative I get a job. Surely you must see that?'

Harold's face screwed up in anger. 'But you must have asked about it before I broke my leg, so you clearly don't think I can cover what this family needs; is that what you're saying?'

'That's just not true, I asked about a job when I knew you were going to be off work.' Ellen wondered if she should leave the room to call a halt to any further discussion until he'd had a chance to think about things properly, but she wanted him to understand. She shook her head. 'Pa, I'm not saying anything of the sort; of course you can cover what we need, but as I said to you before, I'm the one that goes out and does all the shopping. I know how much everything has gone up in price and I want to help.' Ellen spread her arms wide. 'And I'm old enough to help. I don't know why you're so adamant that we can't work, or why you think you must shoulder the burden by yourself. The job in Foyles Bookshop is a safe one. I'm not working in a munitions factory, or any other type of factory, so I'm not putting myself at risk.'

Harold waved his arm in the air. 'Get out of here. I don't want to see you right now.'

'Pa, I'm sorry. Please don't be angry, I just want to help. Ma brought us up to be caring, helpful and to achieve as much as we can while still living our lives. It's what she would have wanted because we are a family.'

Harold tightened his lips. 'You are not your mother and you have no idea what she would have wanted. Your ma and I talked about this on many occasions, and I wouldn't have been defied by her, you or anyone else for that matter.'

Ellen could feel anger and hurt building inside before the words burst from her lips. 'I can't wait to be free of you, to be away from the stranglehold you have on us.' She stepped nearer the door to the front room and scowled at her father. 'It doesn't matter what you say, I know it's what Ma would have wanted.' She hesitated for a moment, before continuing. 'When she gave me *Little Women* she wrote a dedication in it for me. It says, "*Ellen, your life will have times of strife but remember you are stronger than you think. Have faith, be courageous, and strong, the future is yours to build. Your beloved ma.*" Ma wanted us all to live our lives; she made us all strong, including you.'

She walked out of the room and bumped into her grandma.

'Don't worry, Ellen, your ma would be proud of you. Give him time and your pa will get over it. He knows deep down it's the right thing to do, it's just his pride that's all.'

Tears rolled down Ellen's cheeks. She threw her arms around her grandma's small frame. 'Thank you.'

* * *

Ellen gripped her umbrella tight as the wind and rain lashed against it. She marched along Charing Cross Road, weaving between people rushing about their business. The aroma of coffee mingled with the smell of fresh bread as she walked past people and stalls.

An old lady stepped out in front of her, thrusting some dried flowers near Ellen's face. 'They'll bring yer luck, lovey.'

'No, thank you.' Ellen stepped around the woman as she glanced up at the clock outside the watchmaker's shop, which told her it was quarter to nine. Cars chugged along, mixing the rain and the snow into a grey slush, which left ripples in the road.

It wasn't long before the Foyles Bookshop sign came into view. Ellen felt sick with nerves as she read the large black and white sign; she couldn't believe she'd gone against her father's wishes. He hadn't spoken to her for nearly two days, not since their talk about their situation. She couldn't pretend to understand him and was glad to be out of the house. He had eaten his meals with all of them but had only spoken to her sister and grandma. Ellen stopped for a moment and took a breath as she looked at the shop window. She stepped towards the moveable rack of books that had been placed under the shop's awning. Her gaze travelled along the spines, reading their titles. A faint smile played on her lips; how lucky she was to be working in a shop that she loved.

Miss Appleton stepped under the awning and shivered as the cold air cut through her white blouse. 'You can come in out of this awful weather, you know.' She smiled at Ellen's anxious features. 'We don't bite, and it's too cold and wet to stand outside for too long.'

Ellen giggled. 'I know, I'm just feeling a little nervous.'

Victoria reached out and threaded her hand through Ellen's

arm. 'Well, there's no need to be, we are all friends here and if you get lost in the shop you won't be the first or the last.' She chuckled. 'Folklore has it that a man spent the night in here because he got locked in – apparently, he couldn't find his way out. I don't know if that's true or not, but everyone talks about it because there are so many little corners where you can sit with a book, and of course they are everywhere.'

Ellen shook her head. 'I can't believe that. Mind you, this shop does hold a lot of books. My ma used to bring us in here most days, and we'd sit in a corner reading so it's a place I'd be happy to be stuck in overnight. Think of all the books you could read.'

Victoria threw back her head in laughter. 'Let alone the newspapers customers leave behind. You're going to fit in very well here.' She smiled at Ellen. 'Come on, it's freezing and I'm getting wet. Let's get your coat hung up and get you clocked in, otherwise you won't get paid.'

Mr Leadbetter walked towards them as they stepped inside the shop. 'Ahh, good morning, it's good to see you Miss Beckford. I hope you enjoy your time with us.'

Ellen could feel the heat rising up her neck. 'Good morning, Mr Leadbetter, I'm sure I will. I appreciate you taking a chance on me and promise to work hard for you.'

Mr Leadbetter smiled. 'You are in very capable hands with Miss Appleton but please do not be afraid to ask any questions you may have.' He scanned the shop before nodding and walking towards a customer who had a look of confusion about her.

Victoria took Ellen to the rear of the shop and watched her clock in after taking her coat off, noting she was suitably dressed in a black skirt and white blouse. 'I think we'll start you off gently, which means grabbing a rag and dusting the books and the shelves. I've seen you in the shop on a number of occasions so forgive me if I'm telling you things you already know, but the books on the shelves are placed in publisher order and those details can be found either on the back of the book or just inside. Mind you, I would like to change how they are placed on the shelves but changes like that take time. If you come across any queries, please just ask.'

Ellen nodded; she was eager to get started.

'One more thing, if you want to stop for a break at around half past twelve then come in and clock off. Molly and I will be here so you can let me know how you are getting on.'

Ellen frowned. 'Molly?'

Victoria grinned. 'Molly has been here for a long time but now works in the children's section and they love her.'

Ellen laughed. 'Is that the blonde lady I've sometimes seen avoiding Mr Leadbetter?' She lowered her eyelashes. 'Sorry, it's none of my business and it was just an observation from a nosey customer.'

Victoria chuckled. 'No, you have it about right, except she is a hard worker, but she always used to be up to mischief, or be in the wrong place, and Mr Leadbetter almost always caught her, but as I said she's a hard worker and she has a heart of gold.' She pulled open the door of a small cupboard and passed Ellen a rag. 'I hope you get on all right; I think you'll fit in very well, and I'll see you at your break.'

Ellen smiled as she took the rag and almost bounced out of the staff area and into the shop. She worked her way along the nearest bookshelf that was at arm's reach, making a mental note of where she started and the next couple of hours flew by.

'I've been sent to find you.'

Startled, Ellen turned round and stared at a young blonde woman wearing the standard calf-length black skirt and white blouse.

'I'm sorry I didn't mean to make you jump. I'm Molly.'

Ellen shook her head. 'There's no need to be sorry, I'm afraid I was in a world of my own.' She smiled. 'I expect you already know but I'm Ellen.'

'Hello, Ellen, I'm here to make sure you take a break.'

Ellen nodded. 'I've lost all track of time.'

'Excuse me.'

Ellen looked up at a tall, thin, dark-haired man. His hair was shiny and plastered to his head.

Molly turned round to face him. 'Yes, sir, can I help you?'

The man cleared his throat. 'I'm after an information book about London, and maybe other British cities, but there are too many books here for me to know where to start.'

Molly nodded before smiling at the man. 'I'm sure we will have something that will be what you are looking for. Follow me.' She paused. 'Do you mind if I ask where your accent is from? I know I'm being cheeky but it's not very often we hear an accent that isn't from London; yours sounds like it could be from the North or Midlands.' She laughed. 'I'm sorry, I sound like I know what I'm talking about, and I certainly don't.'

The man laughed. 'You're right, my accent gives me away every time, I'm from the Midlands.'

Molly stopped at a tall rack of bookshelves. 'Ahh, I'm better at it than I realised.' Reaching up, she pulled down a couple of books. 'These might help but please feel free to take your time with them and don't forget once you've finished with them you can bring them back and get tuppence return on them.'

The tall man nodded. 'Thank you, I will.' He paused as she moved to walk away. 'Sorry, are they all thruppence?'

Molly smiled. 'Of course.'

* * *

Ellen stared at her father, who didn't look at her. She folded her arms across her body while her glance travelled between her gran and her sister. She shook her head and took a couple of short breaths. 'I loved being around so many books all day and the staff at Foyles seem lovely. I'm going to love working there.' She fidgeted in her chair as she watched her sister painstakingly threading the dark wool around a pair of knitting needles.

Mary smiled, only taking her eyes off her knitting needles for a second. 'That's good, but let's face it, who wouldn't like being surrounded by books all day?' She bit her lip as she stared down at the soft dark wool and her crossed needles.

Phyllis beamed. 'I don't think there was any danger of you not enjoying working in Foyles; it's like a second home to you.'

Ellen quickly nodded and forced a smile before her gaze darted to her father, but there was no reaction. She frowned and glanced back at her sister. 'I'm sorry, I have to ask, what are you knitting and why the sudden interest in it?'

'Grandma was telling me about the socks and gloves she and some of the neighbours have been knitting for soldiers on the front line. I told her I would like to learn so she gave me a quick lesson and a pattern.' She laughed. 'But it seemed like a good idea to try to knit a square first. Grandma made it look so easy and she was so quick, her needles make that clicking noise, but I don't think there's much chance of that happening here.'

Grandma chuckled as her knitting needles clicked away. 'You'll get quicker the more you knit so don't give up.'

Ellen smiled. 'I'm impressed you're even trying. I've never knitted anything but it's fascinating to watch you do it. Keep going, I'm sure you'll soon manage to knit those socks.'

The door knocker thudded three times. Startled, Ellen glanced at the clock on the mantlepiece. 'It's eight o'clock. Who knocks on people's doors at this time of night? Are you expecting someone, Pa?'

Harold had also glanced at the clock. 'No, when do I ever have visitors? Especially at night.'

The knocker thudded down again. Ellen sighed and pulled herself out of the chair. 'Whoever it is, they're impatient.'

Mary put her knitting on the side table and lifted herself out of the armchair. 'I'll come with you; you know, just in case...'

Ellen smoothed down her apron and marched out of the front room and into the hall with Mary close behind her. She took a breath and pulled the door ajar and peered round the small opening. The chill of the evening air hit her face. She smiled at the sight of the two Port of London Authority police officers before pulling the door wider. 'Lovely to see you both have you come to see my father?'

'Good evening, Ellen, er Miss Beckford, I hope you are well.' The constable looked down at his highly polished shoes. 'I'm afraid this isn't a social visit; we have come to speak to Mr Beckford.'

Ellen frowned. 'That sounds very formal.' She hesitated for a moment. 'You had better come in.' She stepped aside and allowed them in, catching a whiff of a woody scent. 'I'll take you to him.'

Mary followed them into the front room. 'Shall I put the kettle on?'

The constable turned to her. 'No, thank you, that won't be necessary. Hopefully we won't take up too much of your time.'

Harold smiled as they walked into the room. 'Hello, fellas, have you come to see how I'm doing?'

The older man looked a little embarrassed as he pulled a notebook and pencil from his pocket. 'Obviously we hope you are doing well, Harold, and your leg is healing, but that's not why we're here.'

Harold screwed up his eyes as he stared at them. 'If it's not a social visit, I take it something has happened?'

'We're not at liberty to say at the moment but we need to talk to you about the break-in at your office.'

Harold scowled. 'Which break-in?'

The constable studied him for a moment before scribbling in his pad. 'You mean there's been more than one?'

Phyllis winked. 'They're on the ball, ain't they?'

Harold stared at his mother-in-law for a moment before turning back to the officers. 'You don't know? The first time I couldn't find anything missing but my office was ransacked. The second time I chased the villain and broke my leg. I think he took photographs because I saw a light flash.'

'I'm sorry, I'd forgotten about the first one because nothing had been taken. We're obviously here about the second one.' The constable paused. 'Are you sure about the flash of light?'

'To be honest, I wasn't at first. I was looking out to the river and saw it from the corner of my eye, but as I walked towards my office the light flashed again. I tried to scare him into coming out, but he threw himself at me and knocked me flying. I couldn't see him. I gave chase but he swung his bag at me. That was when I fell, and my foot got caught up in the chains and ropes – that's how I broke my leg. But he laid into me even when I was on the ground. He gave me a kicking.' Harold paused. 'I stretched out my arm and managed to find a piece of pipe or something and I hit him a couple of times. Then he ran off.'

The constable nodded but didn't look up from his notebook as he made notes of their conversation. 'Did you get a look at him?'

Harold shook his head. 'You can rest assured if I did, you'd have been the first to know.' He looked down at his leg. 'I think he was taller than me, although that's only a guess because I was never standing next to him; he was wearing a big coat, but I think he was quite thin.'

'That could be helpful.' The sergeant hesitated. 'Have you been to the docks since that night?'

Harold screwed up his face. 'Do I look like I've been back? I can hardly walk with this thing on.'

'I'm sorry, but we have to ask, and we are aware you could use crutches, or walking sticks, to assist you.' The sergeant pulled back his shoulders and took a breath. 'We know from our records that your daughter often comes to the docks; why is that and has she been back since you broke your leg?'

Ellen frowned as her gaze moved between her father and the police officers. 'Why are you asking him that question? My father hasn't been outside the house to know where I've been, and what's more I've always told the men on the gate why I'm there.'

The sergeant stared at Ellen. 'So, are you saying you have been back to the docks?'

Ellen shook her head. 'No, I'm pointing out how pointless your question was to a man who can't leave the house, and if you've checked your records, you'll know I haven't been to the docks, so I don't know why you're even asking that question.'

Phyllis rested her knitting on her lap. Her eyes held a steel-like quality. 'You might think it's all right to treat my granddaughter as a second-class woman, but she is an intelligent girl, so if you need to know anything ask her direct – she's quite capable of answering your questions.'

Harold held up his hand to his mother-in-law before looking at the police. 'I'm not sure I like your questions, just tell me what this is about?'

The sergeant glanced between father and daughter. 'You seem reluctant to answer the question, so let me ask it again, has your daughter been to the docks since your accident?'

Colour rose in Harold's face. 'My daughter has not been to the docks since my accident, she has had no need to go.'

Ellen watched the colour deepen in her father's face. 'As you are both aware I only ever came to the docks to deliver my father's sandwiches, and I was never there for more than a few minutes.'

'It only takes a few minutes to hand over information, and I understand you've been working on the tea table at Victoria station, which is a busy station so it would be an easy place to pass on information unnoticed.'

Harold's eyes narrowed. He glanced across at Ellen before giving the officers a scathing look. 'So, let me get this right, my daughter is giving her time to help the injured soldiers on their return so that adds to the evidence that she's a spy? I've never heard anything so ridiculous. Have you asked the gate security? They should be logging everyone that comes and goes.'

The sergeant lifted his chin. 'We have.'

Harold shook his head. 'So, you're testing our honesty? My goodness, I've worked there for years without any issues but I'm certainly seeing another side of it now.'

The constable stopped writing in his notepad and peered across at Harold. 'It's not personal, Harold, you must understand we're just doing our jobs.'

'Then why do I feel like a criminal?'

The sergeant held up his hand to silence Harold. 'You must understand you were cautioned by the police at several peace rallies, and you've not hidden the fact you're anti-war.'

Harold shook his head. 'Other than that, I have never been in trouble with the police. I thought this was a country of free speech.'

The sergeant took a large envelope from inside his uniform jacket. He opened it and watched Harold as he pulled out some papers. 'We found a roll of film and a detailed map near where you broke your leg; we've had the film developed.' He placed a wad of photographs and a drawing mapping out the docks on the side table. 'Have you seen any of this before?'

Ellen stepped nearer, picking them up one at a time to study them. 'They look like they are all places in London, at least I think they are.' She held a few of the photographs in her hand, her gaze moving between them.

Harold studied them and the map. 'No, I haven't seen them before, but I recognise some of the London bridges, train stations and the obvious buildings like the Houses of Parliament.'

They were both watching Harold as he spoke. The constable sighed. 'You know they are more than just photographs of various places in London.'

Harold momentarily looked up. 'Of course, but so do you.'

The sergeant nodded. 'Can you spell it out to us what they are photographs of?'

Harold frowned before shaking his head. He leant forward and picked up a couple of them. 'This is a picture of a timetable of the ships that are due in port and what they are carrying, although some of these won't be coming in on the time it says here; things can change for a variety of reasons.' He glanced down at a couple more photographs. 'This is the entrance to the port itself, along with the security gate.'

The sergeant took the photographs from Harold and handed him three more. 'What about these?'

Harold studied them for a moment. 'These are not such good quality; he was either in a hurry or he has a rubbish camera.' He tilted the photographs towards the light. 'It's hard to say for certain but it looks like these are more of the same, but no one would be able to get any information from them the quality is too poor.'

The sergeant handed Harold the map. 'What do you make of this?'

The paper rustled as Harold opened it and laid it flat on his lap. He smoothed out the folds as he studied it. Taking in the detail that had been drawn on it, he looked up and eyed the two men in front of him. 'What do *you* make of it?'

The sergeant's mouth lifted at the corner. 'It looks to us like it might have been part of a briefing pack.'

Harold glanced down at the map again. 'I agree. Those scrawled circles could mean the person had other targets as well.' He lifted it up for a closer look. 'It looks like my office has one drawn round it so I would say all those areas of the docks were targets, whether that be for bombs or paperwork I have no idea, that's your job to work out.'

The sergeant nodded. 'So, do you think these other photographs are of targets as well?'

Harold's lips tightened as he dropped the map back on to his lap. 'How should I know? Obviously they could be, but they could easily be from someone who likes to take photographs of London.'

'You seem to know a lot about cameras and photographs.' The sergeant stepped forward to study three framed photographs on the wall. 'These are of the docks as well, aren't they?'

Harold followed his gaze. 'Yes, they were taken several years ago.'

The sergeant turned to look at him. 'By you?'

Harold closed his eyes. 'Yes.'

Ellen licked her dry lips and gave the officers a sideways glance. Her hands were shaking. She was tempted to hide a couple of the police photographs in her apron pocket, but she gave them to her father. Her body ached with tension. She glanced around uneasily and turned to sit back down. She didn't like the way this was going.

The constable turned to Harold. 'Do you still have the keys to your office?'

Harold took a deep breath. 'Why do I feel like I'm being accused of something? Here I am, injured at home, with no pay might I add, because someone broke into my office, and you come into my home asking questions as though I have done something wrong when all I did was give chase.'

There was a loud explosion that filled the air around them. Everyone fell to the floor.

Frowning, the constable climbed to his feet and fidgeted from one foot to the other. 'We need to go.' The constable picked up the photographs, while eyeing Harold. 'The Germans are probably on their way; you need to get to a shelter.' He turned to walk towards the hall but suddenly stopped mid-stride. 'I'm sorry but this is important, and we wouldn't be here if it wasn't. Do you still have the keys to your office?'

Harold shook his head. 'No, Bert took them when he came to see me just after the accident.' He raised his eyebrows. 'Has it been broken into again?'

The constable closed his notebook and put it in his pocket, along with his pencil. 'As I said, sir, we're not at liberty to say but an investigation is going on and you will not be allowed to return to work until it's completed.' He turned to Ellen. 'Miss Beckford, you are also advised to stay away from the docks.'

Ellen's palms felt damp. She frowned. 'I have no reason to go there if my father isn't working. Now if you don't mind, I'd like to get us all into the basement.' She stood up and smoothed down her apron. 'If you've finished, I'll show you out, and please be careful.'

The constable nodded. 'Thank you for your time, Mr Beckford, Miss Beckford.'

Mary followed them out into the hall. 'Good night, officers, be quick to take shelter, even if it's only in the Underground stations.'

The door key clattered against the front door as Ellen pulled it ajar and stepped aside. 'Good night.'

The officers spoke in unison. 'Good night.'

The door thudded as she pushed it shut again. 'Mary, I've got to find out what's going on. It doesn't look good for Pa.'

Tears rolled down Mary's cheeks. 'He won't end up going to prison, will he?' she sobbed. 'They shoot spies, don't they?'

Ellen wrapped her arms around her sister and hugged her tight. 'That's not going to happen because Pa didn't do anything.'

Mary pulled back a little. 'So why did they ask all those questions?'

Ellen's lips tightened. 'I don't know, their questions worry me too. Come on, we've got to get everyone down in the basement.'

7

Ellen stood near the entrance of the docks, thankful it was nearly the end of February and spring was just around the corner and the evenings would then turn a little warmer. She looked up at the clear sky, which may well mean a frost could happen later, and of course the Germans liked a clear sky to drop their bombs. Ellen knew she didn't have long.

She breathed in the smell of the river as the sound of chains rattled against the metal posts in the breeze and men's voices shouting instructions to each other carried in the air. The familiarity of it all wrapped itself around her, giving her comfort. Was she foolhardy to come here after the police had been to her home last night? Would they think she was up to no good and just convince them even more that she and her father had something to do with the break-in. Ellen had tossed and turned most of the night thinking about what the police had said. The more she thought about it the more certain she was they were accusing them of spying. Her father would be angry if he knew where she was.

Ellen wrapped her arms around her waist, the softness of her coat giving her little comfort. She didn't know what she was doing there, or what there was to find out but she had felt compelled to come along. Her fingers gripped the woollen material of her coat as she looked over at the security gate. Sam was in the hut reading his newspaper with his hand wrapped around a mug. He had known her since she was a small child so she might stand a chance of getting some information from him, but she would have to be careful.

Ellen took a step forward. Was this really the right thing to do? What if one of the policemen from last night came along? She could end up in prison. She couldn't worry about that. After all, she might end up there anyway. No, she wasn't going to give up without a fight. Ellen took a deep breath and purposefully stepped forward. 'Good evening, Sam, it's lovely to see you again.' Ellen waved as she got nearer.

Sam looked up and smiled, his newspaper rustling as he closed it before folding it in half. 'Hello, young lady, this is a pleasant surprise. How's your father doing?'

Ellen forced herself to smile. 'He's not doing too bad. Obviously he's itching to get back to work, but as you're probably aware, he's not allowed to until his leg has healed and the investigation is completed.'

Sam stood upright. 'Yeah, I've heard something like that.'

Ellen shook her head. 'Do you think they believe my father had something to do with the break-in?'

Sam shrugged. 'I'm not privy to any of that information, and we've been told not to discuss it with anyone. I think they're worried it will get in the papers, but I can't seriously think your father had anything to do with it. I mean, why would he break into his own office? It's all nonsense if you ask me.'

Ellen tightened her lips. 'The police came to our house last night to talk to me and my father, and I can't shake the feeling that they think one of us had something to do with it.'

Sam wrinkled his nose. 'Surely that can't be true. I heard they didn't have much to go on but that's ridiculous. They were looking for evidence where your father got hurt, but I was told all they found was a small piece of brown woollen material attached to one of the chains, which they think could come from a coat or something. They also know about the camera, and that's only because your father said something about flashing lights, and they found a spool of film and a map on the ground where Harold broke his leg, but they don't know how they got there.'

Ellen nodded. 'That's true about the camera; they showed us the photographs last night, but they didn't mention about the piece of material.'

Sam picked up his mug of tea and took a sip. 'I don't think Harold's got anything to worry about; it's just them doing their job and trying to gather all the facts together.'

Ellen sighed. 'I hope you're right. It's a worrying time for us and it's a struggle without Pa's wages.'

Sam put down his cup and studied her for a moment. 'I'm sure it must be because everything is getting so expensive, but I promise to keep my ear to the ground and if I hear anything I'll let you know. I have to be careful, I don't want to lose my job, but your father's a good man and doesn't deserve to have this hanging over him.'

Ellen gave a faint smile. 'Thank you, I'd really appreciate that.'

Sam let out a sigh. 'You do know I can't let you on the docks, don't you? Security was tight before the break-ins but now we are all being watched so even if your pa was here, I wouldn't be able to let you in.'

'I know. I'm not sure why I came here. Pa would be quite angry if he knew.'

Sam laughed. 'I'm sure he would but I won't tell him so your secret's safe with me.'

'Thank you.' Ellen shrugged. 'I just want to do something, but I don't know what I can do to help.'

Sam shook his head. 'It's probably best to let the police do what they've got to do. When you know the outcome, see where you are at; there may not be anything to fight.' He smiled. 'Try and trust the system. I know your father has made no secret of what he thinks of the war but that aside, your father is a good bloke.'

Ellen's lips tightened and she shrugged again. 'I know, but I'm frightened that will all get lost in what's going on.'

Sam shook his head. 'I'm sure he'll be fine. We all miss Harold, hopefully he's a quick healer so he can soon get back to work.'

Ellen nodded. 'I had better get home before he realises I'm late. Thanks for talking to me about it.'

Sam nodded. 'Just take care of yourselves.'

Ellen turned to walk away, when she heard a voice call out. Her head dropped. She took a deep breath. Instinct told her she'd been caught.

'Wait, what are you doing here?'

Ellen glanced over her shoulder, her heart racing when she saw one of the police officers that had been in her home the previous evening. She pulled herself upright and pushed back her shoulders before turning to face him.

* * *

Ellen sat in the break room in Foyles listening to the women chattering around her. Her fish paste sandwich sat on the table unwrapped. She closed her eyes and rubbed the back of her neck. It had been a bad idea to go to the docks yesterday. The police had interviewed her for over an hour before they'd let her go. Her father was furious with her when they brought her home. They made it clear they hadn't believed her explanation of why she was there.

Victoria came over and placed her own greaseproof paper-wrapped sandwich on the table next to Ellen. 'Are you all right? You seem awfully quiet today.'

Ellen breathed in Victoria's floral perfume. 'Everything's good, I'm just tired.'

Victoria studied her troubled expression. 'If there's anything I can do, or if there's a problem, please talk to me.'

As Victoria spoke, Molly also came in to join them for lunch. 'You would think people would be sick of buying books wouldn't you, but I haven't stopped upstairs.'

'At least it keeps you in a job.' Victoria laughed. She nodded towards Ellen who was still gazing down at the table.

Molly had known Victoria for a long time and was used to her not hiding her worries, forgetting that others could see her concern signals. She began unwrapping her sandwiches. 'You're quiet today, Ellen. You're not fed up working with us already, are you?'

Victoria suddenly wondered how far Molly would go – she had forgotten she could be a loose cannon at times.

Ellen's eyes snapped open. 'Oh no, definitely not, I love my job here. Everyone has been so friendly, working here has been everything I thought it would be.' She took a breath. 'While I've been dusting the shelves, I've also been learning some of the publishers' names, so I'll know where to find the books when I'm asked.'

Victoria smiled. 'That's good because you've settled in well.'

Molly studied Ellen for a moment. 'So, what's the problem

then? You know we've all had our share of problems here and if nothing else we've all learnt that it's good to share and maybe get help if you need it. Of course, you may not need help and that's fine but sometimes it's good to just talk about these things.'

Ellen's gaze travelled between the two girls as she wondered if she should confide in them. Neither she nor her father had done anything wrong, but would they understand that? Her lips tightened for a moment. 'I'm sorry, I didn't mean to cause you both to worry; it's just tiredness.' She began unwrapping her sandwich. 'I've had a couple of sleepless nights.'

Victoria's brows drew together. 'Have you heard something that's bothering you? If you have, we can always ask Alice to speak to Freddie; he's a police sergeant so he might be able to offer some help or comfort.'

Molly watched Ellen twist her fingers around her necklace. Molly lowered her voice. 'Ellen, you can trust us, we won't repeat anything you tell us.'

Ellen's gaze moved from Molly to Victoria before sighing. 'You know my father is off work with a broken leg because he chased after someone who had broken into his office in the docks?' She looked up at the girls who were nodding as she spoke. 'I'm concerned, because we had a visit from the Port of London Authority Police, and I think they are of the opinion that my father has something to do with it, or that I do.' Her voice got higher and squeakier the more she spoke. 'I don't understand why they would think that when my father was the one who got injured.' She twisted her fingers together. 'The thing is, I've made matters worse by going to the docks. I don't really know why I went but I needed to do something. It was a waste of time and I got caught by one of the policemen that came to the house, and he didn't believe anything I said. I've been pretty stupid.'

Victoria looked worried as she saw tears in Ellen's eyes. 'They would have to prove your father's involvement; I expect they were just collecting their facts together.'

Ellen scowled. 'It sounded scary, and my father wouldn't have anything to do with something like that. He's always made it clear he was against the war, but he wouldn't do anything to put his family or his country at risk.'

Molly nodded. 'There's a lot of people that think like that, especially as it's gone on for so long, so I don't think that's a basis to accuse people.'

Ellen nodded. 'I know you're right, but I haven't got any evidence to prove he wasn't involved, and you can't just take on the police.' She shook her head. 'I'm sorry, I'm letting my imagination run away with me. I'm sure it's something and nothing and it will all sort itself out in the end.'

Victoria pursed her lips. 'How can you find evidence that someone didn't do something?'

Molly shook her head. 'Unless they were elsewhere you can't so you have to try and prove someone else could have done it.'

Ellen stared down at her sandwich, feeling sick to the stomach. 'Of course you are right, but I don't stand a chance of finding out who did it, particularly if the police can't.'

Victoria reached out and squeezed Ellen's hand. 'We will help you where we can, won't we, Molly?'

Molly raised her eyebrows. 'Of course, although if I'm honest I don't know how we can help.'

Ellen gave them a weak smile. 'That's very kind of you both but you are right, Molly, I don't know how you can help.'

Victoria shook her head. 'I'm not having any of this; if nothing else we can support and advise you.' She paused and looked at both the girls. 'Look, when I was clearing my parents' room I came across some things, you know, paperwork, photographs and money; it was all secreted away. If it hadn't been for Alice and Molly, who knows how far I would have got with finding things out about my family.'

Molly chuckled. 'The difference is you had lots of information, but we didn't know what it all meant, and you weren't being accused of spying.'

Victoria tightened her lips as she glared at Molly. 'That's true.'

Molly studied Ellen. 'Ellen doesn't have anything and for all we know her father *could* be a spy; we need to be careful otherwise we might be accused as well.'

'Molly, I love you dearly but sometimes I wish you would think before you speak.'

Molly shook her head. 'What? I'm sorry, Ellen, but I'm just saying we don't know your father that's all.'

Victoria turned to Ellen. 'Look, why don't you start by talking to your father, see if he can remember any small details that he may have forgotten when he spoke to the police.'

Molly's eyes sparkled. 'Now that's a good idea, and write everything down, although you'll need more than that to prove he isn't a spy.'

Ellen listened to Molly; it was clear she didn't think they should get involved but she didn't want to dwell on that. 'I can do that. At least that will give me something to concentrate on and who knows where that will lead to.'

Victoria beamed. 'Now, eat your sandwich. We've got to get back to work or Mr Leadbetter will be sacking all three of us.'

Ellen picked up her sandwich and took a bite; the bread stuck to the roof of her dry mouth. Molly's words whirled around her head. Would everyone think like Molly? Even if she could prove her father wasn't a spy, would they think there was no smoke without fire?

Molly peered over at Victoria. 'How're things going with Ted and your neighbours gossiping?'

Victoria stared down at her sandwich and frowned. 'It's early days. It's going to take a while for Ted to settle in.'

Molly tilted her head slightly. 'And your neighbours?'

Victoria chuckled. 'I'm not concerned with what the neighbours think.'

Ellen listened to the girls. They were strong in their belief in what they thought was right and that was what she needed to be.

Molly giggled. 'Have you told them you're married?'

Victoria shook her head. 'No, definitely not. I'm not going to lie.'

Molly glanced at Ellen before raising her eyebrows. 'So have you set the date yet?'

Victoria kept her gaze fixed on her sandwich. 'No, but we will, there's no rush.'

Molly eyed her friend. 'Of course not; it's important you take the plunge when it's right for you both.'

* * *

Ellen clenched and unclenched her hands. She took a deep breath and pulled the string through the letter box before the front door key clattered through it. She fiddled with it for a second before inserting it in the lock and letting herself in. She forced a smile and took a deep breath before calling out, 'It's only me.'

Mary was beaming when she came rushing into the hallway. 'That's good timing; I've just set the table and helped Pa into the kitchen.'

Ellen took a deep breath, taking in the smell of the beeswax polish. Her heart was pounding, and heat seemed to burn through her body. Unbuttoning her black coat, she took it off and placed it on the hook in the hall. She pushed her shoulders back. 'That is good timing.'

'You know I'll be glad when the plaster is off Pa's leg; he can't stand or walk and he's getting more miserable every day.' Mary frowned, before turning and heading back to the kitchen. Her slippers scuffed and slid along the floor. Ellen could hear her mother saying, '*Pick your feet up.*'

'Hopefully he'll learn to manage. It's only been a couple of weeks. They said it could be on his leg for nearly two months.' Ellen followed her; the small heels of her black shoes clipped against the tiles as she went. 'Hello, Pa, how are you feeling? Are you in pain?'

Harold didn't look up. 'I'm fine. Don't you go worrying yourself about me.'

Mary took the casserole dish from the oven and placed it in the centre of the table. She removed the lid with a flourish. 'It smells delicious. Ellen, would you like to dish up?'

Ellen smiled. 'You can do it.'

As they ate, Ellen's gaze darted around the kitchen table. Mary was eating the meal with great relish. Ellen watched her father tuck into the sausage casserole she had quickly thrown together that morning. She was waiting for him to complain there were more vegetables than sausages in the dish. He wouldn't be wrong. Perhaps he wouldn't say anything because it would mean talking to her. 'How has your day been, Grandma?'

Phyllis chuckled. 'Well, I've had a very busy day for me.' She winked at Ellen and Mary. 'Let's see, I've sat at this table and peeled potatoes, I dusted the front room while Mary did upstairs, and then I sat down and did some knitting.'

Ellen smiled. 'Oh my, you really have been busy.'

'So, Ellen, how is it going at Foyles, are you still enjoying it?'

Mary crushed some potato under her fork, soaking up the gravy as she did so.

'I'm really enjoying it. The people are very friendly, and I love being surrounded by all those books.'

Mary glanced at a father. 'That's good isn't it, Pa, because we're managing just fine.' She looked back at Ellen. 'I'm not as good as you around the house but I'm not doing too bad, especially with Grandma's help.'

Ellen smiled. 'I'm sure you are, Mary, and I for one am very grateful for all that you and Grandma are doing. I know I'm not earning much but that's because I'm not working full time. I'm going to look for other work to make up the money.' She saw her father wince, but he still said nothing. She lifted her head further and jutted out her chin. 'What do you think, Pa? Any suggestions?'

Harold stopped eating. He held his fork in mid-air for a moment before carrying on as if she hadn't spoken.

'Pa, you can't keep ignoring me.' Ellen felt the frustration rising within her. She tapped her fingers against the side of her skirt. 'You haven't spoken to me properly since we argued and yet you expect me to keep looking after you, cooking your food and making your bed. I'm part of this family and I'm doing the best I can. I know it's not as good as you can do but I'm not putting up with you ignoring me when I'm trying so hard.'

There was a long silence. The air was tense.

Ellen knew she had spoken out of turn; she placed her knife and fork on the edge of her plate. 'Look, Pa, I just want your support, that's all. Is that so wrong?' She leant back in her chair, the wooden spindles pressing hard into her back. 'None of this is easy for any of us, and I know you're struggling with not going to work and providing for your family, but you can provide in other ways.' She looked across at Mary, who had panic written all over her face. Ellen turned her attention back to her father. 'You can provide us with support, even if that's only learning how to peel potatoes.' Ellen chuckled before realising no one else was even smiling. 'Look, Pa, I'm not saying you have to learn to do anything, but you could provide words of encouragement. I accept it's difficult for you but it's difficult for me too. I'm getting to see what you go through every day with trying to earn enough money and look after your family. It's made me realise a lot of things that I took for granted.'

Still Harold remained silent.

Mary's head was bent down as she seemed intent on studying the food on her plate.

Ellen sighed and picked up her knife and fork again.

Phyllis studied Harold; her face was set with tension. 'Come on, Harold, or I'll kick you under the table, and then you'll have your other leg in plaster.' She took a breath. 'Thanks to this blooming war we could all die tomorrow; do you want to survive knowing you didn't speak to your daughter? Stop sulking. Ellen's right. We have to eat and keep a roof over our heads and until you can go back to work your daughter is doing the best she can.'

Harold was silent for a moment before clearing his throat. 'I just worry, that's all.'

Ellen placed her knife back on her plate and reached out to cover his hand with hers. 'I know, Pa, and I know it's only because you love us, but you must understand we love you too. When you were at the docks at night, do you not think we worried you wouldn't come home again?' She paused. 'The bombs always drop under the cover of darkness when you're at work and the docks must be a target for them.'

Harold nodded. 'I suppose I've never thought about it; it was just a job I had to do.'

Ellen tightened her lips for a moment. 'And this is a job I have to do but I want to do it with your support and love. I'll always be home at night so you don't have to worry about any bombing, and I promise I will take care while I'm out and about.'

Harold looked up at his eldest daughter. 'I know you will; you're a good girl and your mother would be proud of both of you.'

Ellen felt the tears pricking at her eyes.

8

Ellen frowned as she tossed her problem around her head. She didn't know how she was going to earn more money and keep her father happy. She wished she had someone to talk to. For the umpteenth time she wished her ma was here to offer her some kind words. Her father ignoring her had put a strain on everyone at home, but thankfully her gran had stepped in the previous evening and they had come through it.

The chill in the air made it a brisk day with the grey clouds making it feel heavy and dull. She crossed the Seven Dials round-about and turned the corner into Little Earl Street. The March cold wind cut through her, taking her breath away, so much for the spring weather. The rain had spiked down earlier, turning the once white snow to a grey slush.

Ellen stood rigid for a moment, pulling her scarf up over her mouth, trying to catch her breath. A couple of dogs barked like they were talking to each other. Paper blew down the footpath towards her, wrapping itself around her ankle boot. She shook it off, wishing she could shake off her problem just as easily. Ellen already loved her job at Foyles Bookshop, and had no desire to give it up, but only working a few days a week would not cover the rent let alone anything else. Sighing, she wondered how she was going to earn more money. Maybe she'd have to look further afield, perhaps even consider going to the munitions factory in Woolwich. Her lips tightened; her father definitely wouldn't like her becoming one of the canary girls making ammunition.

Ellen had always thought there was lots of work available but that no longer seemed to be the case. She had tried on several occasions on her way home from Foyles, stopping at numerous shops, but they had no vacancies. She shook her head. The trouble was, she needed to get work that pleased her father, which meant no factory work, but she knew he wouldn't be happy whatever work she got.

Today, Ellen stopped at the craft shop window and saw the job vacancy sign was still there. She took a deep breath before stepping forward and turning the handle to go inside. A bell sounded above the entrance; its chimes rang again when she closed the door. An elderly lady was standing behind the counter, sorting through reels of thread. 'Good morning, can I help you?'

Ellen smiled. 'I hope so. I've come about the position you've got advertised in the window.'

'Oh, my dear, I am so sorry, I'm afraid the position has been filled.' The lady tilted her head to one side. 'It's a shame because it only went yesterday.'

Ellen nodded. 'I understand, I just thought I'd ask.'

The lady walked around the counter to the window, pulling her knitted blue cardigan around her ample body. 'I best take it down before someone else gets disappointed.' She turned and looked at Ellen. 'I'm so sorry, I should've removed it as soon as the job was filled.'

'Not to worry. I saw it in the window a few days ago and I should've asked then.' Ellen walked towards the door and twisted the handle. 'I hope you have a good day, thank you for your time.' The bell chimed again as she pulled open the door. She took a couple of steps through the doorway and the bell rang again as the door closed behind her. Ellen sighed; she had no idea what to do next except keep looking. Maybe she should ask Mr Leadbetter if she could have more hours. But Ellen didn't want to come across as pushy and lose the job she loved.

She glanced up and down the street, wondering what she was going to do. For the first time, it dawned on her that maybe this was how her father felt, the pressure of bringing home enough money to pay the bills and feed his family. Her throat tightened; was she going to be able to earn enough money and please her father at the same time?

'Get yer papers 'ere, it's only a penny, get up-to-date news of what's 'appening with the war.'

Ellen noticed it was the same lad that she'd bought the newspaper from before. It occurred to her there might be jobs advertised in the paper. She walked over to him and searched in her coat pocket for the penny he required. Pulling out the large copper coin, she handed it to him.

The lad smiled. 'Good morning, miss, it don't get any warmer, does it? 'Opefully, we'll soon get past the bitter cold. It's 'ard standing out 'ere in the freezing cold trying to sell newspapers, especially when everyone's in a 'urry to get inside where it's warm.'

Ellen took the newspaper from him and pushed it under her arm. 'I'm sure you've been freezing; sometimes the wind cuts through me and I'm wearing a heavy coat.'

The lad smiled. 'To be 'onest, yer get used to it.'

Ellen shook her head. 'I'm not sure I would ever get used to it.' She smiled at him. 'But I'm glad you're here today and hope you sell lots of papers.'

'Me too, miss. Me too.'

Ellen chuckled as she walked away. She glanced back at the boy, wondering how old he was. He was probably no more than about eleven. She had never seen him wrapped up against the cold. It was time she got more positive, just like him. She would speak to Mr Leadbetter again and see if there was any chance of getting more hours at the shop.

It wasn't long before she was walking past the butcher's. 'Hello, girl, how's yer father doing? I heard he broke his leg,' Mr Preston called.

Ellen watched him washing down his counter. 'Hello, Mr Preston, my father is doing all right. He did break his leg while he was at work and he's a little grumpy about not being able to get back to work.' She shrugged.

Mr Preston smiled. 'Us men don't make good patients.' He twisted his cloth over a bowl. 'Mary's been in a couple of times; she's grown into a fine young woman.'

Ellen smiled. 'Yes, things have had to change since my pa can't go to work.'

Mr Preston stooped down behind the counter and reappeared with a small package. 'Here, give these to the old man, it might put a smile on his face.' He laughed. 'It ain't much, it's only a few sausages.'

Ellen reached out to take them. 'That's very kind of you, I won't say no, thank you.'

Mr Preston nodded. 'Tell him I'll try and pop in and see him, but I can't say when. I find it hard to leave the shop these days.'

Ellen nodded. 'I'll let him know and thank you again for the sausages. It's freezing out here. I don't mean to be rude, but I must get home before I catch my death.'

Mr Preston waved. 'Of course, you take care now.'

Ellen waved. 'Cheerio.'

* * *

Alan tried to avoid the icy patches of snow that were gradually melting away as he hobbled into Victoria station. It wasn't long before the arches of the imposing building became visible. He hated coming to this train station. It was always so busy, but maybe that was why they used it. It was a good place to go unnoticed.

A train whistled, causing him to jerk round and see the billowing clouds of grey smoke reaching up high into the roof before disappearing altogether. He shook his head. He turned back and saw soldiers walking through the station. He no longer concerned himself about them. Alan pulled on the cuffs of his woollen gloves as he scanned the concourse and platforms. He limped slightly and winced as he weaved between the men and women milling about, trying to avoid the soldiers coming off the trains and the children running around. The tea ladies were there as usual, and everything looked as it did the last time he was there. He spied a couple of police officers standing at the end of one of the platforms. The hairs at the back of his neck stood on end. He wondered who, or what, they were waiting for. Without looking back, he marched past them, wondering if his limp made him look like a veteran of the war. After a moment he glanced over his shoulder and breathed a sigh of relief that their position hadn't changed. A train whistled and grey clouds of smoke filled the roof of the building before it escaped outside.

The grey-haired man he'd been looking for stepped out in front of him. 'You made it then.'

Alan stepped back and cleared his throat. 'I wish you wouldn't do that; it makes me jump every time.' He scraped his fingers through his hair.

The man's eyes narrowed as he stared at him. 'At least you got here on time, so things must be getting better.' He scanned the people around them. 'Was the map useful? I hope you've kept it safe; it might be needed in the future.'

Alan fidgeted from one foot to the other. 'It got lost with everything that was going on.'

'What? Let's hope for your sake it hasn't got into the wrong hands.'

Alan scowled at him. 'You have no idea what I've been through.'

The grey-haired man's tight mouth twisted in disgust. 'There are men dying every day, and yet you are still here.'

Alan snorted. 'Only by the skin of my teeth. Do you know I nearly got killed queuing at the docks? There was no warning, the bombs just started falling. I was lucky to get out of there alive.'

The man shook his head. 'From what I can gather the docks were missed so you were fine, and you're here now so it couldn't have been that bad.'

'Thanks for caring. A man helped me; it was a scary time and I've never been in that situation before.' Alan put down his bag and reached inside his pocket, his face screwed up as he pulled out a crumpled envelope. He stared at it for a moment. His hands worked slowly, trying to straighten out the creases of the thick paper before pressing it to his chest and handing it over. 'Hopefully, this will be helpful.'

The man gave him a disdainful look before taking the envelope, and without opening it, he pushed it into his inside coat pocket. He studied him for a moment. 'Is that where you got those cuts and bruises from?'

Alan shuffled from one foot to the other. 'What?'

'The docks. Was that where you got all your cuts and bruises?'

'No, I slipped on some ice and couldn't save myself; my leg is all bruised as well and it hurts when I walk, so now I'm limping like a veteran.'

The grey-haired man smiled. 'Let's hope they don't scar. After all, you only have your pretty face going for you.'

Alan shook his head. He was tired of this lack of respect when he was doing the best he could and wanted to tell him as much, but he knew it was futile. 'It wouldn't have gone down well if those bombs last night had hit Lord's Cricket Ground.'

The grey-haired man's eyes glinted. 'No, it certainly wouldn't have been cricket.'

Alan's lips tightened. 'I don't know what damage they did but I understand they dropped around Clapham Junction as well.' He bent down to pick up his bag, which burst open.

'You need to be careful; you'll end up breaking that camera and then you'll lose your livelihood and your usefulness.'

Alan gave a wry smile. 'I've got to take some photographs while I'm here for the paper.'

The man frowned. 'What sort of photographs?'

Alan shrugged. 'I don't know.' He looked around him. 'I'll take one of the tea table, maybe of a train coming in and the people getting off it.'

The man smiled. 'If you take one of the injured soldiers that could be appreciated.' He nodded, patting his coat pocket before stepping away and peering over his shoulder. 'These had better be good.' He marched into the crowd.

Alan glanced around before taking his camera out of the bag. He put the strap around his neck and removed the cover, dropping it into the bag. He felt a hand tap him on the shoulder. Startled, he spun round and came face to face with a policeman.

The policeman raised his eyebrows. 'I'm sorry, I didn't mean to make you jump.' He looked down at the camera. 'But I have to ask you why you are carrying a camera at this station?'

Alan forced a smile. 'I work for a newspaper; I have a card somewhere.' He fumbled in one pocket and then another.

The policeman frowned. 'That may be, but I'm asking what you are taking photographs of?'

Alan glanced around; his heart was pounding. 'If I'm honest I haven't decided. I thought I might take one of the tea table, maybe of a train coming in or going out.'

'And what will happen to them?'

Alan shrugged and ran his tongue over his dry lips. 'My editor is doing an article on Victoria station and my photographs are to accompany it.'

The policeman studied him for a moment. 'I'll be watching you, so be careful what you take a picture off and if I think you are up to no good you will find yourself in a different kind of station. Do I make myself clear?'

Alan took a slow breath, trying to calm his nerves. 'Of course, but I'm not here to cause trouble, just doing my job.'

The policeman nodded and stepped aside.

Alan peered over his shoulder at the grey-haired man walking away from him. He breathed a sigh of relief. The last thing he needed was a visit to the police station. That would certainly be looked down upon and take some explaining away.

* * *

Ellen sat in the front room opposite her father. As she fidgeted in her armchair, her gaze wandered between her father and Mary. Ellen closed her eyes and concentrated on the rhythmic sound of Mary's and Phyllis's knitting needles clicking together; it was almost soothing to Ellen's chaotic mind.

The knitting needles stopped. 'Are you all right, Ellen?'

Ellen's eyes snapped open. 'Of course, I'm just a little tired.'

The clicking of the needles started again.

'Wasn't it lovely of Mr Preston to give us those sausages?' Ellen paused. 'Mr Preston said to say hello.' She glanced at her father. 'He said he would try and get away from the shop and pop along to see you, but he didn't know when.'

Mary grinned. 'That's kind of him, isn't it, Pa?'

Their father stayed silent.

Ellen wiggled her pen between her fingers before tapping on the pad in front of her. 'Pa, I think we need to talk about the night you broke your leg.'

Harold screwed his eyes up as he looked at his daughter. 'Why?'

Ellen bit down on her lip. 'We have to try and protect ourselves, maybe figure out what did happen and who it was.'

Harold clenched his hands together and sucked in a breath. 'I know they think I was involved in it and got the same impression as you, but I don't see how we can find out who it was.'

Ellen studied her father for a moment. 'I don't know how either, but I can't do nothing, and I don't see how this can do any harm, so can we talk about it?'

Mary rested her knitting on her lap. Her mouth dropped open a little. 'Does... does that mean you could both go to prison? Do they think you are spies?'

Harold's eyes widened. 'Don't be ridiculous, we're not spies,' he snapped. 'We've done nothing wrong.'

Ellen reached out and squeezed her sister's arm. 'It's not going to come to that, but the trouble is we have no way of proving it.'

Phyllis looked up from her knitting. 'It won't do any harm, Harold; you have nothing to lose.'

Harold shook his head. 'It's madness. I mean, if I was a spy, I didn't need to break in to my own office.'

Ellen took a deep breath and tried to keep her voice calm. 'Of course you're right, but they might think you are working with someone, and your injury is a cover to avoid suspicion at the docks.'

Mary gasped. 'Ellen's right.'

Harold slammed his hand down on the soft arm of his chair. 'This is blooming daft. You two read too many books; no wonder you have overactive imaginations. I told your mother no good would come of it.'

Ellen forced herself to laugh. 'We have nothing to lose by talking about it.'

Harold's hands tightened until the whites of his knuckles were showing through. 'I don't see what good it will do but I suppose it won't do any harm either.'

Ellen beamed at her father. 'Thank you. I'm not sure about any of it but I can't do nothing.'

Harold nodded. 'I don't think I can tell you any more than what I told the police.'

Ellen wrote Harold's name at the top of the paper and the date before looking up at him again. 'Let's start at the beginning. Tell me what you saw.'

Harold released his hands and tapped his fingers on his legs as he appeared to stare at something behind her.

Ellen sat quietly, waiting for his first words.

'I had been out the office checking a ship's load, because there was a query with the paperwork. Anyway, on the way back I stopped and leant on the railings, next to the riverbank, and was thinking about your ma.' Harold paused before clearing his throat. 'I think the first time I was aware that someone was in my office was when I saw a flash of light. I thought I was mistaken but then it happened again.' Pausing, he took a breath. 'When it happened the second time, I went over to my office door and shouted out. I told whoever it was to come out. If I'm honest I was too frightened to go in just in case I got knocked out or worse.'

Ellen nodded as she wrote down everything her father said. 'What happened next, Pa?'

'I'm not exactly sure. The door flew open, and someone threw themselves at me and I ended up on the floor. I was winded with the pain of what had sent me flying to the ground, but I got up and shouted out again before I gave chase.'

Ellen looked up. 'Do you remember anything about what the man looked like? At least, I'm assuming it was a man.'

Harold closed his eyes. 'I'm certain it was a man. He was wearing a hat; I think it was a trilby, and a long coat. But I don't think he said anything, he just ran, and I ran after him, although I couldn't keep up.'

'You're doing well, Pa. Did you go into your office to check if anything had been taken before you raced after the man?'

Harold shook his head. 'No, I didn't.'

'Pa, I don't like to ask but did you have your keys on you?'

Harold gave a wry smile. 'Yes, I did, they were in my trouser pocket, and I know I locked the office door when I left.'

Ellen stared down her notepad as she wrote it all down. 'So, you didn't check the lock, to see if it had been broken before you ran after him?'

Again, Harold shook his head. 'No, I just started chasing him and afterwards I couldn't stand up to check anything.' He screwed up his eyes. 'What are you getting at? Do you think it was someone who works at the docks?'

Ellen shrugged. 'I don't know what I think. I'm just trying to keep an open mind.'

Harold nodded. 'That's the problem, it could be anyone, but I don't want you poking around and putting yourself in danger again. No going back to the docks, do you hear me?'

Ellen smiled. 'All right, Pa, I won't.'

The door knocker thudded several times.

Ellen frowned. 'I think we'll leave it there for tonight.' The door knocker thudded again; Ellen frowned as she glanced towards the hall. 'If you can give it more thought while I'm at work tomorrow, in case you've forgotten anything, and it doesn't matter how small the detail is, it could make all the difference.'

Harold smiled. 'Are you sure you're not going to become a police officer?'

Ellen laughed. 'Definitely not, I just don't want to miss anything that's all.'

The knocker thudded again.

Mary stood up. 'I'd better go and open the front door.'

Ellen closed her pad and placed it under her armchair. It was only then she noticed photographs under her father's armchair. Frowning, she wondered how they had got there, and why Mary hadn't moved the chair to clean under it since the police visit but she decided to say nothing for now.

Mary's voice carried into the front room. 'Hello, Mr Preston, this is a surprise. I'm sure my father will be happy to have your company this evening instead of us three women.'

9

A child's scream rang out in Foyles. Startled, Ellen moved towards the crying child, but Molly got there first. 'Are you all right, little one?'

Before she could answer, a young woman rushed over and knelt in front of the child. 'Sarah, what happened? Are you all right?' She pulled the blue woollen scarf away from her neck.

The girl sniffed and brushed away her tears. 'I slipped.'

'Were you running again? I did tell you not to run because the bottom of your shoes would be wet and slippery from the snow.'

Sarah nodded. 'I know, but I wanted to show you a book I found.'

Molly smiled. 'Would you like to show me and maybe read me a bit as well?' She glanced at the young woman. 'That's if Mum doesn't mind?'

Sarah beamed. 'That's my auntie, my ma is at home having a baby.'

The young woman blushed. 'I'm afraid that's true, and what's more, I'm not a very good aunt because I got caught up with a book I was looking at.'

Ellen smiled. 'That happens to us all.'

Molly jumped up and smoothed down her calf-length black skirt. 'Come on, Sarah, I'm quite excited to see what you've chosen. Maybe your aunt can meet us upstairs in the children's department.'

'Are you sure that's all right?'

Molly nodded. 'It'll be my pleasure. If you're not sure where it is, Ellen will show you.'

Ellen grinned. 'Of course.' She watched Molly take Sarah's hand and disappear up the steps. She turned to the young woman. 'If you need my help, I'll be around here dusting the shelves.'

'Thank you.'

Ellen moved away, weaving between the shelves and the customers.

There were customers queuing with returns to get their tuppence so they could buy more books.

Ellen scanned the shop, trying to find Mr Leadbetter. Her hands felt clammy when she thought about speaking to him about increasing her hours. Should she ask now before he got too busy, or wait until just before the shop closed? Asking him about this felt worse than when she'd asked if there were any vacancies. She knew they were still short staffed but that didn't mean he could give her more hours. She had to stop worrying and get on with the job she got paid for.

Victoria came over to Ellen as she was dusting the books. 'Ellen, I just wanted you to know that I've been very impressed with the way you work, and I saw you just now going to help that little girl.'

Ellen smiled. 'Thank you, but I must admit I don't know what I would have done if Molly hadn't got there first.'

Victoria laughed. 'That doesn't matter, you cared enough to go to her aid.' She paused. 'Anyway, I know you haven't been here very long, but you are already showing a pride in what you do and where you work. I'm going to speak to Mr Leadbetter to see if we can train you either on one of the quieter counters, or the payment kiosk. I'm guessing he won't want you doing the payments quite yet, but you could work behind one of the counters, especially once you know how to fill out the paperwork that the customers take to the payment booth, and I think you'll be able to cope with that.'

Ellen beamed. 'Oh, my goodness, you don't know how happy you've made me. I love working here and I would like to continue and if possible, have more hours.'

Victoria nodded. 'In time that might be possible, but I think at the moment Mr Leadbetter won't be able to give you any more. I'm so sorry, I know we could all do with the money right now, but I think he hopes Alice will come back to work soon. She's so experienced he's waiting to see what her decision is before taking on anyone else full time.'

Ellen's lips tightened. 'Please don't be sorry, I understand and it's not your fault. As you know, my father is off work and that means we have no money coming in but I'm sure I'll find something somewhere.'

Victoria reached out and squeezed Ellen's arm. 'I know what it's like to be responsible for earning enough money so you can feed your family and keep a roof over their heads. If I can help in any way I will.'

Ellen nodded. 'Thank you, I appreciate that. I was intending to ask Mr Leadbetter today for extra hours but considering what you've said, there's very little point.'

Victoria looked sad. 'I will do my best to find you something, so trust me when I say I will help if I can.'

'Thank you, but please don't worry I'm sure something will

turn up.' Ellen forced a smile. 'And it would be lovely to get experience on all the other jobs that comes with working in this wonderful bookshop.'

Victoria nodded. 'And you will. I will speak to Mr Leadbetter to set the wheels in motion. Now I must get on, but maybe I'll see you at lunchtime.'

John was looking up at the books and glanced over at them while they were chatting.

Ellen watched Victoria walk away and knew she was lucky to be working with such a friendly person.

From where he was browsing the books, John looked over at Ellen. He cleared his throat and walked towards her. 'I'm sorry, I don't mean to be rude, but I couldn't help overhearing your conversation. I'm afraid I'm in here rather a lot. I'm book crazy.' He gave a nervous laugh, not taking his eyes off her. 'My name's John and I work as a typesetter for a local paper. If you're looking for work, I might be able to get you a job, but it would probably only be as an office junior.'

Ellen gazed wide eyed up at him. 'I don't know what to say, except: what does an office junior do?'

John chuckled. 'It means you get all the jobs that no one else wants to do, like making the tea.'

Ellen studied him; he wasn't wearing a suit or tie, and his open-neck shirt and black trousers seemed quite casual. She wondered what a typesetter did. 'Well, as you probably heard, I'm not in a position to be picky about what I do but having said that I'm grateful that you're offering me the work, particularly as you don't know me.'

John shrugged. 'The only problem is I'm not in charge so will need to go back and speak to someone, but I can't see it being a problem.'

Ellen frowned. 'Well, I'm very grateful all the same but obviously you need to check first.' She paused. 'If possible, that is, if the work is available, I would love to be able to fit it in around my job here. Being surrounded by all these books is my idea of heaven.'

John chuckled. 'And mine.' He looked at her a bit sheepishly. 'Look, why don't you come along to the office. I'll write down the address, I'm pretty sure they'll take you on.'

Ellen beamed. 'Are you sure? I don't want to get you into trouble.'

John tilted his head. 'Trust me, you won't.'

Ellen couldn't stop smiling. 'I'll come along in a few days when I have a day off, if that's all right, I don't want to miss the opportunity.'

John nodded. 'I'll let the office know.'

'I really appreciate you helping me like this, thank you.'

* * *

Mary looked anxious as she moved her gaze from the large imposing arches of Victoria train station and stared at Ellen, folding her arms around her. 'I don't know.'

'Don't look so worried, you can do it, I know you can, and it's not like you don't know where you are.' Ellen looked around her; she could almost taste the fresh bread she could smell. 'Yesterday I had to pluck up the courage to ask for more hours at Foyles; it's a time when we all have to do things we wouldn't normally do.'

A barrow man shouted to the crowd, 'Get your soup here. Come on now, it's another cold day and nothing warms better than a cup of soup.'

Mary's gaze followed the voice. She took a deep breath. 'I'm not so sure. I'm not as brave as you are.' She jumped when a car backfired, wrinkling her nose as the smoke billowed out from the back of the car.

Ellen reached out and squeezed Mary's arm. 'It's not about being brave it's about doing your bit. You are a kind and lovely person and I know you can pour cups of tea and cut slices of cake.'

Mary gave a wry smile. 'You're not trying to flatter me, are you?'

Ellen giggled. 'I'll try anything, but in all seriousness I'm sure the women that volunteer on that tea table will be glad of your help and the soldiers will definitely be glad of your kindness.'

Mary frowned as she looked at Ellen. 'I'm not afraid of the work, I'm frightened at the thought of seeing all the injured soldiers. I'm not sure I'm grown-up enough to deal with it.'

'None of us know what we can deal with until we have to.' Ellen looked away for a moment. 'Wouldn't you want to hope that someone would look after a brother, father or uncle of yours who had come back from the front? They only want a smile and a hello, and I know you can do that.'

'Ellen, how did you handle it when you helped at the tea table?'

Ellen frowned. 'Trust me, Mary, it will always be hard to see the injured men; some of them are broken both mentally and physically, but once you can see past that it's lovely to be able to help someone by doing something that costs you nothing but your time. Mrs Taylor works on it most days and she is so kind; I've never heard her raise her voice. She will look after you.'

Mary nodded. 'Are they desperate for help then?'

'Yes, they are. I think there's something going around and a few of the women have become quite ill so they are very short-handed.'

Mary looked ahead of her. 'I'll give it a go. I'm sure it will be all right.'

Ellen beamed with pride. 'Well done, I'm very proud of you.' She pulled back her coat sleeve and peered at her wristwatch. 'I've got to go.'

Mary spun round and frowned at her sister. 'What? You're not coming in with me? I thought—'

'Sorry, I have to do some food shopping and then I've got to get to work, I can't afford to be late.' Ellen turned on her heels and marched away before Mary had a chance to respond.

Mary watched her sister get lost in the crowd of people coming and going. The sound of a train whistle snapped her attention back to the station. She tightened her lips – well, she had to grow up some time – and stepped towards the station arches. As she walked under them, she heard a commotion behind her and glanced over her shoulder just as an ambulance was pulling in. A slender young woman climbed out before reaching in to collect a fairly large bag and rushing into the station.

Mary gulped. Did that mean the injured soldiers had already arrived home? She took a breath and followed in the woman's footsteps. Mary coughed as she stepped on to the concourse and the thick grey smoke billowed from the trains, swirling around in the air. She watched as the ambulance driver spoke to the soldiers sitting against a wall; some were holding cups, others had a cigarette between their fingers, and some were flirting with the ambulance driver making her laugh. They were all caked in dried mud and had bandages wrapped around different parts of their bodies. Mary shook her head. She had moaned to Ellen about the war but what they had gone through was nothing compared to these men, and yet they were still trying to help each other through it. Ellen was right, it was time she did something to help someone. No matter how small, and no matter what her father might think. She took another breath, coughing as the smoke filled her lungs, and marched over to the line of soldiers patiently waiting at the tea table.

A stout woman called out as Mary joined the queue. 'Sorry, lovey, this tea and cake is for our boys only.'

Mary felt the colour rush into her cheeks.

'Oh, look you've embarrassed the poor girl, and a sight for sore eyes she is at that.' The soldier who'd spoken had three stripes on the sleeve of his khaki uniform.

A young soldier was standing behind him and had his hand resting on his shoulder. 'Describe her, Sarge; it's been a long time since I've seen a woman and let's face it, I may never see one ever again.'

The sergeant gave the young man a sideways glance. 'Yes you will, boy. Have no worries; the doctors will sort you out.'

Mary called out to the stout woman, 'I'm here to offer my services.'

The blind young man chuckled. 'Are you indeed. Well I'm sure there will be a queue to take up that offer.'

Mary's face turned crimson. 'I meant—'

'Take no notice of the young lad, he's only messing with you.' The sergeant smiled before turning to the young soldier. 'Behave yourself, you've made the young girl blush.'

The stout woman chuckled and walked nearer to Mary. 'Why didn't you say? We need all the help we can get. Come round this side of the table and you can start by keeping the cups coming. I'm Ethel by the way.'

'Hello, Ethel,' the soldiers chorused before turning to look at Mary.

Mary walked around the table and began unbuttoning her coat. 'I'm Mary.'

'Hello, Mary,' the men greeted her.

* * *

Alice unbuttoned the top of her coat as she strolled around Foyles Bookshop. She beamed and turned to her husband Freddie. 'You know, every time I pop in here it feels like I've come home.'

Mr Leadbetter waved and came over to them both. 'I heard you were here; it's lovely to see you again.' He stretched out his hand and shook Freddie's. 'No baby with you today?'

Freddie chuckled. 'No, we've managed to escape for a couple of hours so it's obvious to everyone we would come here first.'

Mr Leadbetter chuckled. 'You just can't stay away, can you?'

Alice laughed. 'I don't think I need to answer that question.'

Freddie shook his head before raising his eyebrows. 'I think she'd move in here if she could.'

Alice nudged her husband. 'Of course I wouldn't, I just miss coming in here every day.'

Mr Leadbetter raised his eyebrows. 'Does that mean you want to come back to work?'

Alice sighed. 'It's not as simple as that; I have two boys to consider.'

Freddie wrapped his arm around his wife's waist. 'Yes it is. Mrs Headley would love to look after Arthur and David.'

Alice glanced at him; sadness swept over her. 'Mrs Headley isn't getting any younger. I don't think it would be right to burden her with it. We've been lucky to keep her while the war has been going on, and she has enough to do keeping house for us all.'

Freddie threw back his head with laughter. 'You don't think your mother and father would let her have all the glory of looking after the boys, do you?'

Alice smiled at him. 'No, probably not, I'm not convinced they will ever approve of us having our own home because of the children. They love us all living in the same house together.'

Mr Leadbetter grinned at them both. 'It sounds like they are very loved, and you are fortunate to have that support.' He gave them a sheepish look. 'However, from my perspective, does that mean I'm getting my wish?'

Alice paused. 'I need to talk to my parents first; it's a big thing to look after the two of them. I won't pretend I'd not love to come back but I also love being with my children.'

Freddie smiled. 'I think it's safe to say you'll be back; the question is more of when and I don't mind either way, I just want you to be happy.'

Mr Leadbetter nodded. 'We have several people going down with a sickness thing that's going around. They are off work so even if you come back to fill those gaps it would be helpful.' He paused. 'Just keep me in the picture. At the moment I'm happy for you to come back whenever you want.' His gaze darted around the shop. 'As you can see, we're as busy as ever. Oh, and we have a new member of staff. Although she is only part time at the moment, she's very good and if the staff keep dropping with sickness, I might offer her full time.' He stretched his arm out and waved at Ellen to join them. 'Although, as you already know the job, that would be easier for me as I wouldn't have to worry about training you.'

Ellen bit down on her lip and stretched out her fingers as she made her way to Mr Leadbetter. 'Did you want me, sir?'

Mr Leadbetter smiled. 'I just wanted to introduce you to Mrs Alice Leybourne and her husband, Sergeant Leybourne. I know you and your sister have always come in here regularly, so you probably recognise Mrs Leybourne.'

Ellen nodded. 'Hello, it's nice to meet you.'

Alice grinned. 'You've done more than that; you recommended I read *Little Women*, and that was before you started working here.' She leant forward and dropped her voice to a whisper. 'And I have to say I love it. It was an excellent recommendation.'

Ellen smiled. 'I'm so glad you enjoyed it. I've read it many, many times.'

Mr Leadbetter looked back at Alice. 'Well, I shall officially introduce you to Miss Ellen Beckford, and she is turning out to be a real asset to us.'

Ellen could feel the colour rushing up her face. 'Thank you, Mr Leadbetter, it makes me happy to know that you're pleased with my work.'

Alice tilted her head slightly. 'You're not by any chance related to Mary Beckford, are you?'

Ellen's eyes widened, and her gaze slipped between Alice and the police sergeant. 'We're sisters. How do you know her?'

Alice laughed. 'Don't look so worried, it's all good. I believe she started work on the tea table at Victoria station yesterday and, my mother, Mrs Taylor, was working there as well. She was singing her praises, saying how good she was for someone so young.'

Ellen's mouth dropped open. 'I had no idea Mrs Taylor was your mother. I worked on the table for a while, and she often told me how proud she was of her daughter and the work you do.'

'She might have meant my sister, Lily. When the war broke out she signed up for the police along with Victoria's sister Daisy.' Alice chuckled. 'And that probably saved the pair of them from going down the wrong path.'

Ellen tilted her head. 'Mrs Taylor did talk about her daughter who joined the police, but I got the impression she was proud of how you manage to deal with the wounded soldiers.' She watched as colour flooded Alice's face. 'I didn't mean to embarrass you, but your mother is very impressed with the ambulance work you do and clearly loves her daughters very much.'

'Thank you, thank you so much. My mother offered great guidance and advice when I took on that role.' Alice took a breath. 'I shall look forward to working with you when I get back.'

Ellen nodded. 'And I you, but talking of which, I had better get back to work.'

Mr Leadbetter grinned. 'So, Mrs Leybourne, did you just pop in for a chat or have you come looking for books?'

Freddie groaned. 'I've told her she can only buy more books if she gets rid of some of those we have at home, whether that means bringing them back here or taking them to the hospitals. I don't mind which, but they really are taking over the house.'

Mr Leadbetter chuckled. 'I think I'll leave you there. I don't want to get involved in a family feud over books, but we are here when you're ready.' He turned away and immediately began chatting to a customer.

Alice turned to Freddie. 'You know I always feel like I'm amongst family when I come in this shop; it would be difficult for me to give it up.'

Freddie took his wife's hand and squeezed it. 'I know, and it's not something I would make you do.'

10

Ellen closed her eyes as she thought about the photographs she had found under her father's armchair. It was from the bundle the police had brought to show them. Had they just dropped to the floor or had her father hidden them? Her eyes snapped open; she couldn't think about her father hiding them on purpose. She glanced across at her grandma before she turned to stare at her father. 'I know we've talked about what happened at the docks before, but we did get interrupted by Mr Preston visiting. I just need to know if the man said anything to you or if there was anything about him that sticks with you. For instance, did he speak with an accent, or did he have a distinctive smell about him?' She sighed. 'I know you don't want to keep talking about it, but I don't want you going to prison, or even worse, getting shot as a spy. We don't stand a chance of finding who did it but at least we can try and prove your innocence.'

Harold curled his lip. 'I know, I know, but I don't know what I can tell you and I've been over it a million times in my head. After all, I can do little else but think about it with this blooming plaster on my leg. I don't even know if I'm remembering it right any more.

It happened weeks ago, back in February and it's March now so it's not that surprising is it.'

Ellen shook her head before taking a deep breath. 'I know but there must be something he said or did that stuck with you.'

'I don't know, I was too busy trying to breathe as I raced after him.'

'Look, Pa, while you were on the ground did you hear him say or mumble something?'

Harold sat in silence for a moment, his fingers tapping his pursed lips. 'He told me to stay down.' He stared at the tiled floor. 'I think he mumbled something about the darkness, you know, not liking it, but I can't remember the exact words.'

Ellen nodded. 'Good, hopefully you'll gradually remember more. It doesn't matter how small the memory, it might be the piece that holds it all together.'

Harold raised his eyebrows. 'I think his bag came undone when he swung it at me because that's when he was mumbling to himself.'

Ellen smiled as she noted it down in her pad. 'That's good, Pa, all these little things might help. To be honest I don't know how yet but we've got to keep trying.'

Harold pushed back his chair. It screeched on the kitchen floor. He stood up and leant on the table. 'I'll keep thinking but I can't promise I'll remember anything else.'

'I know, Pa, but at least you're trying and that's what's important.' Ellen watched him hobble out of the kitchen. She noticed he walked like a man that was beaten and carrying the weight of the world on his shoulders. 'Grandma, please keep an eye on Pa for me.'

Phyllis nodded. 'That's what I've done every day since your ma died. I thought it broke me when she died but your father carries it on his shoulders every day. He loved her so much.'

Ellen's lips tightened. 'And yet there are no photographs of her around the house, nothing to show she ever lived here.'

Phyllis tightened her lips. 'He can't bear to be reminded of what he's lost. He's still grieving every minute of every day, which is why when you mention her, he gets so angry.'

Ellen sat deep in thought at the kitchen table. 'I never realised. I miss her, but I suppose I never really thought about Pa missing her that much.'

Mary strolled in. 'That's it, Pa has his paper so that's him happy for a while.' She glanced at Ellen. 'What are you thinking? Is everything all right?'

Ellen nodded. 'Of course. I'm just chatting to Gran.' She gave her gran a sideways look. 'It's surprising how tiring going to work is.' She laughed. 'But don't tell Pa I said that.' She studied Mary for a moment. 'Are you coping managing Pa and everything that goes with it? I know I'm not doing as much as I thought I would, and I must admit to feeling guilty about that.'

Mary touched Ellen's shoulder. 'Well don't, Grandma helps with her instructions on how to do things properly.' Mary giggled. 'I'm actually enjoying the responsibility and it's made me realise how you held everything together when Ma died. It's now my turn to do my bit.'

'Thank you. Ma would be proud of us.'

Silence sat between them for a few minutes.

Ellen took a deep breath before peering at Mary. 'Three days ago, someone came into the shop and heard me talking to Victoria about getting some extra hours. He suggested I go along to the newspaper office, and I might be able to get a job there.'

Mary smiled. 'He?'

Ellen chuckled. 'Don't start looking for something that doesn't exist. Apparently, he's a regular at the shop and he was just being kind to me.'

'Are you going to go?'

Ellen raised her eyebrows. 'Well, I need the work, so I have nothing to lose.'

Mary grinned. 'I suppose that's true, and I don't want to sound like Pa but please be careful.'

Ellen nodded. 'Everything will work out so don't worry. I'm just going upstairs for a moment and when I come down, I'll make us a cuppa.' Her chair scraped the floor as she stood up. 'I won't be a moment.' Her stockinged feet were silent as she walked out of the kitchen. The creaking of the stairs announced where she was.

Ellen walked into the spare bedroom and cast an eye over it, wondering if she could change the room around. The single bed had long been moved into her bedroom, which Mary now shared with her, so there wasn't much furniture in there. She scanned the room, tapping her finger against her lips. She could move the dressing table to sit in front of the window to give her more natural light, enabling her to use it as a writing desk. The side table that would normally sit next to the bed could be moved next to the dressing table. She knew Mary wouldn't be moving back into this bedroom any time soon, especially not while they were still sleeping in the basement. Although it occurred to her that she should ask her first. On that thought, she turned on her heels and ran down the creaking stairs to find Mary. She headed towards the kitchen and the sound of gushing water bouncing off the inside of the kettle.

Mary peered over her shoulder as she stood at the sink. 'You know I'm sure I spill more water than ever goes in this kettle. My clothes get wet every time.' She giggled. 'The problem is I always put it on too fast to begin with and it's about time I learnt, but when I do it slow the pipes rattle and shake and that always scares me.'

Ellen chuckled. 'You're not on your own; why do you think I wore an apron all the time? If you're making tea though, I wouldn't mind having a cuppa.'

'You're getting cheeky, you know. I thought you said you'd make me one.'

Ellen laughed. 'I could say that's what I came in here to do, and you've beaten me to it, but I would be lying, although I did say I'd do it, you're right.'

Mary giggled. 'At least you're honest.'

Ellen took a deep breath. 'Actually, I came down here to ask you a question.'

'That sounds serious.'

Ellen tilted her head. 'Not really but I want to do something, and I don't think I should do it before I speak to you first.'

Mary turned off the tap before turning round and facing her sister full on. 'Oh no, don't tell me, you're moving out and leaving me here.'

Ellen burst out laughing and shook her head. 'Nothing as drastic as that. I just wondered if I could use your bedroom like an office for a little while? I know it's your bedroom and one day you might want to sleep in it but at the moment when we're not in the basement we're in my bedroom, so I feel it's a bit of a wasted space when I could use it as a writing room, for my stories about Ma and, if I get anywhere, I could keep evidence against Pa in there too.'

Mary sighed with relief as she put the kettle on the stove. 'I'm not leaving your room until you kick me out. I like sharing, and all the time it doesn't bother you I intend to stay there. So, you can do what you like with my room, although I don't want you throwing my things away without speaking to me first.'

Ellen shook her head. 'I have no intentions of throwing anything away; I just want to use the space, that's all.'

'Then feel free. I have no objections to it. In fact, I don't mind helping if you tell me what you want me to do.'

Ellen grinned and immediately turned round and ran back upstairs. She opened her bedroom door and collected her diaries, pencils and notepads. She stared down at the one she'd used when she'd spoken to her father. She bit her lip hard. Did the police have any real evidence against her father? Why was her father being dragged into something that had nothing to do with him? Was she right in thinking they believed she had something to do with the break-ins? She shook her head; she had to act quickly to try and find out what was happening before her father got arrested.

Victoria's words of encouragement came to mind. She needed to keep talking to her father about the night he broke his leg.

* * *

Ellen's heart was pounding as she stood outside the newspaper office. She wiped her clammy palms down the sides of her coat. Had she taken too long to come here? In those three days the job might have gone, but she didn't feel able to ask for time off from Foyles. Taking a deep breath, she pushed open the door. There was a clatter of typewriter keys from around the office as they hit the paper on the rolls. The dings of the bells as the roll reached the end of the line seem to be continuous. Men were sat at their desks, which were laid out in rows. Some were typing, others chatting. Ellen blinked quickly; her eyes were stinging, and she coughed as the cigarette smoke hit the back of her throat. She shook her head. It reminded her of standing in the smog as most of them puffed on their cigarettes and the grey spirals threaded up to the ceiling. Ellen glanced around, wondering who she should speak to but nearly all the men had a cigarette hanging from their lips as they typed away; they all seemed so busy.

'Ah, you must be the new girl.'

Ellen spun on her small heels and stared wide-eyed at the tall, grey-haired man who'd spoken. 'Yes, yes I am, at least I hope I am, although I'm not sure what I'm meant to be doing or who I need to speak to.'

The tall, slim man smiled, before running his fingers through his mass of grey hair. 'I expect John told you we're just looking for someone to do a bit of running around for us. You know, making the tea, taking the copy to the typesetters and any other errands that need doing.'

Ellen smiled. 'I'm just happy to have a job and be kept busy. To be honest I'm surprised you didn't want to interview me first, or at least have a chat.'

The man chuckled. 'It's very hard to get staff these days; no one lasts, everyone wants to earn the big money in the factories so I can't afford to be picky.' He tilted his head slightly. 'I'm sorry, that didn't sound very good, did it? John told me he'd seen you working in Foyles and he seems to think you are a hard worker. That's a good enough reference for me.' The man smiled, tucking a newspaper under his arm before holding out his hand. 'Forgive my bad manners. My name is Mr Williams; I run this paper, so if you have any problems just let me know. I won't introduce you to everybody because I'm sure, if you're like me, you won't remember all the names. I almost forgot, I'll need some home details from you for our files, like your full name and address along with a contact name should we need it.'

Ellen nodded. 'Of course.'

There was a flourish of activity behind Mr Williams. Ellen looked in the direction of the door. A floral scent caught in her throat just as a stunning blonde lady walked in followed by a tall man. She immediately recognised them as the couple who had bought the newspaper outside the craft shop.

Mr Williams glanced over his shoulder and smiled. 'Irene, I'm sure you would like to help our new office junior settle in.' He turned back to Ellen and waved his arm at Irene. 'Miss Beckford, this is our only lady reporter, Miss Walker. The man standing in her shadow is Frank Harris, a very respected reporter, at least in these parts of London.'

Irene's eyes narrowed. 'Beckford, Beckford, that name rings a bell. We haven't met before, have we?'

Ellen peered down at her shoes and cleared her throat. 'No, I don't think so.'

Irene looked pensive for a moment before grinning. 'Hmm, never mind, it will come to me. I don't usually forget a face or a name.'

Frank nodded in Ellen's direction before turning to Mr Williams. 'I see you're reading the *Echo*. Anything decent in there?'

'Not really, I just like to keep up with what our readership rivals are printing.'

Frank unbuttoned his coat, moving the notepad he was carrying from hand to hand as he took it off. 'I don't think you have much to worry about there. Right, I'd better get on, I have a lot to do today.' He turned to stroll towards his desk.

Irene smiled. 'I'll see you at lunch, Frank.'

Without looking back, the man waved and carried on walking.

Mr Williams frowned as his gaze flitted between Frank and Irene. He cleared his throat before speaking to Ellen. 'I feel sure Irene will help you to deal with the men in this office.' He looked around the room. 'As you can see, it is predominantly a man's world but don't let any of them upset you. You need to put them in their place if they speak out of turn.'

Irene giggled; it was a thin, raucous, breathy sound that carried around the office. 'I am sure that won't be necessary. You just have to learn how to deal with it, and let's face it, all the attention is a compliment.'

Ellen watched her closely as Irene removed her coat, revealing a fitted red dress the likes of which she had never seen before. She fleetingly wondered how Irene managed to walk in it as it was so tight.

Irene handed the coat to a man standing nearby. His eyes shone as he leant in to take it. He hugged it close. Irene watched him sniff it before giggling. 'Be a darling and put it on the coat stand for me.'

Ellen couldn't help wondering if her laughter was real. How did anyone laugh like that? A little voice sounded in her head. *She knows your name.* Folding her arms around her midriff, she shifted from one foot to the other. Was Irene working on a story about her father's break-in at the docks? If she wasn't, why would she know her name? If she was working on one, was her situation about to become public knowledge? Did they all know who she was? Ellen could feel her chest tightening.

Irene's eyes narrowed. 'Don't look so worried, I'm sure you'll fit in well. Do you do any writing yourself?'

Ellen chuckled. 'Oh no. Well, I keep a diary, but I've done that for many years. My mother always encouraged me to write down my thoughts.'

Irene studied Ellen for a moment. 'So, I expect you want to be a reporter then.'

Ellen shook her head vigorously. 'Oh, definitely not. I wouldn't know where to begin.'

Irene raised her eyebrows. 'Well, you can begin by making me a cup of tea. I'm gasping.'

Mr Williams chuckled. 'That's all very well but at the moment she doesn't know where the tea things are so you might want to show her around first.' He leant towards Irene. 'How's your story about the docks coming along?'

Irene glanced at Ellen before scowling at him. 'I don't wish to talk about it out in the open. After all, if what I've heard is true then heads are going to roll.'

Ellen dropped her gaze and pretended to be looking for something in her handbag.

Mr Williams' lips tightened. 'All right, but I want to be kept informed, do you hear me? Nothing gets written up until I've heard the facts.' Not waiting for an answer, he turned and walked out of the main office to enter a smaller one at the end of the room.

'If you would like to point me in the right direction, I will happily make you a cup of tea.' Ellen removed her coat. 'But first, can you just tell me where I put my things and then I will get on.'

Irene frowned. 'I believe the desk in front of mine is free so you might as well use that one for now and hang your coat on one of the stands that are around.' She slung her handbag on her desk. 'When you've done that, there is a small kitchen over in the corner.' She pointed to the far end of the room.

Ellen nodded. 'How do you like your tea?'

Irene smiled, her deep red lipstick framing her perfect white teeth. 'I suggest you write it down because by the time you get to the kitchen you will have at least another dozen to make.'

Ellen chuckled and opened one of the drawers of the desk to look for paper and a pen. She wrote Miss Walker's name down, ready to take her tea requirements.

'I like it strong with no sugar and just a splash of milk.' Irene looked down at her own desk and picked up a pen and began scribbling on a notepad.

Ellen weaved between the desks towards the kitchen, and as Irene predicted, she gained several more tea orders for her list.

'You made it then.'

Ellen looked up from the cups she was gathering and saw John leaning against the door jamb, wiping the ink off his hands with a rag. She smiled. 'Thank you for arranging this for me. I've never been in an office before, except my father's at the docks and he's the only one who works in it. Whereas this is so busy.' She glanced over her shoulder. 'It's quite exciting.'

John laughed. 'I expect that will soon wear off. Here, let me help you with the tea. After all, I'm learning how most things work here so I might as well learn about making the tea as well.'

Ellen smiled and passed him a teaspoon and the milk. 'I'm enjoying it but I've only just arrived.' She lowered her voice. 'I've noticed if they're not shouting across the office they're whispering in corners.'

John raised his eyebrows. 'They all think they've caught the next big story that will take them to the big time.' He hesitated before continuing, 'I don't know if you remember, but we met before I mentioned this job.' He paused as he watched her eyes widen. 'I picked up the books that fell out of your arms in Foyles.'

Ellen could feel the heat rising in her face. 'I remember but I wasn't sure you would.'

* * *

Ellen sat in the spare bedroom staring at the notes she'd made when her father had spoken of the night he broke his leg. She tore the pages from the pad before pulling open a dressing table drawer to take out the photographs she had found under her father's armchair. Was there something in the photographs that she was missing? The police thought they were relevant but what wasn't she seeing?

Looking at the notes, it dawned on her that it might be easier to pin some string along the wall and clip everything to where it would fit, if she was able to find any more evidence. Tears pricked at her eyes. What could she do that the police weren't doing? She had so many questions. Had her father seen this man before? Had *she* seen him before? Was there anything distinctive about him? How did he get on the docks? What was he after in her father's office? How was she going to find the answers to all these questions?

Suddenly, she had a thought. She stood up and ran down the stairs, the usual creaking following in her wake. Once in the kitchen, she headed to one of the cupboards and opened it. She scanned the inside, looking for an old box that had been kept for odds and ends that might one day prove to be useful. The thought brought a smile to her face; she couldn't remember the last time the box had been opened.

Standing on tiptoes, she saw the box hidden at the back of the cupboard. Turning round, she grabbed the back of a kitchen chair and pulled it near to the cupboard. The screeching of the legs across the tiles made her wince. The chair wobbled on the uneven floor as she stood on it. Ellen gasped as she grabbed the back of it; her fear of heights froze her for a moment. 'I can do this, it's only a chair for goodness' sake.' Taking a deep breath, she gripped the back of the chair with one hand and slowly raised one arm to reach into the cupboard and slide the box forward to the front. Ellen let out her breath, she hadn't realised until then she had been holding it in. Gingerly, she got herself off the chair before placing the seat back under the kitchen table.

Ellen put the box down on to the kitchen side and teased off the lid. She took a sharp intake of breath as she stared down at the photograph that greeted her. It was familiar to her, but she hadn't seen it since her mother had died. It was her mother and father's wedding day. She picked it up. Tears pricked at her eyes when she saw another one of her mother with Ellen and Mary as children. She blinked quickly, realising her father had hidden them away because they were too painful for him to look at. Maybe it was time she spoke to him about putting the photographs back in their frames for all to see, but not today. She collected them together; she would put them in the spare room so she could look at them and hopefully her mother, with God's help, would help guide her in the right direction.

Taking a deep breath, Ellen replaced the lid before putting the box back into the cupboard. She dashed upstairs clutching the photographs, once again the stairs creaking their objections. Once in the spare room, she sat down, staring at the pictures. Sighing, she realised she hadn't looked for the string. She shrugged. Right now it wasn't important.

Ellen wondered if she could get some information on the break-ins at the docks via the newspaper office without rousing suspicion. The last thing they needed was newspaper reporters hounding her father. Maybe she just needed to go to work and keep her eyes and ears open, but did she have the luxury of time?

Mary pushed the door open. 'Oh, so this is where you're hiding. What are you doing in here?'

Startled, Ellen peered over her shoulder. 'My goodness, I didn't hear you come in. I didn't even hear the creaking of the stairs.'

Mary raised her eyebrows. 'Well, you are clearly in a world of your own.' She pursed her lips as she blinked rapidly, trying to hold the tears at bay. 'Do you really think you can find out who did it?'

Ellen shrugged. 'I have no idea, but I can't do nothing. I

promised Ma I would always do my best to look after the family and that's what I intend to do.'

Mary frowned. 'But you didn't see Ma when she died.'

Ellen's lips tightened. 'No, it was a promise made a long time ago. I remember her getting sick once; she was so ill she couldn't get out of bed.' She paused before taking a deep breath. 'Looking back, I think she thought she was going to die, and to this day I don't know what was wrong with her, but I promised then I would always do my best for you and Pa and that's what I'm doing.'

Mary walked further into the room. She bent down and wrapped her arms around her sister. 'Then Ma would be very proud of you because you've certainly done that.' She stepped away and wiped her eyes. 'You can talk about it with me, and I might be able to think of something that might help.'

Ellen nodded. 'Thank you. At the moment I don't know where to start. I need to talk to Pa again; there must be something more he remembers and for some reason he's just not telling me.'

Mary picked up one of the photographs from the dock. 'I don't understand what this is all about, do you?'

Ellen sighed. 'No, I wish I did. I kept them because I thought they might be useful, but now I don't know.'

'Yes, well, they might give us a clue, but the police know Pa has photographs of the docks, so I expect they think these photographs are his, although these are larger than the ones he took.' Mary took a breath and dropped the photo back on the dressing table. 'How was your first day at the newspaper?'

Ellen laughed. 'It's very different to working at Foyles; it's very noisy and the room is full of smoke because everyone seems to have a cigarette hanging from their lips. There are some characters, and everyone seems to be excited or worrying about the story they are working on.'

'It all sounds very exciting.' Mary turned and walked towards the door. 'I'll go downstairs and see if Pa and Grandma are all right.'

Ellen nodded. 'I won't be long.'

Sitting down at her makeshift desk, Ellen thought about Irene Walker's big story of what was happening at the docks.

11

John walked between the shelves in Foyles, staring up at the many books and not really knowing what he was looking for. He stopped and bent his injured leg back and forth a couple of times; the damp and cold weather wasn't good for it. A child tugged at his trousers. John glanced down at the young boy. 'Hello, and what can I do for you?'

'I can't find me ma; I don't know where she is.' A tear rolled down the young boy's face.

'Don't get upset, she's probably looking for you too.' John frowned. 'I'm sure she can't be far away. Take my hand and we'll go and find her. Can you tell me what she looks like?'

The boy shook his head.

John knelt in front of him. 'Well, can you tell me what colour her hair is?'

The boy nodded. 'She's got brown hair.'

John smiled. 'There you go, you can tell me what she looks like, you're very clever.'

The boy gave a watery smile. 'She's thin and carrying my little sister.'

John ruffled the lad's hair. 'Now that's a good description, that will help us find her quicker.' He took the boy's hand and walked further down the aisle. He saw Ellen tidying up the books on the shelves. 'Ellen, this young lad has lost his mother; can you help us find her?'

Startled, Ellen looked up wide-eyed. 'Oh, you made me jump, I was lost in my own thoughts.'

John chuckled. 'Sometimes that's the best place to be.'

Ellen frowned. 'Not when you're at work. You're meant to be concentrating on the job at hand. Anyway, I didn't quite catch what you said.'

The boy looked up at Ellen. 'I've lost me ma. I can't find her; I don't know where she is.'

Ellen got down on her knees. 'That's all right, don't worry. She won't be far away. I expect she's worrying about where you are too. We'll soon find her.'

John watched her as she comforted the lad. 'Shall I go one way while you go another? If you take the boy with you, it won't look like I'm trying to kidnap him.' He laughed. 'What I mean is, you work here so you'd be expected to be looking for his mother.'

Ellen couldn't help smiling. 'I don't think anyone would think you were kidnapping him, but I'll take him with me.' Ellen looked at the boy. 'Right, can you tell me your name?'

The boy sniffed. 'It's Sam. It's the same as my pa's.'

Ellen smiled. 'Now that's a nice name, and it's even better knowing it's your pa's name. Come on, let's go and see if we can find your ma. I'm sure she's not far away.'

John watched her chatting to the boy. 'I'll go upstairs in case she's looking in the children's department for him.'

Ellen nodded. 'That's a good idea.' She walked a little further to the end of the bookshelves when she glanced down at Sam. 'Do you know your ma's name?'

Sam nodded. 'It's Ma.'

Ellen pushed down the laughter that was threatening to burst from her. 'That's good but do you know what other people call her?'

A tearful lady came rushing towards them. 'Sam, thank goodness you're safe. How many times have I told you not to wander off? I've been going out of my mind with worry.' She bent down with a baby in her arms and hugged Sam close. 'Thank you for looking after him, thank you so much.'

Ellen smiled. 'He's a good boy. He asked a man for help, and he went in one direction to see if he could find you and we went in the other, didn't we, Sam? We've been on an adventure, haven't we?'

Sam beamed up at Ellen.

The lady stood up and rebalanced the baby in her arms. 'That must be the man that spoke to me upstairs. He said he only had the description of brown hair, thin and carrying a little sister.'

Ellen smiled. 'The good news is he never left the shop and he asked for help.'

The lady ruffled Sam's hair. 'That's good but it would have been better if he'd stayed close to me.'

Ellen nodded. 'That's true, but you've obviously taught him well.'

The lady sighed. 'Thank you, I don't know what I would have done if he had left the shop.'

'Well, he was very sensible.' Ellen knelt again to speak to Sam. 'If your ma's not in a rush, why don't you go back to the children's section and ask for Molly? She might even have time to read a book to you.'

Sam grinned at his mother. 'Can we, Ma, can we?'

His mother beamed at her son. 'I'm sure we can spare a few

minutes to do that.' She glanced at Ellen. 'Thank you once again for looking after Sam.' She turned to walk away.

Sam looked over his shoulder and waved.

John walked over to Ellen. 'I'm glad they've been reunited, and all's well that ends well.'

Ellen smiled at him. 'Yes, it's quite a relief.'

John nodded. 'I wanted to ask you how you found working in the newspaper office?'

Ellen's eyes lit up. 'I've never been anywhere like it before, it was all so noisy but exciting as well.'

John laughed. 'Does it make you want to be a reporter?'

Ellen shook her head. 'Miss Walker asked me that, and the answer's no. I wouldn't know where to start.'

'I know what you mean. From what I've seen, you have to be a little bit ruthless to get your story.'

Ellen nodded. 'I can imagine. Miss Walker seemed very protective of her story when she was talking to Mr Williams... I'm sorry, I shouldn't be gossiping.'

John smiled. 'You're not gossiping when you talk to me. Remember, I work there so I know how it is. Miss Walker is glamorous, and some of the men fall over themselves to help her and mark my words it will all end in carnage.'

Ellen giggled. 'I saw a bit of that; a man was smelling her coat when she passed it to him to hang up. I know I've led a sheltered life but it's obviously even more so than I realised.'

John chuckled. 'Trust me when I say that's a good thing.' He stopped laughing and fidgeted a little. 'Perhaps when you've got time we could go out for tea, or lunch, what do you think?'

Ellen half turned away. 'Is that why you got me the job, so I could pay you back in some way?'

John grabbed her arm. 'No, why would you think that?' He

immediately let go of her. 'I'm sorry, I didn't mean to offend you. I just like you so I thought we could get to know each other better.'

Ellen blushed. 'Mr Williams implied that some of the men might act in way that could upset me, so I didn't know...'

'Well, I like to think I'm a gentleman, but it clearly isn't what you want so let's just leave it there.' John turned and walked away.

Ellen watched him leave the shop, wishing she had thought about what she'd said before she'd spoken.

* * *

Ellen sat at her desk staring out of the window, eyeing the early morning sun trying to break through the murky sky. Had it only been three days since she had upset John in Foyles? She felt dreadful for repaying his kindness with mistrust. Glancing round the office, she wondered if she would ever get used to listening to the typewriters and the excited voices of the reporters. It was so different to working in Foyles.

John walked out of Mr Williams' office, but he didn't look her way. She stood up and her chair fell backwards and clattered on the floor. The whole office stopped and stared at her. Immediately flushing with colour, she stooped down to pick it up before walking in his direction. 'John.' She hesitated. His musky, woody scent wafted between them. 'Erm, I just wanted to say I'm so sorry about our... erm... conversation in Foyles.'

John turned round and gazed at her. 'You don't have to be, you made your position very clear.'

Ellen lowered her head, wondering what she could say to make up for it. 'I am sorry, more than you know. I nearly followed you out of the shop, I felt so bad. I was rude and there's no excuse for that. You've only ever been kind to me, so you deserve better than the way I spoke to you.' She wrung her hands together. 'So, if the offer is still on for tea then I would love to go with you.'

John placed his fingers under her chin and gently lifted her head slightly. 'That sounds good to me.' He immediately dropped his hand and examined his fingers. 'Sorry, I hope I haven't left any ink on your face.'

Ellen giggled. 'That will give everyone something to talk about apart from their big stories.'

John nodded. 'That's true. I'm sorry we got off on the wrong foot.'

Ellen tilted her head. 'Let's put it behind us and start our friendship again.'

John smiled. 'That sounds like a good idea and trust me when I say I don't want to cut our conversation short, but I have to get back to the typesetters otherwise I'll be in trouble.'

Ellen nodded. 'Oh, of course. I'm so sorry, I don't want to get you into trouble, it's just I hadn't seen you since we spoke in Foyles.'

John nodded and glanced down at his ink-blotched fingers. 'At least I won't have to worry about all this ink for much longer. I'm having a lesson on looking at photographs through some sort of magnifying glass later.'

'What are you looking for that needs a magnifying glass?'

John shrugged and gave a little laugh. 'I don't have a clue.'

Ellen giggled. 'Well, it sounds interesting.'

'Let's hope so. Anyway, I must go but we'll talk soon and fix a time and day for the tea and cake.'

Ellen watched as he walked away.

'He didn't hang around asking you out. Take care. Irene doesn't miss a trick and I wouldn't like you to get hurt.' He paused, eyeing her as he strolled past. 'By the way, I'm Alan Hutchins.'

Ellen wrinkled her nose at the man's breath. Had he been

eating onions so early in the morning? She peered at him, wanting to know what he meant about Irene but deciding it was better not to ask. 'It's only tea and cake so I'm sure I'll be fine.'

Alan stopped and stared at her. 'You look familiar. Have we met before?'

Ellen shook her head. 'I don't think so, I'm Ellen Beckford.'

Alan frowned but only for a moment before giving her a broad smile. 'That was my line for picking up a pretty girl, but you don't look impressed.'

Ellen blushed.

Frank Harris approached them, carrying a notepad and pen. 'You're not another one throwing your hat at John are you.' He looked her up and down before peering at Irene. 'I can tell you there's no chance, so you might as well give up now and save yourself all the heartbreak.' He carried on walking towards Mr Williams' office. 'I heard he got you the job and the last thing we need is someone else to carry.'

Ellen lowered her eyelashes and cleared her throat. She tried to stave off the embarrassment that was threatening to engulf her. Her hands gripped the side of her skirt; she needed to break the uncomfortable silence. Ellen couldn't bring herself to look at Alan when she spoke. 'Are you kept busy working here? I noticed you have a camera, so I assume you take photographs for the papers.'

'Yes, I do, it keeps a roof over my head, but I can't say it's well paid. Actually, to make my money up I take photographs of families and young women so if you're ever interested let me know.'

Ellen gave a polite smile. 'I don't think I'll ever be able to afford to have my photograph taken with my family – much as I might like to.'

Alan's thin fingers stroked her cheek. 'You are a pretty girl so it may not be as expensive as you think.'

Ellen's body went rigid. 'I'll give it some thought.' She clasped her hands together and stepped back. 'I need to get on with my work.'

'Come on, Alan, stop teasing the poor girl.' Irene slapped his shoulder as she walked past. 'Ellen, take no notice of him, he enjoys creeping women out.'

Alan chuckled. 'That's not true, don't let the green-eyed monster catch you out.'

Mr Williams' raised voice rang through the office. 'Ellen.'

Ellen peered around Alan and saw Mr Williams standing in his office doorway. She breathed a sigh of relief and walked over to him. 'Yes, Mr Williams.'

Mr Williams frowned. 'I hope Alan wasn't bothering you. He thinks he's a ladies' man because he has a camera, although lately his photos aren't as good as they used to be so he'll have to work on his personality a bit more.'

Ellen smiled as she followed him into his office. 'It's not a problem.'

Mr Williams gave a lopsided smile. 'Just be careful and don't get sucked into his rubbish.'

Ellen nodded. 'I won't, sir.'

Mr Williams looked down at his desk and shuffled some papers together. 'Good, now, I want you to take these papers downstairs and give them to John. He'll know what to do with them.'

Ellen reached out and took them from him. 'Yes, sir.' She clutched the papers tight as she left his office. She opened the door to the basement and pulled on what looked like a light switch. The wooden stairway was flooded with light. Her heels thudded on each step as she walked down them. She breathed in the damp and mustiness that mingled with a smell she hadn't come across before. When she reached the bottom step she scanned the room. The large machinery took up most of the space.

John was suddenly in front of her, wiping his hands on a rag that looked like it would put more dirt on than take off. 'Ellen, I hope those papers are for me; we are already behind and might have to work into the night to get the paper out for the morning.'

Ellen nodded. 'This all looks quite interesting, but I won't hold you up.'

John frowned. 'Maybe when I'm not so busy I'll show you around and explain what we do.' He raised his eyebrows. 'But I have to say I'm not sure when that will be.'

'I'd like that, thank you, but I should let you get on.' Ellen smiled before turning to climb the stairs again.

* * *

Mary beamed as Ellen recited her day at the newspaper office. 'It all sounds so exciting.'

Ellen matched Mary's smile. 'It is. It's also very noisy; it's surprising how much noise typewriters make let alone all the people talking above them. Then there's the telephone ringing.' She glanced at her sister. 'The photographer at work told me he takes photos of pretty girls and families to make up his money. To be honest I think he was flirting with me, but I'm not sure.'

Harold frowned. 'I hope you gave him short, sharp shrift?'

Ellen chuckled. 'Well, I said no, if that's what you mean. Apparently, he thinks he's a ladies' man, but he gave me the creeps.'

Mary laughed as Ellen screwed up her face and gave a little shudder. 'Him being creepy aside, it might be nice to have a family photograph, but I suppose that depends on how much he charges.'

Ellen wrinkled her nose. 'You're right of course but I'm not sure I'd want him to take it.'

Mary shrugged. 'Well, you know him so trust your feelings but if we're all in the photograph it should be all right.' She jumped up from the armchair and hugged her sister. 'I'm glad you're enjoying it.'

Ellen wrapped her arms around Mary. 'Yes, it was good.' She pulled back and sighed. 'The only fly in the ointment is a reporter called Frank; he's an older man and he seems to have taken a dislike to me, but I don't know why.'

Harold frowned. 'There's always someone that has an axe to grind, and it probably has nothing to do with you. You're young and a woman so that makes you an easy target, but don't take no nonsense from any of them. When I get this plaster off my leg next week, I don't mind coming to the office and putting him straight.'

Ellen smiled at her father. 'It's all right, Pa, I have to learn to deal with these people because I'm sure there are probably lots of them around. Besides, you and Ma raised us to be strong and stand up for what is right.'

Harold shook his head. 'Trust me when I say I had nothing to do with that; it was all your ma's doing.'

Mary giggled. 'I'll tell you what, I'll go and make a cup of tea to celebrate how well Ellen is doing in her jobs.' She turned to her father. 'Are you going to celebrate with us, Pa?'

Harold gave a faint smile. 'Yes, if only because I could do with a cuppa.' He glanced at Ellen. 'I'm pleased you've settled into both your jobs without too many problems, but don't try and do too much. We will manage one way or another.'

Ellen pushed herself out of the armchair and took the couple of steps to her father. Bending down, she knelt at his feet. 'Thank you, Pa, it means everything to me.'

Harold rested his hand on Ellen's shoulder. 'Please don't take on more than you can do.'

Phyllis, who had been knitting quietly in the corner and listening to the conversation, frowned. 'I'm pleased for you, Ellen, but there's something you need to know.'

'What? Has something happened?'

Harold scowled at his mother-in-law. 'No, it hasn't.'

Phyllis grunted. 'That's not true. Your girls are old enough to know what's going on.'

Harold tightened his lips. 'It's nothing.'

Ellen frowned. 'Will you stop and just tell us? My mind is jumping about all over the place wondering what it could be.'

Phyllis shook her head. 'Your pa had to go to the police station today to answer more questions.'

Ellen's gaze travelled from her grandma to her father. 'What sort of questions?'

Harold shrugged. 'It was nothing, they were just going over the stuff they asked us before.'

Ellen studied her father closely. 'Are you sure that's all it was? I mean, why would they want you down the station just to repeat what you've already said? Are you holding something back?'

Harold scowled. 'No, and I don't need you questioning me as well.'

Tension filled the air. Ellen bit down on her lip as she wondered how far she should go.

Mary wrapped her arms around her waist and hugged herself before taking a deep breath and putting a smile in her voice. 'Well, I have some news, not as big as everyone else's but it's big for me.' She blushed as everyone stared at her. 'I tried to make some biscuits today so maybe you could all try one and give me your honest opinions. Mind you, there wasn't enough sugar, and because I couldn't get any today, I was an egg short so they might not taste that great.'

Ellen and Harold burst out laughing.

Harold shook his head. 'Well, I definitely would be happy to try one.'

Ellen nodded. 'So would I.'

Phyllis chuckled. 'And me.'

Mary clapped her hands together in her excitement. 'I shall go and make the tea and bring them in.'

Ellen smiled as she watched Mary almost skip out of the front room. She stood up and took the couple of steps back to the armchair Mary had been sitting on. 'Mary seems to be very happy. I hope she isn't driving you mad.'

Harold smiled. 'No, she isn't, I've never noticed before how happy she is, it's like being around a breath of fresh air. I suppose I was always too tired or grumpy to notice before.'

Ellen laughed. 'Well, it's nice that you've had the chance to get to know her more. She's a good girl.' She frowned and wrung her hands together as she looked at her father. She had been unsure whether to say anything about what she'd been hearing at the paper but if the police were still questioning him maybe she should. 'Pa, there's something I need to talk to you about...'

'You don't have to look so worried. I've spoken to the rent man, and luckily enough he said he will give us a couple of weeks to sort ourselves out.' Harold smiled. 'That's because we've always been reliable tenants—'

'That's not what I want to talk about.' Ellen took a breath. 'I heard someone whispering at the paper about something to do with the docks. I don't know anything other than that.'

Harold frowned. 'I expect they've just got wind of the break-in but there's nothing to say about it so don't worry. It'll be something about nothing. Things go missing from the docks all the time, that's why the dock police are hot on checking paperwork, and as you know, that's now got even tighter.'

Ellen ran her clammy palms down her skirt. 'I just don't want you getting caught up in anything; we have enough to contend with at the moment.'

Harold chuckled. 'You sound like your mother. Don't worry, I haven't done anything wrong.'

Mary pushed the door open with her elbow, causing the cups and saucers she'd put together on a tray to clatter against each other. She sat the tray on the small dining table tucked in the corner near the window. 'Right, I'll pour the tea and then you can try one of my misshapen biscuits. I hope they taste better than they look.'

Ellen watched Mary pour the dark liquid into the tea strainer. 'I'm sure they will be all right, and remember, they are your first attempt and I think you were very brave to try, especially without all the ingredients.'

Mary glanced at her sister. 'It wouldn't have stopped you from trying, and I expect you'll say it wouldn't have stopped Ma, so I'm just following in the big shoes I have to fill.'

Ellen opened her mouth to speak.

Harold held up his hand. 'You must be your own person just like Ellen is. Your ma wouldn't want you to be held back because of the things she did. Yes, she was a good wife and mother but, as Ellen pointed out to me, she would want you to forge your own ways in life. I know I'm not very good at it but I'm trying my best to be supportive.'

Ellen smiled. 'I know it's difficult, Pa, but we'll get there, you'll see.'

Mary slowly walked over carrying a cup and saucer. The teaspoon rattled against the china. She held her breath as she handed it to her father. 'I'll bring over the tin of biscuits.' She giggled. 'I feel quite nervous.'

Harold sipped the hot tea, gasping as he burnt his top lip in the process. He ran his tongue across it. 'There's no need, I'm sure they will be lovely.'

Mary passed her father the tin and he selected a small biscuit before passing it to Ellen.

Mary chuckled. 'I noticed you pick the smallest biscuit in the tin.'

Harold laughed. 'I don't think so.' He bit into the biscuit; it crumbled on his tongue and crumbs fell on to his shirt. 'It's actually quite good.'

Ellen giggled. 'There's no need to sound so surprised.' She turned to Mary. 'I'm proud of you, you're doing a good job.'

Mary clapped her hands together. 'You mean there's a chance for me yet?'

Harold chuckled. 'I think there is. I might be able to marry you off yet.'

Mary's eyes widened. 'I don't want to be married off, Pa. Ma said we should only marry for love. She also said we should always make sure we vote when we can.'

Harold raised his eyebrows. 'That sounds like your ma.'

12

Ellen pushed open the door to the newspaper office and began unbuttoning her heavy coat as she walked towards her desk.

Alan sidled up to her. 'Have you thought any more about my offer of taking your photograph, or a family one?'

Startled, Ellen frowned, just managing to stop wrinkling her nose before he noticed. 'Thank you for the offer, but I'm afraid my money won't run to such things at this time.'

After pulling a glum face, Alan suddenly smiled. 'Well, how about I do one for free and you can then recommend me to your friends and neighbours.'

Ellen stood still. 'Why would you do that?'

Alan laughed. 'It's what people in business do all the time.'

Ellen nodded. 'My sister was keen when I told her of your offer.'

'That's it then, I'm looking forward to it already.'

Ellen hung up her coat and made her way to her desk. Her chair creaked as she sat down, and she tried to ignore the sight of Irene whispering to Frank. When John walked over to her, she looked up and smiled. 'And to what do I owe this pleasure?'

John chuckled. 'I thought I'd come and firm up that date of ours for tea and cake.' He pulled at a rag that was hanging out of his overall pocket. 'I'm sorry I didn't get back to you yesterday about it.'

Ellen watched as he tried to wipe the ink off his hands and on to the cloth. 'That's all right.'

John peered over at her. 'I've been doing a bit of typesetting and I love it but getting the ink off my hands feels like a full-time job on its own.' He looked back at his black ink fingertips. 'Are you free over the weekend?'

Irene stopped talking to Frank and glanced in their direction. 'I trust you aren't stopping her from working. She has a lot to do.'

John looked up. 'Sorry, Irene, were you talking to me?'

Irene ran her hands down the sides of her fitted blue dress. 'I'm sure you, John, understand better than anyone here that we have deadlines to meet. This is no time to be arranging your social life.'

John smiled. 'My goodness, Irene, I never realised how dedicated you are, but this is a private conversation just like the one you were having with Frank before you thought it was all right to interrupt us.'

Frank shook his head. 'I have no desire to be dragged into this, but I can tell you we were talking about work.'

John nodded. 'I don't doubt you were, Frank, but by the nature of the whispering it was clearly a private conversation, and I wouldn't dream of joining in without being asked to.'

Frank nodded. 'Well, I have work to do.' He picked up some papers from Irene's desk and walked away.

Ellen shuffled some papers around her desk. She had no desire to get involved in a spat she didn't understand. She wondered if there was history between them. Irene had never called out anyone else who had stopped to speak to her.

John touched Ellen's arm. 'I'm sorry about that. Where were we? Oh yes, we were talking about the weekend.'

Ellen didn't look up. 'Erm, maybe we should talk about it another time.'

John frowned. 'Don't let Irene spoil the day.'

Ellen took a deep breath. 'No, you're right, it's just embarrassing.'

John smiled. 'I know. Let's talk about happier things like you being free over the weekend.'

Ellen couldn't resist smiling, but she had a feeling if her father knew she was meeting a man it would be a problem for him. 'I could meet you somewhere?'

'Doesn't a gentleman usually pick up a lady from her home?'

Ellen tightened her lips. 'That sounds very old-fashioned when you put it like that. I'm quite happy to meet you somewhere this time.'

John tilted his head slightly. 'That implies there could be another outing for us.'

Ellen shook her head vigorously. 'Oh no, I wasn't assuming anything, honestly I wasn't.'

John threw back his head and laughed. 'If I have my way there will definitely be another outing so don't worry yourself.' He paused. 'How about I meet you at Foyles, and in the meantime, I'll find a nice place for us to go. Are you working Saturday at the shop?'

'No, but if anything changes it will only be until two o'clock.'

John frowned, while his finger tapped his lips. 'How about I meet you outside Foyles at two but if you're still working, I'll come in and have a look at the books? That sounds like my ideal day.'

Ellen nodded. 'I shall look forward to it.' She couldn't help smiling as she watched him walk away. His overalls were smudged with ink. She caught a whiff of floral perfume from behind her.

'He's a ladies' man. You need to be careful you're not his latest conquest.'

Ellen peered over her shoulder to see Irene looking at her with concern. 'We are just friends. I'm not anyone's conquest.'

Irene raised her eyebrows. 'We all are, dear. You have to learn to play the game, especially if you want to get on in this business.' She arched an eyebrow. 'Do you want to be a reporter?'

Ellen shook her head. 'You've already had the answer to that question.'

'Do you write at all?'

Ellen smiled. 'The only writing I do is my memories of my late mother.'

Irene's eyes narrowed as she studied her. 'Well, I can give you some tips to deal with these men; they all think they are better than us, but they aren't.' She paused. 'You need to laugh at their jokes so they will start confiding in you. Remember, you will always have the upper hand because you have something they want.'

Ellen frowned; her confusion was plain to see.

Irene giggled. 'You're so sweet. I've forgotten what it was like to be so innocent, but the world will eat you up if you're not careful.' She walked to her side of the desk before leaning over and dropping her voice to a whisper. 'Watch and learn.' She dropped a wad of papers on the floor.

Ellen didn't know what to say so she lowered her head and pretended not to hear.

Irene held her hands up to her red lips. 'Oh no, what a mess, I don't know how I'm going to get all of this in any kind of order.'

A couple of the men came rushing to her aid. One stooped down and scooped up the paperwork and the other put his arm around her while offering to make her a cup of tea.

Irene looked over at Ellen and winked. 'Thank you so much,

you are real gentlemen. I'm sure I'll be all right now but I do appreciate your help.'

Both men smiled at Irene; one squeezed her arm as he walked away.

Irene slowly lowered herself on to her desk chair. 'See how easy it is; you can have them eating out of the palm of your hand.'

Ellen blushed. 'I'm not sure I could. You are a beautiful woman, and I wouldn't have the confidence to do anything like that.'

Irene raised her eyebrows. 'This is a man's world, so you have to use the tools God gave you to get ahead, otherwise you'll always be making them cups of tea.' She pulled a cigarette from the box on her desk and placed it between her red painted lips and lit it. She stared at Ellen and blew the smoke in her direction. 'No woman should be tied to the kitchen sink.'

Ellen thought about it for a moment. 'That's true. My ma was excited about the suffragette movement. I remember her telling us life would be different when women got the vote but surely there are other ways to get on in this world.'

Irene chuckled. 'You are young and so naive, but you'll change because you'll have no option if you want to survive and do something with your life.' She gave her a sideways glance. 'Don't worry, you'll soon pick it up.' She reviewed the paperwork the men had picked up off the floor and began arranging the pages.

Intrigued, Ellen watched Irene. She had never met anyone like her before. Had John hurt her and that was why she was warning her? Why she'd had a problem with John talking to her earlier?

Irene suddenly looked up and scanned the office before looking at Ellen. 'Have you seen Alan? He was here earlier; I need to see if he has taken some new photographs for me.'

Ellen looked around her. 'No, I haven't.'

Irene pursed her lips together. 'That man is never around

when I need him.' She held up a photograph of Victoria station. 'Apparently, this one isn't up to standard so if you see him tell him I need to speak to him urgently, otherwise this article is never going to get into print.'

Ellen nodded. 'I will. Why isn't it good enough?'

Irene raised her eyebrows. 'I have no idea; I just got a note from John to say the quality wasn't good enough. He's proving to be quite picky since he's started dealing with the photographs before they go into print. Someone said he's looking at them through a magnifying glass or something. I'm going to need all my charms to loosen him up a bit otherwise nothing is ever going to get printed.'

'I thought he was a typesetter.'

Irene's eyes narrowed. 'He's been promoted to do the photographs as well.'

Ellen grinned. 'That's good news, he never said about the promotion, but I'm sure he's pleased about it.' She glanced in the direction of the picture. 'I don't know anything about taking a photograph, but can I see it?'

Irene shrugged. 'Of course, but it's just a boring picture of the station.' She passed it over to Ellen.

'I wonder what John's looking for when he's studying them?'

Irene watched Ellen closely. 'God only knows.'

Ellen studied it closely before shrugging. 'It looks all right to me,' she said but the process interested her so she resolved to ask John about it later.

* * *

The two adjacent pyramid signs of Café Monico were just ahead; people were milling around outside. John pushed the wooden door, which opened into a large room filled with round wooden tables and matching chairs. Arched mirrors on the wall gave the illusion of space, while the white roman pillars gave it grandeur. The panelled ceiling was edged with Victorian scrolled mouldings. Large potted palms were strategically placed around the room.

Ellen's jaw dropped. 'This is beautiful.' She looked around her. 'I haven't been here, or anywhere like this, before.'

John smiled as he watched Ellen's eyes moving around the room. 'I'm surprised it hasn't been damaged with all the bombs dropping in London, but I don't think Regent Street has been hit in the same way as other roads.'

Ellen's heels clattered on the tiled floor as they were shown to a table. 'I feel a bit underdressed in this blue dress.' She patted the back of her hair. 'It's all so beautiful, which probably also means it's very expensive.'

John nodded at the waitress, dressed in a floor-length black dress with a pristine white, frilled-edge apron tied around her waist. Her brown hair was topped with a white cap. 'Do you know what cake you want, Ellen? You don't have to have cake; they do meals here as well as sandwiches.'

John pulled out her chair and Ellen sat down. 'Oh no, a cup of tea and a slice of cake is fine.'

The waitress smiled. 'Shall I give you a few minutes?'

Ellen's eyes shone. 'Oh no, I'm sure it won't take us long to decide.'

The waitress glanced at them both. 'Is there any particular cake you'd like? We have chocolate, lemon, coffee and Victoria sponge.'

'Hmm, there's so much choice, but I'll have a slice of lemon cake please, and—' Ellen looked at John as he sat down opposite her '—a pot of tea please.'

John nodded his agreement. 'I'll have a slice of Victoria sponge please.'

The waitress looked at her pad. 'That's tea for two, a slice of lemon cake and a slice of Victoria sponge.'

Both John and Ellen nodded before the waitress smiled and stepped away. Her black dress and white apron rustled together as she weaved between the tables.

Ellen stared down at the gleaming cutlery, straightening the knife. She picked up the monogrammed white napkin, shook it and placed it on her lap. She glanced around her and was surprised to spot Victoria and Molly a couple of tables away.

Victoria looked up and smiled and waved when she saw Ellen.

Molly turned round in her seat and did the same.

The waitress returned to the table and unloaded her tray of matching floral china cups, saucers, milk jug, and teapot. Her fingers gripped the sugar bowl. 'Do you take sugar in your tea?'

John looked at Ellen, who shook her head, before glancing up at the waitress. 'No, thank you.'

The waitress smiled and took the sugar bowl away with her.

John watched her go. 'There must be a real shortage if they don't want to leave it on the table.'

Ellen smiled. 'They probably need all they can get for the cakes.'

John laughed. 'That's true.' He paused. 'How are you finding working in the office and sitting opposite Irene?'

'It's certainly lively.' Ellen raised her eyebrows. 'Irene's definitely interesting and has been giving me some tips on how to use the tools God gave me to get what I want.' She giggled. 'She certainly comes across as a woman of the world.'

John chuckled. 'Yes, I've seen her in action; she can be quite provocative when she wants to be. She's ambitious, as indeed most of the reporters are; they see us as a stepping stone to working for the nationals.'

Ellen tilted her head and once again wondered if there was history between them. 'How long has the photographer worked there?' She giggled. 'He seems to think he's a ladies' man.'

'So, I've heard.'

Ellen looked at John from under her eyelashes. 'I got told to watch myself because you are also a ladies' man, and I could end up as one of your conquests.'

John burst out laughing. 'That sounds like someone who is jealous about us having tea and cake together.' He reached over and put his hand over hers. 'I'm not going to ask who said it, but I want you to know it's far from the truth.'

Ellen studied him for a moment.

John tilted his head slightly. 'I hope you will come to trust me and realise I'm not a womaniser.'

Ellen smiled. 'I plan to just enjoy your company and this wonderful tea and cake.' The lid of the teapot chinked against the china as Ellen lifted it. She placed her spoon in the dark liquid and stirred it. She glanced into the whirlpool she had created before trying to replace the lid; it took a couple of turns to put it on correctly. Lifting the tea strainer, she placed it on John's cup. 'Are you happy for me to pour?'

John smiled. 'Of course.'

Ellen tipped the teapot over his cup. She watched the tea leaves slowly fill up the strainer before the dark brown liquid drained into his cup. 'I'll let you add your milk.'

John added a splash of milk to his tea. 'It looks a fine cup.'

Ellen gave a wry smile. 'I was always told it's all in the brewing.'

The waitress stopped at their table and placed the plates of cake in front of them in turn.

John nodded. 'Thank you.'

They peered over at each other's plate.

Ellen laughed and picked up her cake fork. She prised off the thin end of the slice and popped it in her mouth. 'This is delicious; so light.' She scooped up another piece. 'I like Victoria sponge but this lemon one is lovely. My mother used to make it so it's a bit of a weakness of mine.' She laughed. 'Mind you, cake is a weakness full stop.' Ellen looked around as the constant buzz of conversation filled the room. 'I love this place.' She frowned. 'Although I'm not sure I like seeing myself in the arched mirrors on the wall.'

John followed her lead and looked around. 'It does feel very grand, probably too grand for me.'

Ellen giggled. 'Why did you pick it then?'

John shrugged. 'It's obviously a popular place and we all deserve to be spoilt now and then.'

'I understand you've been promoted and you're now a type-setter and checking photographs with a magnifying glass before they get into the newspaper.' Ellen chuckled. 'Sorry, that's my own ignorant description of how these things are done. That must be worth celebrating.'

John shrugged. 'I suppose it is. I enjoy being a typesetter, despite getting the ink all over me.'

Ellen laughed as she picked up her cup. She went to take a sip, but the steam warned her it was too hot. A shadow passed over her eyes as she returned her teacup to the matching saucer. She glanced around the room. 'My ma would have loved this.' She smiled. 'Not so much my father; he would see it as a waste of money but it's a welcoming place.' Ellen looked round at the waitresses weaving in and out of the tables delivering the food orders.

John laughed. 'That sounds familiar. What does your father do?'

Ellen raised her eyebrows as she stared into her cup of tea. 'At the moment he's off work, but he normally works on the docks.'

John nodded. 'That's right, I remember that was the conversation I overheard in Foyles.'

The door to Monico's swung open. Ellen glanced over and saw Mrs Leybourne talking to a waitress. She watched as the waitress led her between the tables.

Molly's voice carried across the restaurant. 'I was getting worried.' She jumped up and hugged Alice.

John followed Ellen's gaze. 'They are clearly good friends outside of working at Foyles.'

Ellen realised she was staring as Alice embraced Molly and then Victoria. 'Yes, they are, they are lovely people.' Her lips tightened as she watched them, realising she would have loved to have a friendship like that. 'They seem to be very happy about something.'

* * *

Alice walked through the open door of Foyles to be greeted by a smiling Mr Leadbetter. 'Welcome back, Mrs Leybourne, it's lovely to see you.'

Alice smiled. 'It's lovely to be back, even if it is only for a couple of days. I can't wait to get started.'

'I appreciate your help.' Mr Leadbetter bowed his head slightly. 'Well, I don't have to tell you where everything is, at least I hope I don't, so I shall let you go and meet the girls. I'm sure they will all be pleased to see you.'

'I can't believe how excited I am.' Alice stepped further into the shop and made her way into the staff room to clock in. She walked into a chorus of greetings.

Molly rushed forward and threw her arms around her. 'I'm so

glad you're back. You coming back to work makes it easier all round to keep up with each other and what's more, we can go back to having lunch together.'

Alice giggled. 'That's it, you tell it as it is but don't get carried away because I'm not coming back permanently for some time yet. I shall enjoy this time catching up with everyone, but I'm not prepared to give up my time with my boys yet.'

Molly pulled back and looked at her friend. 'You know what I mean, I'm always full of good intentions but nothing ever seems to work out as I think it will.'

Victoria stepped forward to give Alice a hug. 'It's lovely to see you back working here, we're like the Three Musketeers, and when one of us is missing it just doesn't feel right.'

Alice beamed at her friends. 'I know exactly what you mean.' She unbuttoned her coat and hung it on the hook nearby. 'I suppose I had better clock in otherwise I won't get paid.'

Ellen walked into the staff area and took off her coat.

Victoria waved her over. 'Alice is officially back at work for a few days and we couldn't be happier.'

Ellen smiled. 'Welcome back. I know you've missed it because of your visits here and you obviously have a love of books.'

Alice nodded. 'I know it's a strange thing to say but I have missed it. My mother was so excited at looking after the boys she couldn't get me out the door quickly enough this morning.'

The girls laughed.

As the laughter died away, Molly cast her eyes over Ellen. 'I saw you in Monico's on Saturday; you were with... I can't remember his name, but he comes in here quite a lot.' She watched Ellen closely. 'Are you two stepping out together?'

Victoria nudged Molly, meeting her look of innocence with a scowl.

Ellen blushed. 'Of course not. I saw you all as well. I've never

been there before, it's a lovely place but too expensive for my
pocket.'

Victoria shook her head. 'Forgive Molly, she can't keep her
thoughts to herself sometimes. It is lovely there. We only go there
when we have some exciting news to share and then it turns into a
celebration because of where we are.'

'That's right, that's where I told the girls I was getting married.'
Alice laughed. 'It's good to know nothing's changed; Molly has
always been the one to blurt things out without thinking first, but
we still love her.'

Molly wrinkled her nose at Alice. 'We've all shared good news
there; it's become a special place for us.'

Ellen raised her eyebrows. 'Were you celebrating then?'

Victoria grinned. 'Alice told us she was coming back to work,
which we were thrilled about, even if it is only temporary.'

Alice chuckled. 'And Victoria told us that Ted, her boyfriend,
was finally settling in her home without too much of a problem.'
She gave Victoria a mischievous look. 'So, we were trying to get
her to commit to a date for her wedding, but we failed.'

Victoria blushed. 'I just want him to get used to being out of
hospital and living at home first. I don't want to scare him off and
I've waited this long so a few more weeks isn't going to make that
much difference.'

Molly looked over at Ellen. 'Is that why you were there, were
you celebrating?'

Ellen gave a nervous laugh. 'I don't know really, John asked me
to go. I had been rude to him. I did apologise but I think it was his
way of showing he forgave me, not that it was necessary.'

Molly nodded. 'So, it was a celebration then. It's definitely the
place to go; the food is divine, if a little expensive.'

Ellen laughed. 'Yes, but I can't say I enjoyed seeing myself in
all those mirrors.'

Victoria nodded. 'I know exactly what you mean.' She reached out for her clocking-in card and placed it in the machine and listened for the click that told her it had been stamped before pulling it out again. She peered over her shoulder before turning back to Ellen, whose bright smile had been chased away by a frown as she fingered the necklace she was wearing. 'That's pretty.'

Startled, Ellen dropped her hold on the necklace. 'I'm sorry...'

Victoria smiled. 'There's no need to be sorry, you were in a world of your own and I didn't mean to startle you.' She paused before speaking in low tones. 'Do you want to talk about it?'

Ellen glanced at Alice and she forced herself to smile. 'There's nothing to talk about.'

Victoria followed Ellen's gaze. 'You don't have to worry about Alice, she's a true friend and wouldn't hurt a fly.' She rested her hand on Ellen's arm. 'Did you manage to talk to your father about what happened when he broke his leg?'

Ellen's lips tightened. 'Yes, but he doesn't seem to remember anything about the man who attacked him. Also, we didn't get very far, we only got to where he fell backwards and broke his leg.'

Molly frowned. 'Was your sister there when you were talking to your father?'

Ellen nodded.

Victoria raised her eyebrows. 'Maybe he didn't want to talk about it in front of her.'

Ellen looked thoughtful. 'You could be right; I'll try and talk to him again when Mary isn't around.'

Victoria smiled. 'It's worth trying. I know I said very little about my concerns to my younger brother and sister when we were going through things.'

Alice glanced at her friend. 'You didn't say much to us either, and we're your friends.' She turned to Ellen. 'I don't know what you're all talking about but if I can help, I will. No one should go through troubled times alone.' She glanced at Victoria. 'Should they?'

Victoria smiled. 'No, they shouldn't, and I learnt that the hard way. Everyone needs a helping hand sometimes.'

Molly chuckled. 'Ellen may not want to tell you anything because your husband's a peeler.'

Alice shook her head. 'Yes, he's a policeman but he is honest and if he can help to unravel or give you some advice I'm sure he would. I assume you haven't broken the law and that's what you're worried about?'

Ellen's eyes widened. 'No, I don't think I've ever done that, at least not knowingly.'

Victoria rested her hand on Ellen's arm. 'Don't look so worried, I'm not sure who Molly is teasing, you or Alice, but you have nothing to worry about where Freddie is concerned, he's a lovely man.'

Ellen breathed a sigh of relief. 'I have nothing to tell anyway.' She looked at Alice. 'It's just my thoughts running riot around my head, and I don't mind telling you when we have more time, especially if it helps.'

13

Ellen put one of the photographs from the police visit on the dining table. Once again she stared at it, picking it up for a closer look, turning it to the bright light to see if there was any detail she hadn't seen upstairs. It was clearly a picture of the docks, but was the ship in it important? She sighed. She had no idea. The clock in the hall chimed seven times. Ellen placed the photograph back down on the table.

'I love spring, what with the promise of days getting longer and the sun slowly getting brighter and stronger.' Mary squealed. 'He'll be here in a minute; are you ready, Ellen?'

Ellen smiled as she moved over to the sofa to plump up the soft red cushions before glancing round the front room. She stood up straight and smoothed down her blue floral calf-length dress before patting the back of her hair, which she had left hanging loose over her shoulders. 'I think the room is tidy enough, although I think you went overboard with the beeswax. I can almost taste it.'

'I'm sorry, I just wanted to make a good impression.' Mary

beamed from ear to ear. 'I'm so excited, I can't believe we're going to get our pictures taken.'

Harold sat in his armchair scowling at his daughters. 'I'm not happy about this. If you'd just said you wanted it done, I would've taken it. Although, it won't be the same without your ma in it.'

Ellen shook her head. 'We know that Pa, but Ma loved a photograph, so she would've been the first to say yes, let's have it done.' She paused for a moment. 'And you haven't taken one since she died, at least I don't think you have.'

Harold stared down as his hands resting on his lap. 'No, I haven't, but if you'd asked I would've taken one for you.'

Phyllis was sat in the other armchair, her knitting needles clicking away as usual. 'You know as well as I do, Harold, it would've been a fight to get you to do it.'

There was a thud at the front door as the knocker slammed down. 'Pa, try and look happy about it. I know it's hard for you, but your plaster has finally been removed so that's something to be happy about. I don't want you looking grumpy in the photograph. One day it will be shown to your grandchildren, so we don't want them to get the wrong impression about you, do we?'

Harold laughed. 'Nice try.'

The door knocker thudded again.

Ellen sighed. 'I'd better go and answer the door. Remember, I have to work with this man so please behave yourselves.' She marched out into the hall, her footsteps clattering on the tiles as she went.

Mary listened intently as Ellen opened the front door and greeted Alan.

'Good evening, Alan, please come in. It's good of you to come; everyone is looking forward to having their photograph taken.'

Alan grinned. 'Hopefully we will get some good pictures. Where would you like me to take them?'

Ellen smiled, wondering if she had misunderstood his friend-liness in the office. 'We thought about having it done in the front room but see what you think.' She shut the front door behind him. 'Let me take your coat.'

Alan nodded and began unbuttoning his brown winter coat. 'I know it's March, and it should be getting a little warmer, but I haven't been brave enough to move to a jacket yet.'

Ellen chuckled. 'I know what you mean, the great British weather is so unpredictable.' She took the coat from him. 'It's lovely and soft so I assume it's wool, is it?'

Alan shrugged. 'I have no idea. I only know it keeps me warm.'

Ellen hung it on the hook by the door. 'Well, it's a lovely colour. I tend to stick to black coats; maybe I should be more adventurous.' She smiled. 'Follow me. The others are already in the front room. My sister is very excited about it all.' She stepped into the room and stretched out her arm. 'Allow me to introduce my father, Harold, my grandmother, Phyllis, and my sister, Mary.' Each person nodded in turn as they were introduced. 'This is Alan. As you know, he's a photographer at the paper and offered out of the kindness of his heart to take a family photograph of us all.'

Mary beamed as she jumped up. 'Can I make you a cup of tea while you're thinking about where you'd like us?'

Alan nodded. 'That would be very kind of you.' His eyes followed Mary as she gracefully left the room. He scanned the room before walking to the table and momentarily stopping to stare at the photograph. Clearing his throat, he picked it up and studied it. 'I see someone likes to take a photograph. Who has the camera?'

Ellen bit her lip as she reached out and took the picture from Alan and put it in the drawer of the dresser, which housed all her mother's best crockery. She blinked rapidly and cleared her throat. 'My father.'

'I need to make sure I do a good job then.' Alan laughed. 'No one likes to be judged and found lacking by someone who is good with a camera. Is it all right if I put my bag on the table or would you rather I put it on the floor?'

Harold watched him closely, his eyes narrowing as he studied his movements. 'Do whatever you're comfortable with.'

Alan cleared his throat and placed his bag on the floor. The clasp sprung open. 'Thinking about it, I'll leave it here; I wouldn't want it to scratch your table.'

Harold nodded. 'It looks like it's seen some action in its time.'

Alan laughed. 'It certainly has. I've had it for many years. I should treat myself to a new bag really but I'm kind of attached to it. Good job it can't talk because it could tell a story or two.' He bent down, pulled the bag open and lifted out his camera.

The sound of crockery rattling could be heard from the hall. Mary came in carrying a tray and placed it on the table. 'I'll pour, but I'm afraid we don't have much sugar.'

Alan smiled. 'That's fine by me, I don't take sugar.'

Harold frowned as he eyed the open bag, before turning his attention to Alan who was fiddling with his camera.

Alan looked up. 'Do you have a preference on your positions? I mean, would you prefer to be sitting or standing?'

* * *

Irene's eyes sparkled as she ran her hands down the sides of her tight-fitting black dress, smoothing out the creases that had formed when she had sat down earlier. 'I've heard a whisper that the Port of London Police are closing in on who broke in to one of the offices at the docks.'

Ellen's head snapped up. Her gaze travelled around the office, wondering who she was speaking to. She waited for someone to respond.

Mr Williams moved closer to Irene. 'Do you have the full story, or even enough to write about their investigations?'

Ellen held her breath.

Irene shook her head. 'Not yet, but I will do.'

Mr Williams tightened his lips. 'Are you sure? I can always ask Frank to cover it.'

Irene glared at him. 'No, this is my story. Don't make me regret telling you. I'm sick of covering shows and tea tables at train stations; I'm better than that.' She collected her bag before picking up her pad and pencil. 'I'm going to see if I can get any more information.' She turned and walked towards the door before looking back over her shoulder and giving Mr Williams the benefit of her smile. 'Don't worry, if I get stuck, I'm sure Frank will help me.'

Mr Williams raised his eyebrows as she walked out of the office. 'I'm sure he will, as indeed will most of the men in this office.'

It was only then that Ellen saw John standing there. He was watching her closely; he took a step towards her. She lowered her head again. Her mind was in a whirl. Did Irene think her father was responsible? Ellen reminded herself that Irene had recognised her surname when they were introduced. Had she made the connection and was that why Alan had insisted on the family photograph, because they were working together? Ellen had to find out what she knew, but how?

Irene suddenly came rushing back to her desk and picked up a wad of papers. 'Ellen, will you do me a favour and type these notes up for me? It's only on a show I'm reporting on but the typesetters will need them by the end of the day and I'm not sure I'll be back in time to get it done.'

Ellen nodded. 'Of course. It might take me a while though. I'm afraid I've never typed so it will probably take me most of the morning, but I'm happy to learn. I'll need to sit at your desk and use your typewriter.'

Irene hesitated for a moment before giving her a smile that didn't reach her eyes. 'Of course, sweetie. You don't have to do anything except hit the right keys and when you get to the end of the line, pull the lever and you'll get a new line to continue on. The ink on the ribbon shouldn't be a problem. Try not to move anything on my desk.' She eyed Ellen. 'I'm surprised your mother didn't want you to learn; it's what most mothers see as a step up, you know, getting a job in an office. I know my grandmother did. She never wanted me to be in service or taking in other people's washing.'

Ellen sighed. 'My mother wouldn't have wanted that either.' She sat back on her chair, wanting to end the conversation. 'I'll start now and then I'll know it's done.'

Irene nodded. 'Right, I must dash.' She walked as quickly as her tight skirt would allow towards the door.

Frank rushed over, bumping into a chair and just managing to catch it before it thudded to the ground. He called out, 'Irene, wait. While you're out and about, would you go to the craft shop in Little Earl Street, the one that's near where we bought the newspaper with your article in it?' He stopped for breath. 'It would do me a massive favour because I forgot to pick up the wool for my mother. She's knitting socks and gloves like the wind.'

Ellen watched them talking, wondering about their relationship. Frank didn't fawn over Irene like some of the other men did, but they seemed close, although he was old enough to be her father.

Irene's eyes widened as she stared at him. 'You know I would, darling, but I truly don't have time today. Perhaps you can get it on your way home later.'

Alan watched them both. 'You should buy it while it's light. Personally, I hate being out at night; what with no street lighting, you can't see the hand in front of your face.'

Irene glared at Alan before turning back to Frank. 'Look, darling, I must go; I'm already going to be late if I don't hurry.'

Frank watched her leave before turning to scowl at Ellen and Alan. 'What are you both looking at? Have you got no work to do?'

Ellen squirmed inside as she lowered her head. 'I'm sorry, Frank, I didn't mean to stare. It was very rude of me.'

Alan laughed. 'Don't take any notice of him, he's just in a bad mood because Irene wouldn't do what he wanted. He's yet to realise Irene beats to the sound of her own drum.' He was shaking his head when he walked away, still chuckling. 'You men are sucked in by her. You're all fools.'

Ellen ignored Alan's insensitive comments and was glad he had moved away. As she made herself comfortable in Irene's chair, John appeared at her side. His woody fragrance filled the space between them. 'I want to talk to you, but not here. Perhaps later we'll have a cuppa.'

Ellen stared down at the paperwork Irene had told her to type up. 'You make it sound important, almost urgent.' Frowning, she looked up at him.

John lowered his voice. 'It's important to me. I know some-thing's bothering you, and I'm guessing it has something to do with Irene.'

Ellen forced herself to smile and looked up at him. 'No, really, nothing is bothering me. I love my job here.'

John shook his head. 'I know that. Look, I'm not going to let it go so you might as well have the cuppa with me, even if it's only to put my mind at rest.'

Ellen looked back down at the papers on the desk before sighing. 'All right, but I must get on.'

John nodded. 'I'll come back at five. We don't have to go far.'

Ellen watched him walk away. Frowning, she wondered what he wanted to say to her. Her lips tightened. She had to get on. She stared back at the desk that was littered with paper and photographs. Picking up the papers that Irene had left her, she began reading before she thought about typing the notes up. As she concentrated, her other hand moved slowly over the paperwork on the desk. Pushing pieces aside, she hoped no one would notice what she was up to. Ellen took a sharp intake of breath when she noticed a piece of paper with her father's name on it. She fought the urge to pick it up, and turned her head slightly instead, trying to read it. Ellen sighed; Irene's handwriting was all over the place, it was unreadable without drawing attention her way. Her gaze travelled across the desk and she saw a photograph with a small circle drawn in ink close to the edge of it. Ellen picked it up to take a closer look, wondering who had drawn on it and why. Shrugging, she dropped the photograph back on the desk.

'Is everything all right?' Alan stood next to Irene's desk and began riffling through her paperwork.

Startled, Ellen licked her dry lips, wondering if he had noticed she'd been trying to read the papers on Irene's desk.

'Irene said she left me a list of things she wants photographed; it's probably buried amongst this lot somewhere.' He looked up and stared at Ellen. 'Good luck trying to read Irene's handwriting. She's developed her own shorthand that no one understands.' He bent over her shoulder. 'Were you admiring my photograph?'

Ellen took a calming breath and picked up the picture again. 'I was just wondering where it was taken. Is it Victoria train station?'

Alan nodded. 'Yes, Irene is doing a piece on the tea table there. It's about how busy it is. I took a couple of the injured soldiers as well the ladies working there but goodness knows when it will be in the paper. Those types of articles are fillers for when they are short on items to fill the columns.'

Ellen smiled. 'My sister helps out on the table from time to time. I used to too. It's a very busy station.' She put the photograph down. 'It's quite interesting.'

Alan gave her a winning smile. 'I can always teach you about photography if you're interested.'

Ellen nodded. 'Thank you, but my father would want to teach me. After all, in the past it was his passion.'

Alan gently brushed her brown hair off her shoulder. 'That's a shame. I would have enjoyed it.'

Ellen blushed with discomfort at his boldness. She paused to pick up the photograph again. 'This captures the heart of the station and the war.'

Alan tightened his lips. 'That's not one of my best and Irene won't be able to use it because it's already been checked and found to have something wrong with it, that's what the circle is saying.' He took it from Ellen and stared at it. 'In fact, I've a good mind to throw it away.'

Ellen watched him study it before reaching up and taking it back. 'I hope you don't do that; it tells a story. You've managed to get the steam from the trains, the tea table, with the ladies and the injured soldiers all in one photograph. I believe I can even see an ambulance through the arch of the station. It would be a shame not to use it.' She placed the picture back with the paperwork. 'Well, I must get on. Irene's asked me to get this item typed up as it's needed downstairs before the end of today and I don't want to let her down.' She purposely looked down at the paperwork and started typing and was relieved when Alan walked away.

* * *

The bell above the door to the tearoom rang out as John pushed it open, to allow Ellen to walk in ahead of him, and again when the door closed behind him.

A middle-aged woman wearing a jaunty white cap and a long black dress with a white apron stepped forward. 'Can I help you, sir?'

John smiled. 'Have you got a table for two, perhaps in the corner somewhere?'

The waitress nodded. 'Of course, sir. It's the quiet end of the day so please pick the table you would prefer. We are fortunate to be busy at lunchtime and in the early afternoon; we get a lot of business from the newspaper office next door.'

'Of course, it must be very convenient.' John frowned. 'What time do you close?'

'Ordinarily six o'clock but if we still have customers then we just keep it open.'

Ellen smiled at the waitress. 'Well, hopefully we won't keep you waiting.'

The waitress smiled. 'Don't worry, lovey, I have nothing to rush home for.' She turned and walked towards the counter.

John pulled out a chair at the table in the corner for Ellen to sit on. As he watched Ellen sit down, he pulled a chair out for himself. 'What would you like? I hear they do some nice sandwiches here and the cake isn't too bad either so please feel free to have whatever you wish. I assume you would like a pot of tea.'

Ellen looked around the tearoom. It was clean but very old-fashioned. There were floral curtains at the window and the wall behind the counter was covered with shelves filled with white teapots along with plain white cups and saucers. Not the floral china ones that they used at Monico's, but it still looked nice enough. 'I don't wish to have anything to eat, thank you, but a cup of tea would be lovely.'

The waitress came over carrying a notepad and pen. 'What can I get you? I'm afraid we don't have much cake left but I do have some Victoria sponge.'

Ellen laughed. 'Just tea for me, thank you.'

'That will do for me too, thank you.'

The waitress nodded. 'No wonder you're so slim.' She chuckled as she walked away.

Ellen blushed.

John laughed. 'There's nothing like a compliment from the waitress when you pop out for a chat.'

The waitress was soon back with the pot of tea along with the crockery and began placing them on the table.

Ellen nodded. 'Thank you.'

'You're welcome.' The waitress strolled back to the counter.

Ellen watched her before turning back to John. 'What did you want to see me about?'

John was silent for a moment. He lifted the teapot lid; it clanged against the pot. He began stirring the hot water, staring at the tea leaves swirling around.

Ellen watched his concentration and wondered what was so terrible that he wasn't answering her.

John cleared his throat. He replaced the lid and began pouring the tea into the cups. 'I'm... er... I'm sorry, I don't mean to be mysterious about things.' He looked up and studied Ellen for a moment.

Ellen raised her eyebrows but waited for him to finish.

'I... er... the thing is, I noticed your reaction when Irene said she had a story about the docks. You were clearly worried about what the story was.'

Ellen gazed down at the table before closing her eyes. 'No, you must be mistaken.'

John gave a wry smile. 'I know I'm not.' He waited but Ellen said nothing. 'Look, I like to think we are friends, and in time I'd like us to be more than that.'

Ellen's eyes widened as she looked up at him. She opened her mouth to speak but he held up his hand to stop her. 'That's not a conversation for now because I know you don't know me very well so I don't expect a great response from that, but I'm trying to let you know in my own clumsy way that you can trust me. You can tell me anything and it will go no further, and if I can help I will.' He sighed. 'I've laid my cards on the table, do you think you can do the same?'

Ellen took a deep breath. 'I don't know because you work at the newspaper so you might have the urge to get a story in print and I don't know if I can risk that.'

John shook his head. 'Yes, the paper is important, but I would never put any friendship at risk. I promise. Get me a Bible and I'll swear on it. I just want to help if I can.'

Ellen nodded.

John picked up his cup and took a sip of his tea. 'You didn't hide your fear very well in the office; the others may not have noticed but when I see you, I can't take my eyes off you, so I notice everything.'

Ellen blushed as she tucked a loose strand of hair behind her ear. 'You promise it won't go any further?'

John lifted his hand and drew a cross on his chest. 'Cross my heart.'

Ellen frowned. 'My father, and me to a point, have been accused of being involved in the break-ins on the docks. He's not allowed back to work until the investigation is complete.' She stared at John, waiting to see how he reacted but his face gave nothing away. 'The thing is, my father has made no secret of the fact that he doesn't approve of the war but that doesn't mean he would be a spy for the enemy. I want to try and prove he isn't but I'm struggling to gain any meaningful evidence.'

John nodded. 'That I can understand, but why do they think you could be the spy?'

Ellen gave a humourless laugh. 'Because my father kept forgetting his sandwiches, so I used to take them to the docks, to his office. I can quite honestly say I was never there for more than a few minutes and if I saw anything on his desk, I probably wouldn't know what it was, let alone the importance of it.'

John frowned. 'I take it security must have let you on the docks?'

'Of course. I've known most of them since I was a little girl.' Ellen could feel the tears pricking her eyes. 'I just can't stand by and let them put my father in jail for something he didn't do. He may not believe in the war, but he loves his country and he's a very proud man.'

John took another sip of his tea. 'Don't let your tea get cold.' He placed his cup back on to its saucer. 'When you last went to the docks, did you meet anyone? That is, anyone you wouldn't normally meet?'

Ellen shrugged. 'No, it was always so dark and sometimes foggy so you couldn't see much at all.'

John glanced down at his cup. 'There must be something. When you have time, sit down and think carefully about each time you went and any conversations you might have had. Write it all down so you have all the information, no matter how trivial it might seem, and it might trigger something you have forgotten.'

Ellen nodded. 'I will. Thank you for wanting to help me.' She frowned. 'When I sat at Irene's desk I noticed my father's name on a piece of paper but I couldn't read what else she had written.' She paused. 'You won't let anyone know at the paper, will you?'

John smiled. 'Your secret's safe with me, and I shall keep my eyes and ears open for any information. We will get to the bottom of this, I promise. But one thing is for certain: Irene won't be able to keep it to herself if she has a story like that.'

14

Mary glanced up at the clock on the kitchen wall when she heard a thud at the front door. She frowned as she stared at her grandma. 'Who's that at this time in the morning? It's not even nine o'clock yet.'

Phyllis looked over at Mary. 'Maybe it's the postman.'

Mary dried her hands on her apron, before marching out of the kitchen and into the hallway, arriving just as another thud came down on the front door.

Harold appeared in the hallway at the same time. 'Are you expecting someone?'

Mary shook her head. 'Of course not – it's not even nine o'clock yet, and anyway, since when do I have visitors? It's more likely to be for you.'

Ellen appeared on the landing. 'Is everything all right?'

Mary shrugged. 'I'm sure we'll find out in a minute. I hope it's not someone who wants to come in; I haven't done any tidying up yet.' The lock on the door grated as Mary twisted it and pulled the door open. The March sunshine was trying to break through the gloom of the cloudy day. She clenched her jaw as she faced three policemen. 'What can I do for you?'

The police officer who was standing just in front of the other two spoke first. 'You might want to invite us in rather than discuss it on your doorstep for the neighbours to hear.'

Harold stepped forward. 'What's going on?'

The police officer took a breath. 'I didn't want to do this on your doorstep but you're not leaving me any choice. Harold Beckford, I have to take you in for questioning and I need to search your property.'

Mary gasped; fear trampled over her face as she looked over at her father.

Harold frowned. 'What do you mean take me in for questioning? Am I under arrest? I've already told you everything, I don't know what more I can say.'

The police officer lifted his chin slightly. 'I have to take you in for questioning and I think it's fair to say you won't be coming home again for some time. There's evidence that you were part of the break-in.' The police officer walked across the threshold and the other two followed him. 'I need your camera and any photographs you might have of the docks.'

Mary sobbed. 'No, he's innocent.'

'What evidence?' Harold stepped forward, putting his arm around his youngest daughter and shaking his head. 'I can't believe this, I haven't used my camera in years, not since my wife died. You're welcome to take it, although I don't know what that will prove.'

Ellen caught her breath as she stood on the upstairs landing. On the tips of her toes, she ran back into her room and collected all the notes she had made, along with the photographs. Scanning the room, she wondered where she could hide them. Panic rushed over her as she stepped this way and that. Her heart was racing.

She needed to get into the basement without being seen because then she could hide everything under her bed. Stay calm and think. Taking a deep breath, Ellen shook her head; that would probably be the first place they would look. She listened at the doorway; everyone was still in the hall.

'Mr Beckford, you need to understand you will probably be arrested for spying.'

Ellen could hear Mary crying.

Her grandmother's loud voice bounced off the walls. 'How can you say he will be arrested for spying? You have no evidence! Why would he break into his own office?'

The policeman's voice was calm when he spoke. 'We believe that he may have been working with someone. The lock of your office was not damaged in any way, although there are some scratches around it, which implies you either gave someone the key or you left it unlocked.'

Harold tutted. 'But I didn't and I've told you that a hundred times, but you clearly aren't listening and just want a scapegoat.' He paused. 'After the first break-in the window of my office was open. I remember closing it when we all walked in there; maybe that's how they got in. Perhaps you should fingerprint it.'

'Is that so? You've never mentioned that before, so why now?'

Harold shook his head. 'I didn't think it would come to this, I thought you'd find the person who did it because it wasn't me.'

'Well, you could be making it up. We have to take you in for questioning. You withheld the detail about the window and you've made it known that you do not believe the war is right and therefore you don't support it.'

Harold raised his voice. 'What, because I don't like seeing good kids losing limbs or, even worse, dying, that makes me a spy?' He tightened his lips. 'And for your information I wasn't the only one in the office when I shut the window.'

Ellen edged along the landing and into her own bedroom. She looked around, trying to decide where to put the paperwork, but nothing came to her. Would it be dangerous to put it in her father's bedroom? At least he had more furniture than she did. She poked her head out the door and listened to the silence. Should she risk the basement if they weren't in the hallway? She shook her head. What would she say if they suddenly appeared? Ellen walked along to her father's bedroom and scanned it. She didn't have long; she knew questions would be asked if she didn't go downstairs soon. Her eyes rested on the oil lamp her mother had loved but never used. Her heart was pounding as she unscrewed the lower half of the lamp before folding and rolling the paper in her hands and stuffing it inside. The creak of the stairs warned her someone was coming. She thrust the glass top back on the lamp and moved to the window just as the bedroom door swung open.

Ellen peered over her shoulder and saw the police officers standing there. 'Ahh, that's what I need, a strong man to help me.' Flush-faced, she turned to face them. 'I've been trying to open this window, but it appears to be stuck.'

The policeman eyed her. 'You do look rather flushed.' He marched over and pushed the sash window up.

Irene suddenly came into Ellen's head. 'What can I say, I'm clearly not as strong as you, but then I suppose you wouldn't expect me to be.' She reached out and rested her hand on his arm. 'Thank you so much, your timing was excellent, and you helped get some air into this stuffy room.'

The policeman bowed his head. 'I'm glad I could be of assistance.'

Ellen smiled. 'Excuse the mess, I'm afraid my sister and I have been slow to make the beds and tidy up this morning. May I ask what brings you up here?'

The policeman cleared his throat. 'I'm looking for your father's camera and any photos he has taken with it, particularly of the docks. I also need to look in his wardrobe to see if he owns any brown woollen clothing or a scarf and hat.'

Ellen nodded. 'I don't recall seeing anything brown but feel free to look in his wardrobe.' She walked towards it. The floorboards creaked and the wardrobe wobbled as she pulled the heavy wooden door open. 'I expect his camera is packed away in the basement; I'll take you down there when you've finished looking at his clothing.' She pulled open the drawers of the chest so the police could riffle through them one at a time.

The policemen nodded to each other. 'Well, there doesn't seem to be anything here, perhaps we'll go down to the basement.' He turned to walk out of the room.

Ellen breathed a sigh of relief. 'Do you seriously believe my father is a spy, or working with the enemy?'

The policeman raised his eyebrows. 'We have found a photo of the docks in the front room cabinet, and it's the same size as the others that were on the roll of film we found.'

'What, how can that be?' Ellen feigned her astonishment as guilt washed over her. Tears pricked at her eyes, she swallowed hard to try to move the lump forming in her throat. Was she going to be the cause of her father's downfall? Why hadn't she moved the photograph she had hidden away from Alan?

'Who knows?' The policeman shrugged. 'But maybe he's guilty.'

Ellen stood rooted to the spot and stared after him as he walked down the stairs.

Ten minutes later, with the camera and photographs in a bag, Harold was being escorted out of the house and into a police car. He looked back with fear in his eyes. Mary broke down and sobbed at the front door.

Ellen stepped forward and gave her father a hug. 'Don't worry, Pa, somehow I'm going to prove you had nothing to do with it.' She stood there biting her lip until it hurt and the iron taste of blood seeped into her mouth. She watched the car pull away, before turning to her grandmother. 'I can't believe it has come to this. How am I ever going to prove he's innocent?' Ellen wrapped her arm around Mary as they all went inside.

Phyllis pulled herself as upright as she could. 'Come on, it's time for a cup of tea and a council of war.'

Ellen frowned. 'A council of war?'

Phyllis nodded. 'Yes, we need a plan if we're going to get your father out of this mess.' She turned to Ellen. 'And it's not something you can do on your own.'

They entered the kitchen and Mary picked up the kettle before turning on the tap and spraying everything around her. The water bounced loudly off the inside of the kettle.

Ellen scraped a chair along the floor tiles as she pulled it away from the table for her grandmother to sit on. She closed her eyes for a moment. 'I don't know what more I can do.'

Phyllis shook her head. 'Look, you need to involve others, perhaps your friends at Foyles or the newspaper office.'

Ellen's eyes snapped open. 'I can't do that; they are reporters, and it would soon be all over the front pages.'

'You know your ma was a strong woman but even she knew you need good friends when times get tough. It's those times you discover the quality of those friends. This is something you can't do on your own; you are too close to it so you have to figure out who to trust to help you.'

* * *

Irene sidled up to a man in a black suit wearing a trilby hat. 'Good morning. You found it then?'

The man didn't look at her as he tapped the end of a cigarette on the box it came from before putting it to his lips. 'I'm a reporter, aren't I? And let's face it, it's not hard to find anywhere in London.' He slipped his hand into his trouser pocket and pulled out a box of matches. Opening them, he took a single match out and struck the red tip along the side of the box. The smell of sulphur filled the air around them. He sucked in his cheeks as he drew on the cigarette, before blowing the grey smoke rings out into the air. 'So, the story you're trying to sell me is a bit sketchy. I need more details.'

Irene gave him a wry smile. 'You have to make it worth my while. It's worth a lot of money.'

The man gave her a sideways glance. 'If the story is that big, why aren't you writing it for your own paper or selling it yourself to the nationals?'

Irene scowled up at him, before remembering she wanted to keep him sweet and keep the wrinkles at bay. 'Mr Williams won't want to rock the boat, especially as his son John has been out a couple of times with Harold Beckford's daughter. Your paper is different, the *Echo* doesn't have anyone to protect in the same way.' She looked scathingly at the man standing beside her. 'What's more, Mr Williams certainly wouldn't pay me what it's worth.'

The reporter stared at her for a minute. 'Or do you mean you can't write it well enough to do it justice and therefore not get paid the money you think it's worth?' He took a breath. 'Let's face it, you could write and sell it to the nationals, making a big name for yourself along the way.'

Irene's eyes narrowed. 'I don't know why you think I can't write it. I'm more than capable of writing such a story. I want to earn from my hard work, which won't happen if it's left up to Mr

Williams. I'm tired of not being paid what I'm worth, but if you don't want the gift I'm giving you for the price that I suggested then I'll go elsewhere. Plenty will bite my hand off.'

Frank stood outside the craft shop looking in the window. He had been about to go in to buy the wool his mother wanted when he caught Irene's voice. He'd peered over his shoulder when he'd heard the man talking to her and couldn't resist staying put and listening to their conversation.

The man chuckled. 'I'm sure they would.' He hesitated. 'What about Frank? I hear he rewrites most of your articles, you know, makes them punchier, but doesn't get any of the credit.'

Irene's eyes widened. 'I can't believe what I'm hearing. That's just not true. Everything that has my name attached to it is all my own work. When I find out who's spreading such scandalous reports I'll take them down, and that's a promise.'

The man threw back his head and gave a hearty laugh. 'I'm sure Frank will be pleased to hear that; you know he's one of the good ones?' He took another drag on his cigarette. 'Right, I've obviously got the notes you dropped off, but I need to go through them again and to ask if you've checked your facts.'

Irene nodded. 'The police have arrested Harold Beckford for spying at the docks and they think his daughter, Ellen, is involved but she hasn't been arrested yet. Apparently, she used to go to the docks most days under the guise of dropping off her father's sandwiches, but they think she might have been collecting information to give to the other side.'

The man nodded. 'Yeah, but neither of them have ever broken the law before, at least not from what I could find out.' He studied Irene. 'Are you sure you don't have your own motive for bringing them down? I mean, have you added your own bit of embroidery around the story to make it look worse than it is?'

Irene gave him a long look. 'Have you never embroidered a

story to make it sound more sensational than it is? We both know it's not always about the facts.'

The man chuckled. 'Ain't that the truth. I've done some checking and the old man is at the police station, but the daughter works in Foyles Bookshop and at the same newspaper as you. I understand she's a pretty young thing, and impressionable, so could she be stealing your crown and you're just trying to get rid of her? Let's face it, you've been the queen bee there for a long time now and yet you haven't moved on in what you report on.'

Irene spluttered. 'No one could ever steal my crown, and that naive scrap of a girl will never have the wherewithal to know how to do it. I have them all eating out of the palm of my hand, trust me, and for your information I choose what I report on.'

'Sometimes it's the naive ones you have to watch out for.' The man lifted his trilby and ran his fingers through his dark hair before putting his hat back on. 'I'm sure you have the men all wrapped around your little finger, but does that include John?'

Irene fidgeted, moving her feet from side to side. 'Look, I don't want to stand here chatting in these heels. If you want to keep talking, let's get a cuppa somewhere.'

'No, I've heard enough. I'll speak to my editor and get back to you.' He walked away without a backwards glance.

Irene gave a sideways smile before opening her own box of cigarettes and walking in the opposite direction.

Frank scowled as he turned round to see her walking away. Shaking his head, he pushed open the craft shop door, and the bell rang out.

* * *

Ellen wrapped her arms around Mary and closed her eyes as her sister sobbed. She was glad she had been home when the police had arrived to search the house that morning. The tension had been tangible as everyone tried to not voice their worries about how things were going with the investigation. She was beginning to think they weren't even looking for anyone else but kept that thought to herself as she rubbed her sister's back to try and give her some comfort.

Phyllis tutted. 'It's no good crying, Mary. We need to find a way to prove his innocence. You would be better off praying because God only knows how we do that, especially now they've found that photograph.'

Ellen tightened her arms around her sister. 'It'll be all right Mary, you'll see. I don't know how yet but we'll figure something out and we'll do it together.'

Sniffing, Mary leant back and, with watery eyes, peered up at Ellen. 'How? The police took his camera and any photographs he'd taken. They even looked to see if he owned a brown coat.'

Phyllis stopped knitting; her hands were almost transparent as she gripped the needles. 'Ellen, did they find the notes you made of that night and the photographs you held on to?'

Ellen gave a wry smile. 'No, they didn't thanks to Ma.'

Mary wiped away her tears. 'I don't understand.'

Ellen's gaze travelled between them. 'Do you remember the oil lamp Ma had but never used because she didn't want it to get black with smoke and soot?'

They both frowned but nodded at the same time.

'Well, I was frantically looking for somewhere to hide everything when I went into Pa's bedroom, and I remembered the lamp had never been used so I rolled it all up and pushed it into the base of it.' Ellen reached down the side of her bed and lifted the oil lamp to show them. 'It's all still in there in case they come back looking for something else. I never thought I would say this, but I was thankful for the creaking stairs; they told me someone was coming up so I moved towards the window and pretended I couldn't open it.' She laughed. 'I didn't think I would be willing to act like a helpless female, but I can see there are times when it comes in handy.'

Phyllis chuckled. 'Well done for thinking so quickly, I'm sure the distraction helped.'

Ellen nodded. 'Irene – she's a reporter at work – uses her feminine wiles all the time but I have to say I never thought I would.'

Phyllis nodded. 'Sometimes you've got to do what you've got to do, and no one should sit in judgement of that, as long as you're not using people for your own ends.'

Mary sniffed. 'I don't like the idea of Pa being locked up, or us being in this house by ourselves.' She looked up at Ellen. 'I'm more than a little frightened.'

'I know.' Ellen squeezed her hand. 'Just remember you're not on your own; there are three of us; we have to stick together and try to come up with a plan.' She picked up the soft-bristled hairbrush. 'Come on, let me brush your hair like Ma used to.'

Mary gave her sister a watery smile before removing the clip from her hair and turning around.

Ellen gently brushed the ends before working up to the top of her head. 'We need to get some sleep soon otherwise we won't be able to think straight tomorrow.' She glanced over at her grandma and smiled at the comforting sound of her knitting needles clicking together. 'I'm surprised you can see anything in this light.'

Phyllis laughed. 'I don't need to be able to see much to knit, but I must admit I don't like sleeping down here in the basement, it always smells of damp and it's not like we can open a window, so I'll be glad when we can get into our bedrooms again.'

Mary laughed. 'I know what you mean, Gran, I always think it's creepy down here sleeping amongst the storage boxes that haven't been opened for goodness knows how long, and my imagination runs riot seeing things that aren't there, even after four years.'

Ellen put down the hairbrush. 'Sorry, I know I haven't done it for as long as Ma would have done but I've done my best.'

Mary reached out and gave her sister a hug. 'It was lovely, thank you.'

Ellen pulled back the blanket and sheet on her bed and got under the covers to keep warm.

Suddenly she heard a noise. Was that the door key clanging against the front door? She stiffened but didn't say anything. Clutching the blanket close to her chest, she looked up at the ceiling of the basement, straining to hear any movement.

Mary got into her bed. 'I suppose it's—'

'Sshh, listen.' Ellen's heart was pounding as she pointed to the ceiling.

Mary frowned. 'What am I listening for?'

Phyllis put her knitting down and looked up.

Ellen's whole body tensed as she peered into the shadows of the dark corner where the stairs were. She sat still, afraid to break the silence as she listened intently.

Upstairs, the floorboards creaking echoed down in the basement.

Mary gasped before whispering, 'There's someone in the house. Do you think they've released Pa?'

Ellen glanced at her grandma and whispered, 'What do you think we should do? I mean, should we stay put and hope whoever it is doesn't come down here or should we go and find them?'

Phyllis frowned and bit down on her thin lips. 'I think we would be safer to stay here. I mean, we don't know who it is or how many of them there are. If it's your father, he will come down here to make sure we are all right.'

They all sat in silence, listening to cupboards and drawers being opened and shut again. As whoever it was moved around the house, the floorboards creaked and groaned.

Ellen tightened her lips before whispering, 'What are they looking for? It's not like we have money.' She paused, listening again, trying to guess which room the burglar was in. 'I never thought I'd ever say that I was happy to hear the floorboards, but I must admit to being grateful for it tonight.'

All three of them sat in silence once more, hoping they would hear the front door shut again soon.

15

Ellen hadn't slept all night. She'd kept her gaze fixed on the basement door and stairs. Her eyes had felt heavy and a couple of times her head had dropped and her chin had hit her chest, but both times she'd woken up with a start. She swung her legs out of bed and listened for any sign of movement upstairs. The noise of someone in the house had stopped in the early hours of the morning, but she hadn't been brave enough to go upstairs and check. It was only then that her grandmother and sister had given in to tiredness and fallen asleep, and she didn't have the heart to wake them now.

She took a deep breath, the stale air hitting her throat, and grabbed her dressing gown from the bottom of her bed. Standing up, Ellen quickly threw it on along with her slippers. She crept on tiptoes towards the stairs, trying to remember if any of them creaked, but nothing came to mind. Reaching out, she placed her hand on the banister and decided to keep as close to the edge of the stairs as she could, hoping there would be less chance of the step groaning underfoot. Without realising it, she held her breath as she climbed them, and when she reached the top she screwed up her face as she turned the handle. The grind of the lock screamed out in the silence. She quickly glanced over her shoulder but there was no movement, Mary and her grandmother appeared to be still asleep. Ellen breathed a sigh of relief and pulled open the door. Early morning light shone into the basement. She stepped out and pulled the door to behind her. She could hear her blood pulsating in her ears as her heart pounded in her chest. She stood still for a moment, straining to hear any noise, but the house was silent.

Ellen jumped as the door behind her suddenly flew open.

Mary was frowning as she whispered, 'What on earth are you doing coming up here on your own?' She handed Ellen an old frying pan while she gripped the handle of an iron.

Ellen looked down at the items and tried to hold in the laughter that was threatening to bubble to the surface.

'Don't laugh, I found it in the basement when we first started sleeping down there. You might be glad of it; you don't know if someone is still in here.' Mary scowled. 'If we make it to the kitchen, I'll grab the rolling pin as well.'

Ellen shook her head but held the pan up near her shoulder, ready to swing it if needed. 'Come on then, let's go slowly and quietly.' She took a deep breath before she took a step forward along the hallway. Her gaze latched on to the front door; she couldn't remember hearing it shut after the creaking floorboards, so did that mean someone was still in the house?

Mary followed close behind Ellen.

They came to the kitchen first. Mary gasped at the sight of the open kitchen cupboards and drawers. Ellen stood guard in the doorway while Mary tiptoed in and grabbed the rolling pin from one of the drawers and quickly returned to the doorway. Ellen stepped further into the hall. The floorboard creaked. She turned to look at Mary, who looked terrified. 'We need to get this over and done with before we both have a heart attack.'

Mary nodded. 'Just run into the front room and I'll be close behind you, then we'll go upstairs.'

Ellen sucked in her breath and ran forward, trying to ignore the bouncing floorboards. She held back the scream she felt rising inside her as she faced the devastation; the floor was covered with papers and photographs. She stepped further into the room and noticed some of the pictures were of their mother and the River Thames. She turned to look at her sister and saw her tears were threatening to spill over. Ellen grabbed her hand and squeezed it tight. 'Don't worry, we'll tidy up in a minute.'

'What's happened here?'

Startled, the girls turned to face the doorway.

Ellen's lips tightened. 'Grandma, someone was clearly in the house last night. We haven't checked upstairs yet so you need to go back downstairs to stay safe and we'll come and get you when we've done that.'

Phyllis raised her eyebrows. 'I might be old but I'm not hiding away from whoever the coward is; let him face us.'

Mary shook her head. 'Grandma, I couldn't stand it if something happened to you, it's bad enough Pa isn't here.'

Phyllis shook her head. 'I'm not hiding away. Now get upstairs while I start tidying up the kitchen.'

Ellen shrugged, knowing it was pointless to argue with her gran. She took Mary's arm and they walked back into the hall.

Mary looked up. 'Do you think someone is likely to still be in the house?'

'I don't know but we need to feel safe so let's just get it over and done with.' Ellen tentatively stepped on to the bottom step. She took a breath and ran up them, trying to ignore the creaks that followed her and shrilled out as Mary ran behind.

Mary was breathless as she reached the top and stood next to Ellen. 'Well, no one has come rushing on to the landing so that's a good sign, right?'

'Let's hope so.' Ellen stepped towards her father's bedroom. She shook her head at the sight of his bedding on the floor and his mattress hanging off the bed. His wardrobe was open, as were the drawers. 'Someone was definitely looking for something and didn't mind ransacking the place to find it.'

Mary sighed and turned back to the landing. 'I think whoever was in here has gone but I expect Grandma's room and ours will be in the same state.'

Ellen nodded. 'Thank goodness I moved my notes on what happened at the docks.' Her mind immediately went to the photographs she'd held back from the police. Was that what the person was looking for?

* * *

The early morning sunshine was trying to break through the grey clouds, offering a promise of spring warmth. People smiled as they went about their business. Children's voices could be heard in the distance as they played their war games. A baby cried nearby.

Mary sighed as the Victoria station arches came into view. 'I feel too tired for this, and I feel bad leaving Gran on her own in the house.'

Ellen walked alongside Mary. 'I know what you mean but it'll be good for you to get out of the house, and Gran's made of stern stuff. Try not to worry, we'll finish tidying up when I get home.'

Mary shook her head. 'I just can't believe it happened, especially while we were in the house.'

'At least we were in the basement and the burglar didn't come down there. It was lucky Pa wasn't in the house. Who knows what would have happened if he had been?'

Mary stopped walking and turned to Ellen. 'Do you think it was someone who knew he'd been taken away by the police? Because if so, it's someone who knows us and that makes it even worse.'

Ellen took Mary's hands in hers. 'We may never find out who it was so try not to keep thinking about it.' She pulled her sister into her arms. 'At least nothing of Ma's was taken.'

Mary pulled back and forced a smile. 'That's true.'

They carried on walking into the station, which was as busy as always. The smoky atmosphere made Ellen cough as they strolled towards the tea table.

Mary turned to Ellen and laughed. 'I'm all right, you don't have to deliver me.'

'I know but I want to—'

'Isn't that the man who came round our house? You know, the one who works at the newspaper?'

Ellen peered over her shoulder. 'Where?'

'I don't want to point but he's near platform three and talking to a grey-haired man.'

Ellen scanned the concourse. 'Oh yes, I see them, that does look like Alan. I wonder who the older man is?'

Mary shrugged. 'Maybe it's his father.'

They stood and watched them both for a minute or two.

Mary shook Ellen's arm. 'I think Alan has just given the older man something.'

Ellen smiled at Mary's excitement. 'It might be photographs he has taken; you know, family pictures like he took of us.'

Mary didn't take her eyes off him. 'Maybe, but they don't look like they are father and son, do they? I mean, they aren't smiling or laughing.'

Ellen shrugged. 'That's true. Perhaps you could try and get nearer to hear what they are talking about.'

Mary looked horrified.

Ellen laughed. 'Well, I can't; he sees me most days at the paper.'

Mary gave her sister a wry smile. 'I suppose that's true. All right, I'll try, but I can't promise anything.' She stepped forward, lifting her head confidently. Peering over her shoulder, she saw Ellen nod in her direction.

Mary walked closely behind two women and their children, her gaze fixed on Alan and the older man. The two women stopped without warning and Mary collided with one of them. 'I'm so sorry, I wasn't looking where I was going.'

The woman rubbed her arm. 'That's all right, I did just stop, thanks to these two here.'

Mary looked across at the two young children. 'I hope you're all right.' She glanced across at Alan, who was still chatting to the older man. 'I'm sorry I must go, or I'll miss my train.'

'Of course.' The lady stepped aside.

Mary marched ahead until she was within earshot of the two men. She opened her handbag and pretended to rummage around inside while she listened intently to their conversation.

Alan shook his head. 'I don't know what else you want me to do; you are never happy with me.'

The grey-haired man glanced down at the ground for a moment before looking up again. 'We just want you to do what you're told and stop messing things up, I can't keep covering for you. You've had a lot of help with money and cover stories, and it's time you showed the respect that help deserves.' He straightened his lips. 'I have to go, otherwise I'll miss my meeting. Just remember what I said, we're all accountable for our actions.'

Alan nodded. 'I will but it's not as easy as you think.'

'Nothing we do is easy thanks to this war. If you have anything to say before our next meeting then use the newspaper, if you still remember how.'

Alan gave a wry smile. 'I know I haven't used it yet, but I don't want to draw attention to myself.'

The older man nodded. 'Right, I have to go.' Without another word he turned and walked further up the concourse.

Mary quickly snapped her bag shut and turned away. Her heart was racing as she sped towards Ellen, trying to avoid people walking towards her.

Ellen rushed forward to meet her. 'Are you all right?'

Mary gasped for breath. 'Yes, but I was scared he would see me and then recognise me from when he came round.'

Ellen grabbed her arm and pulled her aside, near to the edge of a platform. 'He's coming.'

Both girls immediately turned around, while trying to peer over their shoulders at him.

Mary held her breath as he got nearer, hoping he would turn and go under the arches and onto the street beyond. 'Shall we follow him?'

Ellen watched him leave the station. 'No, he's probably doing something for the paper and we're just getting carried away with ourselves.'

Mary sighed. 'I expect you're right, but you must admit they did look suspicious. Although on the face of it they didn't seem to talk about anything important, but they also didn't seem like they were related to each other. I can't explain it, it's just a feeling I have.'

Ellen nodded. 'You were very brave to get that close.'

Mary bit her lip. 'The older man said something about "we just want you to do what you say you will". He also talked about cover stories and respect.' She shook her head. 'None of it made much sense to me.'

Ellen frowned. 'If you can, write down what they said, and we'll talk about it later. Something isn't right, I just don't know what it is yet.'

* * *

Ellen's damp palms clutched the straps of her handbag. Her brow creased. She knew she had to report the break-in last night to hopefully prove someone else was behind the break-ins at the docks, but she was running out of faith that the police would do anything, let alone believe her. She paced up and down the pavement, unaware of the looks she was getting as people walked by.

'Yer all right, lovey?'

Ellen stopped pacing and stared at the grey-haired lady, who was stooped over a walking stick.

'Is there anything I can do to 'elp? I mean, yer getting some strange looks from everyone; 'ave yer broke the law and yer to scared to give yerself up?'

Ellen frowned as she stared at the woman. She shook her head before quickly looking around her. The old lady was right, people were staring at her. 'No, I'm just trying to decide what's the best thing to do.'

The old lady gave a toothless grin. 'I figured yer already decided that because yer 'ere. I fink yer just got cold feet.'

Ellen swallowed hard. 'You're right, I'm scared because it could all backfire on me.'

The old lady shook her head. 'Trust yerself, trust what brought yer 'ere in the first place.'

Ellen looked up at the police station sign, focusing on it for a moment before peering back at the lady. 'You're right, I know what

I must do, regardless of the outcome. Thank you.' She turned to face the closed door, startled when it suddenly swung open, and a policeman walked out.

The policeman nodded. 'Everything all right, ladies?'

The old lady cackled. 'It's more than all right. Who doesn't love to see a man in uniform? If only I was fifty years younger.'

The policeman tipped his hat and gave her a big smile. 'If only all the ladies were like you.'

They watched him stroll down the street, stopping to talk to people as he went.

The lady kept her eyes focused on the policeman. 'Go on then, girl, get yerself inside and do what yer gotta do.'

Ellen nodded. 'Thank you.' She walked purposefully towards the black polished door and pulled it open. Stepping through the doorway, she saw an officer at the counter.

He looked up from his paperwork. 'Hello, miss, and what can I do for you?'

Ellen took a deep breath and stepped nearer to the counter. 'I need to speak to someone about a break-in at my home last night.' She took a breath. 'I'm Ellen Beckford, Harold Beckford's daughter.'

The policeman raised his eyebrows. 'I'll get someone to come and see you.' He walked to a closed door and opened it. 'I'll take you to an interview room.' He shut the door behind him and opened another adjacent to it. 'Follow me.'

Ellen did as she was told and was immediately shown into a room, which housed a table and four chairs.

'Take a seat while I try to find someone.' The policeman paused. 'You do know this is really a Port of London Authority case?'

Ellen nodded. 'What I have to say isn't directly about the case against my father. Our home was broken into last night, and I do believe it is linked to it.' She shook her head. 'The trouble is, I feel they have already made their minds up and I believe my father isn't guilty.'

The policeman raised his eyebrows. 'Everyone thinks their family member is innocent, but I'll find someone to help you.' He turned and closed the door as he left the room.

Ellen pulled a chair away from the table. She glanced around. She had never been in a police station before, and she suddenly doubted whether she had done the right thing in coming to one now. She wiped her damp palms down her lap. Her heart was racing. What if it all went wrong? What if they didn't believe the burglary was connected? Where could she go from there?

The door swung open, and the desk sergeant walked in. 'I'm afraid I'm the only one available to take the details of what you want to say.' He flung a pad of paper on the desk and took a pen out of his top jacket pocket. 'Let's get started.' He pulled out a chair opposite Ellen and sat down. 'Right, Miss Beckford.'

'Someone broke into our home last night after my father was arrested. You can't tell me that's a coincidence. The person was clearly looking for something specific because every room was ransacked but no money or jewellery was taken.'

The sergeant studied her for a moment. 'So that's why you're here?'

Ellen nodded. 'I did think at first there seemed little point in coming as nothing appeared to be taken, but what if it was the spy looking for something they think my father had?'

The sergeant raised his eyebrows. 'You have quite an imagination. Tell me what evidence you have to say your father's innocent of the break-ins at the docks?'

Ellen sighed. 'It should be me asking you what evidence you have to say he did do it; I don't believe you have anything.' She sighed. 'Look, my father got beaten black and blue and broke his leg chasing this man; does that really sound like someone who is involved in it? I'm telling you, someone came to our house looking for something last night.' Ellen released her grip on her handbag and undid the clasp. She hesitated for a moment. 'My father isn't a spy, so can I ask that you please approach this with an open mind?'

The sergeant shook his head. 'It's very hard to do that when all the evidence is stacked against him.'

Ellen's face flushed with colour as she raised her voice. 'What evidence? He works at the docks, which he's done for most of my life, and to my knowledge he never got into trouble. He chased the person that broke into his office and broke his leg in the process, but in the eyes of the police he was running away with some photographs. I must ask, why would he do that especially as he could take them from the docks at any time? And the thinnest of evidence is that he owns a camera and has taken photographs of the river before. Have I forgotten anything?'

The sergeant smiled. 'No, you seemed to have summed it up quite nicely, except for the photograph that was found in your home when your father was arrested.'

'I don't know how that got there but you must admit it's all very flimsy, especially as he has never been in trouble with the police before.'

The sergeant leant back in his chair. 'Now that's not strictly true.'

Ellen jerked her head back and gasped. 'What?'

'Well, he got arrested a couple of times at the peace rallies in Trafalgar Square. I understand he was a little exuberant in expressing his anti-war feelings.'

Ellen shrugged. 'I don't suppose he was alone and he's very passionate in what he believes is right, but that doesn't make him a spy otherwise all the other people on the rallies would have been arrested too.'

The sergeant chuckled. 'Is there anything else?'

Ellen hesitated before sliding her hand inside her bag and pulling out one of the photographs that were in her possession. She put the postcard-size picture down on the table.

They both stared at it without saying a word.

The sergeant looked up, his eyes narrowed. 'Where did you get this from?'

'I found it at home this morning, among all the paperwork that had been thrown on the floor from our cabinet in the front room.' Ellen sensed this conversation wasn't going to end well. 'I assume this was what the person who broke in was looking for. I think it's from the film the police got developed. They must have dropped it in their hurry to leave.' She took a breath. 'When they came, with the photographs, to question my father the rockets went up to warn us of a possible attack, so they quickly left, and we went down into the basement; none of us realised the photograph had been left behind.'

The sergeant tightened his lips but said nothing.

Ellen rubbed her hands over her face. 'Look, I know I can't prove that but if the officers had counted how many they had before they came round and then counted them after they left, they would know they left some in their hurry to leave.'

'You do know that bringing it here makes it look like it's your father's.'

Ellen stared at the sergeant. 'I know how it looks, but surely someone has to start believing me otherwise how am I ever going to prove his innocence?' She picked up the photograph. 'It's important someone compares the photographs in your possession, and this one, with the ones you took from our home, which my father took with his own camera.' She took a breath. 'There

must be some way of proving they came from different cameras.'
She picked up the photograph and moved it this way and that.
'This one is bigger than the ones we have at home so could that
mean something? My father might be able to answer that
question.'

The sergeant's lips thinned as he sucked in his breath. 'I will
have to get someone who knows about these things to look at it,
but I have to say it doesn't look good – after all, you could have
taken this picture to get your father off.' He studied the young girl
in front of him for a moment. 'I admire you for coming here to
defend your father, but he has taken pictures of the docks before.'

Ellen vigorously shook her head. 'Not since the war began.'
She took a breath. 'My mother died just before the war started
and my father hasn't touched his camera since she passed away.
Check your records. It was packed away in the basement when the
police came to search our home.' She could feel the tears pricking
at her eyes and she blinked quickly. 'I knew it was a mistake
reporting the break-in last night, let alone bringing the photograph to you, but I was brought up to believe in the police and
that honesty always pays off.' She sniffed. 'I never thought I would
say this, as my ma was a strong woman, but she was wrong about
honesty always paying off. You have all decided my father is guilty
and as far as I can tell you haven't bothered looking for anyone
else.' She scraped back the chair on the wooden floor and stood
up. 'You've just made the evidence fit an innocent man while the
true spy is still working against this country. You tell me how you
are not all being done for treason.' She paced across to the door
and flung it wide open before stepping outside to let the tears roll
down her cheeks.

Alice was back on her normal counter. She beamed as she watched the customers milling around Foyles Bookshop. She could hear children giggling upstairs and wondered if Molly was putting on her funny voices as she read books to them.

An old lady gave her a toothless grin. 'It's good to see you back.'

Alice smiled. 'It's good to be back. I'm enjoying the few days' work when I'm needed, a lot of staff seem to be going down with some sickness or other.'

'We've got to look after ourselves, so you take care.'

Alice nodded. 'And you.'

'How is that handsome husband of yours? I do love a man in uniform, even if it's a police one.'

Alice chuckled. 'He's doing fine, thank you.'

'Well, it's good to see you, and hopefully one day I'll be here when he pops in.' She turned and hobbled away with a wave.

Alice tidied up her counter, moving books that had been returned to the far end of the table behind her. It had been a long, but wonderful day. She took a deep breath, knowing she would sleep well after such a busy day. Looking out across the shop, she noticed Ellen on her knees talking to a little girl, who was clutching a rag doll in one hand and a book in the other. Ellen tweaked the girl's pigtails. The child giggled and Ellen took her hand and walked towards the children's department. Alice shook her head; it was amazing how many children lost their parents up there.

Victoria strolled over to Alice. 'Are you all right?'

Alice smiled. 'I'm more than all right, I feel like I've come home. I was just watching Ellen with a little girl who looked like she had lost a parent.'

Victoria nodded. 'Yes, she's very good with them.'

Alice glanced across at Victoria. 'She seems a lovely, but troubled person. There's a sadness about her.'

Victoria walked around the counter to the stack of returns. 'Yes, I know what you mean. I'd like to help her if I could but I'm not sure where to start, apart from offering an ear when she wants to talk. She's a hard worker and gets on with everyone; at least, I've not had any complaints about her.'

Alice listened to her friend and smiled. 'Well, we do like a lost cause.'

Victoria giggled. 'Why do you think we are all friends? I'm happy to admit our friendship, and probably our arguments as well, have saved me at times.'

'Ahh, that's a lovely thing to say.' Alice reached out and hugged Victoria tight. 'Then we must help Ellen in any way we can.'

Victoria stepped back. 'I'm not sure Molly would say the same, I know she has a heart of gold, but I do have concerns about her abruptness with Ellen. I know we are used to it but sometimes I think she goes too far.'

'Then we need to talk to Ellen and see what we can do to help, and I'm sure Molly will want to help too. Perhaps when we close, we can take five minutes to sit down with her.'

Victoria nodded. 'That sounds like a plan. I'll speak with Molly and then maybe we'll grab Ellen at the end of the day.' Looking down at her wristwatch, she smiled. 'Well, actually that's in about ten minutes. I hope we can help her in some way.'

Alice smiled. 'I'm sure we will. There isn't a problem that can't be solved; at least, I hope there isn't.' Alice picked up some paperwork on her counter. 'Well, I'd better get tidying up.'

Victoria picked up the books from behind Alice's counter. 'I'll take these down to Albert for checking and I'll see you in the staffroom.'

It wasn't long before Mr Leadbetter was standing by the door and wishing everyone good night. Once the shop was empty of customers and the door was locked, all the staff made their way to clock off.

Ellen waited in the queue with her clocking out card in her hand. The chime of the clock sounded every time a card was put in and pulled out again. She hadn't been able to stop thinking about who had broken into her home all day; what were they looking for? Surely, they wouldn't come back. She hadn't wanted to leave her grandma on her own, but she was so independent she had insisted that Ellen still had to work and she'd even talked about taking in washing or doing sewing for people to help bring in some money.

Molly called out, 'Ellen.'

Shouts of good night and laughter filled the room as everyone left the shop.

Ellen reached the clock and put in her card and pulled it out again.

'Ellen.' Molly reached out and rested her hand on Ellen's arm.

Startled, Ellen looked up.

Molly smiled. 'I'm sorry, I didn't mean to make you jump. I've been calling you, but you've clearly been in a world of your own.'

Ellen blushed. 'Sorry, I have a lot on my mind.'

Molly nodded. 'Yes, it's obvious you are troubled, and we want to help if we can. I assume it's to do with your father?'

Ellen felt the tears pricking at her eyes. She nodded, not trusting herself to speak.

'Come on then, it might help to share what's going round and round in your head.'

Molly led her to the table where Victoria and Alice were already sitting. 'I'm just going to get a drink of water. Does anyone want anything?'

'No, thank you,' the three of them said in unison.

Victoria cleared her throat. 'Ellen, we are all quite worried about you; you've been very subdued today and I know you have a lot going on with your father, but we wondered if we could help at all.'

Ellen sat in silence; her fingers intertwined as her hands rested on the table.

Alice leant forward. 'Sometimes it helps to talk about these things, and you can trust us.'

Molly pulled out a chair, the legs scratching at the floor, and sat down. She sipped the water from the glass and placed it in front of her on the table.

Ellen peered at them watching her. She took a deep breath. 'My father has been arrested, and someone broke into our home last night. Whoever it was searched through every cupboard and drawer while we were in the basement.' A tear rolled down her cheek. She quickly brushed it away. 'I don't know what they were looking for, or if they found it.'

Alice gasped. 'Have you told the police?'

Ellen nodded.

Molly leant forward. 'It sounds like someone thinks you have something they want or need. Was any money, jewellery or anything that could be sold taken?'

Ellen shook her head. 'No, thankfully even my ma's wedding ring and other bits of jewellery were not touched.'

Molly frowned. 'Then that tells you it wasn't a burglary; it was someone looking for something specific and it could be related to your father's arrest.'

Victoria nodded. 'Last time we talked, you were going to have a chat with your father and take some notes about what happened at the docks. Did you do that?'

Ellen sighed. 'Yes, I did. I've been trying to gather information but I'm no nearer to proving my father's innocence. Thankfully, whoever broke in didn't get that.'

Molly took another sip of her drink. 'If they went through everything, why didn't they find it?'

Ellen smiled. 'My ma was watching over us.' She paused and glanced at Alice, suddenly remembering her husband was a police officer.

Alice tilted her head. 'Don't worry, Freddie won't get to hear about anything that is said here, unless you want him to.'

Ellen bit down on her lip. 'When the police came for my father, I hid everything in the base of an oil lamp my mother had never used, and thankfully they didn't search there. I've kept everything with me ever since.'

Victoria clasped her hands together. 'Do you have it on you now?'

Ellen nodded.

Alice, Victoria and Molly all looked at each other before nodding.

Victoria pursed her lips. 'We're in here on our own. Mr Leadbetter has left me the keys to lock up, so why don't we go through it all now?'

Ellen's eyes widened. 'Are you sure? I mean, aren't your families expecting you home?'

Alice laughed. 'Mine will just think I'm too busy chatting with these two and lost track of time.'

The girls laughed.

Molly chuckled. 'And that's not strictly a lie.'

Ellen pushed back her chair, wincing as it scratched across the floor. 'If you're sure, although I'm not sure if it will help and I won't be wasting your time.' She took the couple of steps to her coat and bag. Unclipping the handbag, she rummaged around and pulled out a roll of paperwork. 'I don't know why I'm keeping it with me, but something tells me I should.'

Victoria watched Ellen sit back down at the table. 'It's instinct; you should always trust it. We have it for a reason.'

Ellen nodded and unrolled her notes and the photographs she'd held on to when the police had come to the house.

Alice's eyes narrowed as she tried to study everything. 'Why don't you talk us through it all.'

Ellen smoothed out the papers in front of her and spread the photographs around them. 'I don't know where to start.' She took a deep breath. 'The security man at the docks told me the police had found some brown material that had caught on the chains or posts, I can't remember, but they think it could be from a coat or a scarf. My father said when he was attacked the man used a bag, which came undone when he swung it at him, and that also explains why the police found a camera film and a map strewn on the ground nearby. It would have been too dark for the person to see to pick them up before the police got there.

'My father also said he mumbled something about the dark, but he couldn't catch what he said.' She paused. 'John told me to write down anyone I had seen or had a conversation with at the docks that shouldn't have been there.' She frowned. 'At first, I didn't think there was anyone at all but then I remembered I bumped into someone on the docks the night my father's office was first ransacked. It was so foggy and dark I just didn't see him, but he did apologise and say something about not being able to see a hand in front of your face it was so dark. Oh, my goodness, I've just remembered his bag came undone as well when it accidentally hit me. I wonder if that was the same man that attacked my father? Do you think it could be?'

Molly put down her glass and picked up the photograph. She stood up and paced around the table as she examined it. 'It sounds like it could be.' She put the picture down and took another sip of her water before putting the glass down again.

Victoria nudged Molly. 'You've put your glass on the photograph; that's evidence, so be careful.'

Molly grimaced. 'Sorry.' She glanced at the glass before picking it up. 'How strange is that?' She picked up the glass and looked at the picture before putting it back down on it again.

Victoria tutted. 'Don't put it back on there again, you'll ruin it.'

Molly shook her head. 'I don't know what I'm looking at, or even if it's important, but take a look, am I seeing things?'

Ellen jumped up to stare into the glass. 'I don't know but John might, he examines photographs all day.'

Alice and Victoria each took a turn to look in the glass but said nothing.

* * *

Ellen walked into the newspaper office and felt eyes boring into her back. The hair on the back of her neck stood on end. She looked round but everyone was silent. There weren't the usual raised voices or the clatter of typewriter keys. Had everyone heard her father had been arrested? She frowned; this was exactly what she hadn't wanted. Ellen tightened her lips. She was relying on the photographs, but she didn't really hold out much hope. News about her father was always going to come out but she had hoped to prove his innocence before that had happened. She unbuttoned her lightweight jacket and placed it on the hook. Smoothing down the blue floral skirt of her dress, she saw John walking towards her. 'John, do you have a minute?'

John looked through the glass door of Mr Williams' office. 'I have to be quick because I'm wanted, and don't want to keep him waiting.'

Ellen nodded. 'Of course not. When I was going over my notes and information with the girls at Foyles, Molly accidentally put her glass of water on one of the photographs and thought she could see something, which we couldn't see when we lifted the glass off, so we checked all of them and they were all the same. I just wondered if you would have a look at it with whatever you use to check photographs.' She paused. 'John, I know I shouldn't be asking you, but it could mean the difference between my father being locked up or being allowed to come home.'

John glanced over at Mr Williams' office again before taking a deep breath and taking the picture from her. 'Of course.'

'Please tell me if you can find anything. I must admit I don't know what I'll do with the information, but it might at least be able to prove it didn't come from my father's camera.'

John looked pensive. 'I promise I will do my best.' He reached out and took her outside the office to stand on the pavement, where they couldn't be overheard. 'Did you manage to come up with any other information?' He squeezed her hand and whispered, 'Look, I'm sorry and don't mean to rush you but I don't have much time.'

Ellen's eyes widened. 'Erm, the man's bag kept coming undone. I say that because I probably bumped into the same man on the docks the first time my father's office was ransacked.' Her gaze darted left and right. 'The security man said they found some brown woollen material, which might have come from a coat or a scarf.' She paused. 'I think the man also said something about hating the dark and not being able to see anything. I'm sure there's more but my mind is racing.'

'Try and think.'

'Oh, the other thing is the photographs on the roll of film were the size of a postcard whereas my father's are much smaller. I don't know what that means but it could be a different type of camera, couldn't it?'

John's lips tightened. 'Maybe.'

'There's something else you should know, but I don't know if it's connected to all of this. We were broken into, and someone was clearly looking for something.'

John shook his head. 'Did they take anything?'

Ellen shrugged. 'I can't be certain they didn't, but my ma's wedding ring was still there and there was a little money in the house and that wasn't taken either.'

John stared at her. 'So that implies they were looking for something specific.' He forced a smile. 'Please try not to worry.' He turned to walk back into the office. 'I'm sorry, I have to go, but please remember I'm on your side.'

'John, there's a strange mood in there, has the news of my father got out?'

Alan smiled as he sauntered past Ellen and John to get into the building. 'Boy, are you in trouble.' He carried on walking.

Ellen stared after him, wondering what she had done wrong. Her stomach churned.

Alan glanced over his shoulder. 'I'll leave your family photograph on your desk. Let me know what you think.'

Ellen looked back at John. 'Why am I in trouble?'

John closed his eyes for a moment before taking a deep breath. 'You and your father are front page news.'

'What? How can that be...?' Tears began to roll down Ellen's cheeks.

John pulled her close, wrapping his arms around her. 'Don't worry, we're going to sort this mess out.'

Ellen snuggled in, realising how reassuring it was to be in his arms. She looked up, her face blotchy with tears. 'I don't think we can now, and he'll end up getting shot in the Tower for being a spy.' She sniffed. 'This is all such a mess.'

John ran his hand over her cheek, wiping away the damp trail, before kissing her on the forehead. 'No, it's not over yet.'

Mr Williams came outside and eyed John with his arms around Ellen. 'I need to see you both in my office.' He turned and walked back inside.

John hugged her tight before they followed Mr Williams to his office. 'It's going to be all right.'

Mr Williams sighed as they walked in. 'Shut the door.'

John did as he was told.

Mr Williams stood tall. He thrust his hands into his suit trouser pockets. 'Ellen, first I want to say I'm sorry about the action I must take in light of this newspaper article.' He picked up a rival newspaper before throwing it back down on his desk.

She heard John gasp.

Ellen's eyes welled up again as she peered at the headline dominating the front page. *Dock Spy Sensation*. Was this the beginning of the end? Was she about to get the sack, and because of that lose their home? She blinked rapidly as she tried to hold it all together.

Mr Williams walked around his desk and perched on the edge of it. 'I'm afraid in light of this article I have no choice but to let you go.'

John stepped forward, his anger bubbling to the surface. 'But none of it is true.'

Mr Williams folded his arms and looked at Ellen. 'Is your father still under arrest?'

Ellen nodded, taking a deep breath as she tried to calm herself. 'He's not a spy, any more than I am. I've been trying to prove his innocence, but I haven't got very far.'

John reached out and took her hand. 'Something is definitely not right about all of this because someone has broken into Ellen's home clearly looking for something. Her home was ransacked but no money or jewellery was taken so that must tell you something isn't right.'

Mr Williams nodded. 'I'm not saying the story is true, but I can't employ someone that has now been publicly linked to spying. I mean, that must be treason, especially when we're at war.'

Ellen gripped John's hand. 'I understand, Mr Williams. It was good of you to take me on without knowing me.'

John raised his voice. 'I can't accept this. It's not fair on Ellen when she's trying to keep a roof over her family's heads. Talk about kicking someone when they're down—'

'It's all right, John, Mr Williams has to think of his business and how it looks, and it's exactly why I wanted to prove my father's innocence before anyone realised he had been arrested.'

John shook his head. 'It's not right.'

Ellen gazed up at John. 'Don't worry, I'll be all right.' She looked over at Mr Williams. 'Thank you for the opportunity of working here, I've enjoyed it. I'll get my things and leave immediately.' She pulled back her shoulders and lifted her chin before walking out of the office.

Irene smirked at Ellen as she walked to her desk. 'So, you're out then?'

Ellen looked at her and shrugged. 'You obviously look pleased about it. What's the matter, couldn't you cope with having another woman in the office?' She picked up the family photograph Alan had left on her desk without really looking at it and put it in her handbag.

Irene laughed. 'You were never any competition for me, darling.'

Ellen shook her head. 'And yet you are happy to see me get the sack.' She walked away from her desk and picked up her coat and left the office.

John glared at Mr Williams before turning to open the door. 'Wait, Ellen, come with me to my office.'

Ellen turned round. 'No, John, please don't get yourself into trouble. I would hate for you to lose your job as well.'

John took her hand and gave a humourless laugh. 'There's no chance of that happening.' They walked into his empty office. 'Come in and sit down.' He moved past her to shut the door before walking over to his desk. Opening a drawer, he pulled out a small eyeglass. He placed the photograph down on his desk, and without a word he put the glass monocle to his eye. He stared down, moving his gaze slowly across the picture.

Ellen sat quietly, watching John examining the photograph.

John looked up. 'You need to leave this with me. I'm almost certain I've seen this mark before, but I can't be sure without checking first.'

Ellen was silent for a moment before standing up. 'Thank you, thank you for trying, I really appreciate it.' She stood up and walked out of the office. It was hopeless. Every time she thought she was getting somewhere the door was slammed in her face.

* * *

Tears ran down Ellen's face, leaving a salty taste on her lips as she walked along Charing Cross Road. People were staring at her as they approached.

An old lady called out to her as she walked by. 'It'll be all right, lovey, you'll see.'

Ellen shook her head. She wanted to scream that nothing was ever going to be all right ever again. If she didn't get work, they would lose everything.

She heard a paper boy shout out, 'Get yer paper 'ere. Read all about the dockworker locked up as a spy.'

How was she ever going to face people again? And what about Mary and her grandmother? She put her head down and picked up her pace. Perhaps she should have just gone home but she had to get work and her first stop was to ask Mr Leadbetter if he could give her more hours in Foyles.

The large white lettering of the bookshop came into view. Ellen stopped, wiped her hands across her cheeks and took a couple of breaths. Would they sack her too? She sniffed, trying to hold back the tears that threatened to tumble down again. What would she do if that happened? Did it mean no one would employ her again? Everything she had been working for was now lost. She stood outside the bookshop and took another couple of deep breaths. Working in Foyles had been a dream job for her and now she was terrified of walking inside and losing everything. But she sucked in her breath and blew it out again. Standing there wasn't going to change anything; she had to just get on with it.

Ellen stepped inside the shop.

Victoria smiled as she walked her way. 'It's your day off and here you are.' She laughed. 'You're as bad as the rest of us.'

Ellen blinked quickly but it didn't stop the tears from tripping over her eyelashes again.

Victoria stepped forward and wrapped her arms around her. 'What's happened? Come on, let's go to the staff area where we can talk in private.' She led Ellen to the back of the shop.

Molly came running in holding a newspaper. 'Look at this...' She stopped dead. 'Oh, Ellen, you've already seen it.'

Ellen shook her head. 'Only the headline.' She sniffed. 'I know about it because I've been sacked from the newspaper.'

Victoria reached out to take the paper from Molly. She looked at it but didn't say anything for a while. 'This is such nonsense; how do they get away with printing such rubbish?'

Molly lowered her head. 'It says you're—'

'I don't want to know what it says. It doesn't matter,' Ellen said, and Molly sucked in her breath. 'That's why I'm here. To see if I can get more hours to make up my money.'

Mr Leadbetter's voice came from the doorway. 'That won't be possible. I'm afraid I have to take the same line as the newspaper office. We can't be seen to be employing someone who is linked to a spy, or possibly spying herself.'

Victoria rested her hand on Ellen's shoulder. 'Mr Leadbetter, Ellen is innocent.'

Mr Leadbetter frowned. 'You don't know that any more than I do.'

Molly stepped nearer to Victoria. 'But that's just it, we do; Ellen has been trying to gather information to prove her father is innocent. This article is nothing but lies. I'd like to know where this reporter got his facts from because he certainly hasn't checked them.'

Ellen shook her head. 'This morning I had two jobs and in less than a couple of hours I have none.' Tears rolled down her cheeks again. 'I've let my father and my family down. We will be starving and living on the street within a couple of weeks.'

Victoria shook her head. 'It's not going to come to that. There must be something we can do.'

Molly shrugged. 'Ellen, I hope it won't come to this but on a practical level, there's somewhere called Helping Hands. I can't remember the road it's on but it's around the Seven Dials area. Anyway, they will give you a bowl of soup and some bread if nothing else.'

Ellen nodded. 'Thank you.'

Victoria raised her voice and repeated, 'It's not going to come to that.' She paused and gazed at Ellen. 'Look, if things get that bad you can come and live with me at least until something is sorted out. I don't have much room but I'm sure we'll manage.'

Ellen shook her head. 'That's a lovely thing to say but I have my grandma and sister to think about.'

Victoria smiled. 'I'm including them, silly.'

Ellen took a deep breath. 'I can't believe this is happening.'

Mr Leadbetter stepped nearer. 'I'm truly sorry, Ellen, but I have no choice.'

'Don't worry, Mr Leadbetter, I understand it's not good for business.'

Mr Leadbetter nodded before turning around and leaving the girls alone to comfort Ellen.

Molly's eyes narrowed. 'Did you go to the police and tell them about the break-in and about the different sized pictures? They'll know then that they're not linked to your father's camera.'

'Yes, I did that.' Ellen frowned. 'I also gave one of the photographs to John. He made noises about having to check something, but I don't think he meant it. He was just trying to let me down gently.' Ellen shrugged.

Molly's eyes widened. 'It's no good sitting there feeling sorry for yourself. If you do nothing, then nothing will change, and your father could be shot for spying. You must keep fighting. Tell the police whatever you must but you have to keep fighting. You achieve nothing by giving up. Pray that God will show you the way.'

Ellen sighed. 'I don't think it will do any good.'

Molly shook her head. 'Well, if you don't try you will never know, will you?'

Victoria frowned. 'I don't agree with the way Molly has put it, but that's Molly, but I do agree with the sentiment behind it. You can't give up.'

* * *

Ellen sat in the bedroom she had used to think about the evidence she'd collected. She sighed, opened her handbag, and began searching for one of the photographs that she had held back from the police. She was disappointed John hadn't been able to give her more information before she'd left the newspaper office, but maybe deep down he thought she, or her father, was guilty.

Putting the picture on the makeshift desk with all her notes, she held her head in her hands. It was all too late; the police weren't interested in the photograph. Ellen had sobbed until her eyes hurt; the salty taste of her tears stayed on her lips until she had no tears left to shed. She rubbed her eyes and took a deep breath; she hadn't told her family yet that she had lost two jobs, or about the newspaper article. Resting her hands on the desk, Ellen pushed herself up and her chair thudded to the floor. She pulled herself upright, catching sight of her ashen features and red eyes in the mirror. Shaking her head, she lifted her chin before marching out of the bedroom. She clung to the banister as she slowly walked down the stairs.

Mary appeared in the hall carrying a tray of tea things. 'I was just about to call you; I've just made a cuppa.'

Ellen forced a smile. 'Thank you.'

Mary stopped in her tracks and studied her sister. 'Are you all right? You're looking very pale; have you been crying?'

Ellen shook her head. 'Mary, you should know me better than that. Go and put that tray down before you drop it.' She followed her sister into the front room and slumped down on to an armchair.

Phyllis watched Ellen closely. 'What's going on? And don't say nothing, because something clearly is.'

Ellen stayed silent, concentrating on the clatter of the teaspoon stirring the tea in the pot. She watched her sister pour the tea into the china cups.

Mary handed them all a cup and saucer before sitting down with her own. 'I'm afraid there's no biscuits this time.'

Ellen peered down into the dark tea still swirling in her cup. She took a breath, realising her thoughts were also swirling round in her mind and there seemed no end to it. 'I have something to tell you both and I'm afraid it's not good news.'

Phyllis stared at Ellen before placing her knitting on the floor by her chair. 'What is it?'

Ellen kept her head down. 'I've lost both my jobs today.'

Mary almost sprayed her tea out as she tried to control herself.

Phyllis sounded calm when she spoke. 'How did that come about?'

Ellen could feel the tears pricking at her eyes. She blinked rapidly. 'Someone has written an article, it's actually front-page news. It's about Pa being a spy, and I'm mentioned in it.' She paused for breath. 'It seems no one wants to employ someone that's linked to a spy, or even a potential spy.'

Mary put her cup on to the matching saucer. 'That's why you look so dreadful. I'm sure you will get other work.'

Ellen stared at her sister in disbelief. 'You don't understand. No one is going to want to give me a job because it will be bad for business.' She shook her head. 'That means we are going to lose our home.' Her tears began to fall. 'And have no money for food.'

Phyllis let her gaze travel between the girls. 'We will have to go back to cleaning other people's homes and taking in washing and clothing repairs. I know you've never had to do it, but I did when your ma was small, and your ma took on similar work when her father died. It was the only way we could bring money into the home.' She shook her head. 'We will survive this, the truth will out, and your father will come home again, you'll see.'

Ellen gave her grandma a watery smile. 'You sound like some kind of fortune teller. Please forgive me for not having your confidence.'

Phyllis shook her head. 'No, I have my faith.'

The door knocker crashed against the front door. Mary jumped out of her chair; her footsteps clipped along the floor in the hall. Ellen didn't want to see anyone, but she couldn't leave Mary to deal with the fallout from the newspaper article. She strained to hear the muffled voices. 'Mary, who is it?'

The front door shut with a click. Mary entered the front room and gave her sister an anxious look. 'It's the ladies from Foyles. They've come to see you.'

Ellen stood up and with a heavy heart, took a deep breath.

The girls followed Mary into the room.

Phyllis eyed the girls as they filed in.

Victoria stepped forward. 'We've been worried. You didn't come back to the shop to tell us how you got on. Did you go to the police? Did you show them the mark on the photograph? What did they say?'

Ellen lifted her hand. 'Please, one question at a time.'

Alice watched Ellen closely. Her pale features told them all something had happened.

Ellen indicated the chairs around the room. 'Please take a seat.' She suddenly felt unsteady on her feet. 'I need to sit down.'

Mary took Ellen's arm. 'Come on, once you're comfortable I'll go and make another cup of tea.'

Ellen slumped down in the armchair her father normally sat in.

Mary frowned at her grandmother before turning to smile at their guests. 'Please sit down. I'm afraid apart from Ellen losing her jobs, I don't know what's happened to cause you to be concerned but I'm sure Ellen will let you know.' She moved to walk out of the room.

'Mary, stay, you need to hear this as well.' Ellen sucked in her breath. 'I'm sure everyone can wait a few minutes for a cuppa.' She kept her eyes fixed on her hands that were clenched in her lap. 'I went to the police station, but they weren't interested in the mark on the photograph; they implied it could have happened anywhere at any time and it just made me look like I was in on it all. They have already made their minds up, even though I told them they were all letting the real spy run free by making the evidence fit an innocent man.'

The room was silent.

Molly stared at the crestfallen faces in the room. 'Did John come back to you after we spoke?'

Ellen shook her head. 'No, and I couldn't face going to the newspaper office again to check.'

Molly shook her head. 'You trust John, don't you?'

Ellen nodded. 'I don't have many people I trust with this information, but he was one of them.' She fought the urge to scream.

The door knocker came down hard on the front door.

Alice looked at Ellen; she was pale and broken. 'I'll go and get rid of them.' She walked into the hall.

Ellen covered her face with her hands as she strained to hear what was being said at the front door.

The clipping of Alice's heels announced she was coming into the front room.

Ellen looked up and saw Alice's husband follow her in.

Alice's lips tightened. 'I'm sorry, I had no choice. He's here on police business.' She stepped back as her husband stepped forward.

Ellen stood up. Fear ran across her face. She reached out and grabbed Mary's hand. 'What is it?'

Freddie cleared his throat. 'I'm afraid it's not good news, but I asked to come and tell you myself.' He took a breath. 'Your father will be charged and there will be a trial. If he's found guilty of spying, he'll probably face the death penalty.'

Mary dropped to the floor like a stone, taking Ellen with her.

Victoria ran towards the hall. 'I'll get some water.'

Freddie lifted Mary into the armchair, and Victoria ran back with a full glass. She stepped towards Mary and knelt on the floor, offering the glass to her lips.

Mary's eyes opened and closed again quickly.

Ellen wrung her hands in front of her. 'I didn't think this day could get any worse but how wrong I was.'

Phyllis looked at her granddaughters. 'The truth will out, you'll see.'

Ellen shook her head. 'I've let everyone down by not being able to prove Pa is innocent.' She glared at Freddie. 'My father is not a spy. I can't prove it, but I refuse to believe it.'

17

Frank Harris knocked on Mr Williams' office door.

Mr Williams didn't look up. 'Come in.' The sun battled with the grey clouds, its rays of light came through the office window, warming everything they touched. The room gradually grew darker as the sun disappeared behind the cloud.

Frank opened the door and stepped inside, shutting it behind him.

Mr Williams looked up and frowned. 'Hello, Frank, it's unusual to see you in my office.'

Frank smiled. 'You know me, I like to keep my head down and just get on with my work.'

Mr Williams nodded. 'You are a credit to your profession; in fact, I wouldn't be at all surprised if you haven't come in here to tell me you've been offered another job at one of the nationals.'

Frank laughed. 'No, it's nothing like that, but I want to talk to you about something serious. In fact, I should have come forward before.'

Mr Williams' eyes narrowed. 'That sounds ominous. Take a seat.'

Frank's eyes darted from side to side before he sat down on the cushioned chair opposite his boss.

Mr Williams watched him fidget in his seat. 'What is it, Frank? I don't think I've ever seen you look so uncomfortable.'

Frank cleared his throat. 'I don't really know where to start.'

Mr Williams smiled. 'You've worked here for a long time so just spit it out.'

Frank's lips tightened. 'I've been a fool and allowed Irene to use me like she does most of the men here.'

Mr Williams' face gave nothing away. 'Right, I know Irene has half the men twisted around her little finger, but I need you to put some flesh on that statement.'

Frank looked down at his hands. 'Irene has had me rewrite a lot of her articles for a long time and I never really minded.' He glanced up and gave a wry smile. 'All right, I did sometimes.'

Mr Williams laughed. 'I've always known that, Frank; you have a unique writing style.'

Frank frowned. 'And yet you said nothing?'

Mr Williams shook his head. 'If you chose to help Irene then that's your business, I just thought you might be helping her, and to be honest as long as I get a decent article for the paper the rest is none of my business.'

'I understand what you're saying, Mr Williams, but I've created a monster.' Frank stared at his boss. 'There was never anything going on between us. I thought we were friends but above all else I thought she wanted to learn the trade and I admire that in a person.'

Mr Williams arched his eyebrows. 'Go on.'

'I was out on the street, and Irene didn't see me when she stopped nearby to talk to another reporter about the front-page story that got Ellen the sack.' He paused. 'I believed Irene's lies about that poor girl, but I realise now that Irene had her own agenda.'

Mr Williams studied Frank. 'And that is?'

'I assume you know she's after John; he would be a real catch for her.' Frank paused. 'I don't want you to think that anything I'm saying comes from jealousy because it doesn't. I'm old enough to be her father.' He smiled. 'Well, that is if I started young. I used to admire her drive to succeed in a man's world, but she has gradually stopped learning and decided marrying someone of status is more important, which is why she took a dislike to the young girl.'

Mr Williams frowned. 'I don't understand. I thought Ellen kept herself to herself.'

Frank smiled. 'She did but John would come and say hello most days and I think she could see them getting closer and didn't like it. I'm ashamed to say I didn't realise how far she would go to get rid of her and break up their friendship.'

Mr Williams stood up and walked around his desk. 'If it's any consolation, she hasn't succeeded. I think John is quite smitten with Ellen. He was quite angry with me for letting her go.' He chuckled. 'And he let me know it. I had to warn him about overstepping the mark.'

Frank stood up and paced around the office before stopping by the window and staring out at the street. The rain was now pouring down and umbrellas were clashing against each other as people rushed to get out of it. 'That whole article is a lie. Irene got paid for it and she didn't care if she took that family down. She had no evidence, apart from the father being at the police station. In fact, she admitted to embroidering some of it to make a better story; she even implicated John because he had been on a couple of dates with Ellen.'

'Are you sure? I don't remember reading anything about John.'

'Then I guess the reporter, or his editor, decided to leave him out of it but I can tell you I heard the whole conversation.' Frank looked straight at Mr Williams. 'The paper boy who stands outside the shop every day would have heard it too.' He hesitated. 'I feel like I'm partly to blame because I really believed she wanted to learn but actually she just wanted the attention and a great catch of a husband.' He took a breath. 'I know we must have a ruthless streak in us to get the story, but we should also have a moral one as well, and I don't think Irene has that. I've thought about it a lot and want you to know I won't be editing any more of her articles.'

Mr Williams nodded. 'Thank you for coming in here and being so honest with me, that took courage. You are respected in your field because you have integrity and that's a good thing. I will speak to that reporter and Irene, and if what you say is true, she won't be working here any more. I don't hold with that kind of reporting as I'm sure the owner of the *Echo* doesn't either.'

* * *

Ellen stood outside Foyles, staring at the familiar rack of books. Sadness washed over her. She had loved working in the bookshop; it had brought back happy memories of her mother and sister. She thrust up her chin. She wasn't going to hide away; she had done nothing wrong.

'Hello, Ellen.' Victoria frowned as she watched Ellen enter the shop. 'How are you and your family?'

Ellen gave a weak smile. 'I'm sure we'll get through all of this but I'm just not sure how at the moment.' She paused. 'I hope it's all right I'm here, it's just a good place for me and I feel close to my ma here.'

Victoria reached out and squeezed her arm. 'Of course it is, silly, and if I can help in any way please just say.'

Ellen nodded. 'Thank you.' She moved to step around Victoria when Molly came bounding towards them. Ellen wasn't sure she could take Molly's hard-hitting words today.

Molly eyed Ellen. 'Has anything changed?'

Ellen shook her head.

Molly sighed. 'Have you done anything to try to change things?'

Ellen shook her head. Her shoulders hunched over as she stared down at her feet.

'What's the matter with you? You know the real spy is out there and yet you are letting him get away with it and that begs the question: is it because you and your father are part of the whole mess, and you are protecting the person who broke into your house?'

Victoria snapped, 'Enough, Molly. You need to be more careful with your words.'

Molly's lip curled. 'Oh yes, because that has helped. Look at her, she's broken. She's never going to prove her father's innocence because she hasn't got it in her. If I was in that position, I wouldn't leave any stone unturned.'

Ellen's head snapped up. 'If you must know, I'm riddled with guilt. I told him I wanted to be free of his hold and now I am. I feel like I wished it and it's happened.'

Molly stepped forward and put her arm around her. She spoke in soft tones. 'That's not how it works, otherwise there would be a shortage of fathers around the world.' She laughed. 'Do you not think every son and daughter wishes all kinds of things on their strict mothers and fathers? That's normal, but it doesn't mean it will happen.'

Victoria shook her head. 'Molly, take her out the back and please try and be kind to her.'

Molly turned and saw Mr Leadbetter watching them. He

nodded, but he didn't step forward. 'Come on, I'll make you a cup of tea.'

They walked to the back of the shop in silence. Molly pulled out a chair for Ellen to sit on and walked over to the sink to fill the kettle up. She looked over her shoulder at Ellen's pale features. 'Look, I know I come across like I'm the enemy but I'm not, I'm just convinced the answer is here somewhere but that you're not thinking straight.' She turned back and switched on the kettle before returning to sit with Ellen. 'I suppose I'm all about the tough love.'

Ellen didn't look up. 'Do you think it's someone I know? I mean not many people knew my father had been arrested, or what for, and whoever broke in was clearly looking for something specific as nothing appears to have been taken.'

Molly stood up to get a couple of cups and a teapot. She began spooning the tea leaves into the pot. 'I've wondered that myself. Although I expect the neighbours have probably had a field day about it, so everyone probably knows by now but perhaps not why. Why don't you think about the people you know; is there anyone who is either super nice or really awful to you? They could be your suspects.'

Ellen laughed. 'You girls have been super nice to me, so does that mean you are all suspects?'

Molly chuckled. 'Well, I don't think I come under the super nice heading but the other thing to remember is it's a man you are looking for, so unless you or your father know lots of men that should give you a short list to think about.'

Ellen nodded. 'I could probably ignore the men that work at the docks. They wouldn't have to break in to my father's office because they can go in there anytime.'

Molly filled the teapot with boiling water. 'That's it. Now you're thinking. Doesn't that make you feel better? It's about trying to take control of it all.' She walked over with the cups and the teapot and placed them on the table. 'Although, if they are security, they might have their own set of keys.'

'That's true. I don't know why I didn't think of that.' Ellen sighed. 'I suppose I should think about the reasons why they think my father's the spy.'

Molly walked back over to the side to pick up a couple of spoons and a bottle of milk. 'That's good. Go on then, list them. Saying it out loud can help.'

Ellen was quiet for a moment.

Molly sat down and waited for Ellen to speak.

'Well, I suppose it's mainly because he works there and he has a camera and has taken many photos, although not since my ma has died.'

Molly nodded. 'And you said he didn't believe in the war.' She chuckled. 'Mind you, on that basis they would have me arrested as well.'

Ellen was silent again; her mind was in turmoil. 'When the war first began, he apparently went on some anti-war demonstrations in Trafalgar Square, but he's never talked about it.'

Molly raised her eyebrows. 'Do you think he got arrested, or had a run-in with the police and that's why they think he's a spy?'

Ellen shrugged. 'The police say he did.'

Molly's lips tightened as she used the teaspoon to swirl the dark brown liquid in the teapot. The spoon chinked against the inside of the pot. With a clatter, she replaced the lid. 'Right, so talk about the other evidence.'

'I've been over it so many times and I don't seem to get anywhere.'

Molly rested her hand on Ellen's arm and sighed. 'I know but perhaps if we go over it again, something will suddenly fall into place, and everything will become clearer to you. Let's face it, it's all you have; the alternative is to do nothing.'

Ellen shrugged before taking a deep breath. 'There's the brown piece of woollen material, the bag that came open. That happened when I bumped into a man at the docks just after the first break-in, and again when the man swung the bag at my father. Of course, what I don't know is whether it's the same man or not.'

Molly nodded. 'For now, let's assume it is. What else is there?'

'He's got a camera and I'm not sure many people would own such an expensive item. I believe my father's belonged to my grandfather; he would never have spent the money on such a thing.'

Molly smiled at her as she picked up her cup. 'That's quite a specific thing: do you know any other men with cameras?'

'The only other person that jumps to mind is Alan, the photographer at the newspaper, but I'm not sure he has it in him to be a spy.' Ellen took a gulp of her tea, immediately regretting it as it burnt her mouth and throat as she swallowed. 'That was a mistake.' She laughed. 'Thank you for helping me to see through the fog. I think I've just got myself in a state over it and therefore haven't been able to think clearly.'

'Don't dismiss Alan because he might be putting on some sort of act.' Molly stood up and wrapped her arms around her. 'I truly want you to succeed, which is probably why I've been so hard on you. We all need a bit of tough love from time to time but I'm sorry if I was too tough on you.'

Ellen smiled as she enjoyed and returned the hug. 'I must admit there were times when you scared me.'

* * *

Ellen slumped down on the dining chair and spread her rough notes and the photographs on the polished table. She took a deep breath, breathing in the beeswax Mary liked to overuse when she was doing the housework. Molly's words flooded her mind as she thought about the men she knew. There were the security men on the docks; they had access to all areas but why would they run away? And did they own a camera? She didn't know the answer to that. Ellen frowned. Of course, they could be trying to frame her father for spying, but why would they do that? Wouldn't they have preferred to carry on without anyone noticing? Sighing, she decided to set aside the security men for now; there were more questions than answers. She picked up the photographs she hadn't given to the police.

Ellen pushed back her chair. Leaving the room, she walked into the kitchen and opened a cupboard to collect a glass.

Mary was standing at the sink; she looked round when she heard Ellen's footsteps. 'Is everything all right?'

Ellen frowned. 'The honest answer is I don't know, but Molly's right, I need to take the emotion out of my thinking and just look at the facts logically and then I might find the answer I'm looking for.' She turned and walked back into the front room to find her grandmother peering over her notes.

Phyllis dropped down on to a chair near the table. 'Do you think you can solve this, Ellen? You've always been a clever girl, but I know it's hard on you, what with it being your pa and all.'

Ellen smiled at her. 'I don't know, Gran, but I can't just give up. It's Pa's life that's at risk.'

The door squeaked as Mary pushed it open with her elbow.

Ellen turned round to see Mary drying her hands on her apron.

Mary groaned. 'I've only come to offer my support. I'm not sure I'll be much help.'

Ellen reached out and clasped her hands around Mary's. 'You know what they say, two heads are better than one.' She turned back to her notes. 'Molly, at Foyles, suggested I think about the men I know because whoever broke into our home was looking for something specific and not many people would have known Pa wasn't here.' She glanced up to see Mary and Phyllis nodding their agreement. 'Now, I don't think it's any of the reporters at the newspaper office. The obvious person with a camera is Alan but... oh I don't know, maybe it's not someone I know.'

Mary looked at her intently. 'I only remember you mentioning Alan and John from the newspaper office to us, apart from Irene, and surely you can't think it's John. You really like him.'

Ellen's eyes narrowed. 'I don't want it to be him. After all, I've told him everything. The one thing that makes me wonder is that he hasn't come back to me about the photograph I left with him.'

Mary nodded. 'What about that Alan?'

Phyllis watched the two girls as they talked it all over. 'There was something about him when he came round to take our photograph.'

Ellen smiled at her gran. 'Like what?'

Phyllis shrugged. 'I'm not sure but I thought he was a bit shifty. He looked around the room.'

Ellen laughed. 'I think he's shifty too, Gran, but for different reasons.' She paused. 'Mary and I saw him talking to an older man, and there was something strange about the way they were acting.'

Mary nodded. 'Yes, there was definitely something going on there and he wears a brown coat.'

'You're right, Mary. I've never really paid attention at work, but I remember saying something when he came to the house and I was putting it on the coat hooks in the hall.' She looked down at her notes.

Phyllis watched for a moment. 'Come on, girl, you're getting there, so don't start doubting yourself.'

Ellen forced a smile. 'I was just trying to think about the bag he carries his camera in. I have a feeling the clasp came undone when it was passed to him and when he was here taking our photograph. If that's true, that could make him the man who bumped into me on that foggy evening at the docks when Pa's office was ransacked.'

Mary nodded. 'And Pa said when the man swung the bag at him the clasp came undone and that's how the roll of film dropped out of it.'

Ellen turned to look at her sister. 'Pa said he also mumbled something about the dark and not being able to see the hand in front of your face, and I'm almost certain I heard him say the same thing in the office.' She shook her head. 'If it's that easy, why didn't I see it before? I'm not sure it's enough to prove he's a spy though.' She picked up one of the photographs and placed the glass over it. 'I wish I knew what that mark meant. If only John had come back to me about it.'

Mary stroked her sister's back. 'You don't think John is in on it too, do you?'

Ellen sighed. 'I hope not. He's a lovely man and I really like him.'

Phyllis studied her granddaughter. 'If he's a good man, he won't be part of it and there will be a reason why he hasn't got back to you. If he is part of it, you are well shot of him before you gave him too much of your heart.'

Ellen could feel the tears pricking at her eyes. 'I think it's too late for that, Gran.'

Phyllis shook her head. 'Don't think about it; you have no evidence to say he's involved in it so let's assume he's innocent for now.'

Ellen nodded. Moving the glass, she picked up the photograph again. 'I wish I knew what this mark was.' She sat silently, staring at the photograph for a moment. 'Of course. Why didn't I think of it before?' She jumped up; the chair toppled backwards.

Mary just caught it before it hit the floor. 'What is it?'

'If it's Alan, the photograph he took of us might have the same mark on it.' Ellen rushed to the wooden mantlepiece and picked up the photograph. She stared at it but couldn't see anything wrong with it. Carrying it over to the table, Ellen picked up the glass and placed it on top of the picture. She took a breath before staring into it.

Mary gasped. 'Is it the same? Are we right?' There was a thud at the front door. She spun round on her heels. 'Let's leave it. I want to know whether you are on to something.'

The door knocker thudded down again.

Mary sighed. 'I'll go and see who it is.'

Ellen peered over her shoulder as she heard a commotion behind her.

John came rushing towards her. 'Are you all right?'

Ellen shook her head. 'I don't think I'll ever be all right again. The police have charged our father and if he's found guilty, he faces the death penalty.' Her body shook as she tried to control herself. Molly's words rang in her head again. 'When I went to the police, they weren't interested in the marks on the photographs. They said they could have happened at any time.'

John nodded. 'I expect that's true in some cases but not in this one, and I can prove it and so can you.'

Ellen's eyes widened. 'I know it's only been two days but when you didn't get back to me about the photograph, I had a moment when I thought you might be protecting someone.'

'I had to find someone who could give me a proper opinion and I'm afraid that took time.' John pulled her close. 'You're the only one I want to protect. I'm sorry it's taken me this long to let you know. I should have told you what I was doing, and now it's all kicked off at the newspaper, but we'll talk about that later.'

Ellen pulled back and stared up at John. 'You might be shocked to know that I think it is Alan.' She stepped away and picked up the family photograph. 'I think this has the same mark on it as the others and it's about the size of a postcard, which I'm hoping means it's a different camera to the one my father has.'

John took the photograph. He studied it for a moment. 'If my sources are correct, it will be a Kodak Folding Brownie Camera No. 3A. Apparently, they have a wider back because the film it takes is bigger.' He pulled his magnifying glass out of his pocket and examined the picture. 'The mark is the same, and Alan took this, didn't he?'

Ellen nodded.

John put the photograph back on the table. 'I've been told that the mark on the photograph comes from a damaged lens.'

Ellen pondered for a moment. 'If he is the man that bumped into me at the docks, he dropped his bag and the clasp opened so it could have got damaged then. Mind you, according to Alan, it was always coming undone so the camera could have been damaged at any time.'

Mary beamed as she clapped her hands together. 'Ellen, don't forget about him talking to that grey-haired man at Victoria station.'

John's glance travelled between the sisters. He frowned. 'Did you see him hand over any envelopes or papers?'

The girls both shook their heads.

Mary's eyes narrowed. 'No, but there was something that wasn't quite right about the way they spoke to each other.'

There were a couple of raps on the door.

Ellen sighed.

Mary went to answer it. Ellen could hear the girls' voices in the hall.

Molly ran in. 'Mary said you know who it is?'

Ellen laughed. 'Well, I think I do but we still have to satisfy the police so my father can come home.' She lowered her eyelashes. 'I'm still not confident they will believe me.'

Alice looked at Freddie. 'Can't you do something? We can't let an innocent man take the blame for this, let alone get shot.'

Victoria nodded in agreement. 'There must be something we can do.'

John looked at Freddie and the girls. 'I have a plan, but I'll need your help.'

18

John looked at his father expectantly. 'Well, what do you think?'

Mr Williams watched Irene collect her things from her desk. 'I've always known about Irene's faults, or at least I thought I did, but I never realised how far she would go. She left me no choice but to sack her. I suppose that's what you get if you dance with the devil.'

John nodded. 'Yes, and she knew her story wouldn't get printed in our paper. At least not without a lot of fact checking first.' He paused and followed his father's gaze. 'She was happy to sell her sources down the river to save herself though, including Alan's meanderings about being at the Beckfords' family home and the photographs he had seen. From what Irene said he was clearly passing on information to her.'

Mr Williams tightened his lips as he glanced back at John. 'Do you really think it's Alan?'

John nodded. 'I have no doubt.'

Mr Williams eyed his son. 'I need to be sure what you're planning is for the right reasons.' He paused. 'I know you're smitten with Ellen...'

'I'm more than smitten with her, I'd like to ask her to marry me, but now isn't the time.' John smiled. 'I don't want to frighten her off by getting ahead of myself.'

Mr Williams nodded. 'That sounds like a sensible approach, and I can see why you want to be careful with her.'

'The problem is, Pa, we haven't spent any real time together where we haven't been talking about her father, so we still have a lot to learn about each other.' John lifted his chin. 'To answer your question, I am doing it for Ellen, but I also want to do it for us and our country. If the police find evidence that he is a real spy, he could be putting our country at risk, let alone the people he has probably helped kill, especially if he's given information about potential bombing targets.'

'I couldn't agree more, it's just difficult to believe.' Mr Williams shook his head. 'I always had a tendency to think of him as a bit lacking in graces and personality but then it shows, what do I know?' He placed his hands on his hips.

John shook his head. 'Don't forget Irene said Alan told her about seeing the dock photographs when he went there to take their family photograph. I know she might have been trying to save herself, her credibility and her job today, but, let's face it, if he's been feeding her with information, it will be to take the attention away from him.' He took a breath. 'Also, Ellen's sister, Mary, was saying they saw him meet a man at Victoria station. That could be the person he passes his information to.' John paced around the office. 'Look, we need to get him to a specific place at a specific time so the police can search where he lives and do whatever it is they do.' He paused. 'Also, if he's doing a job for us he'll have his camera with him so he can't deny it's his and hopefully his lens will show the damage that causes the marks on the photographs.'

Mr Williams pursed his lips. 'I don't want to put any lives at risk. How do we know he won't be carrying a weapon of some sort?'

John shrugged. 'Obviously we don't but he doesn't strike me as the sort who would do something that stupid. Do you think he would?'

Mr Williams shook his head. 'I've never really thought much of him. To be honest, I can't imagine him being much of a spy.'

'Well maybe he's had us all fooled.'

Mr Williams nodded. 'All right, tell him tomorrow he has to go to the Foyles Bookshop in Charing Cross Road. We want lots of photographs of the outside of the shop as well as inside, explain that we are doing an article on them and the success they've had with their tuppence for returned books policy. If he asks who's covering it tell him Frank; I can trust him, and I'll have a word with him later.' He took a deep breath. 'I hope you are right, and we don't come out of this looking like fools.'

John studied his father for a moment. 'Pa, I saw some terrible things at the front, and I lost a lot of friends. Some would say I was lucky to come back alive but that's not always how it feels in my head so I can't sit back and do nothing.'

Mr Williams stepped forward and wrapped his arms around his son. 'I know. I know it's not been easy for you but I'm very grateful you are here.' He stepped back. 'Let's do it. Let's catch him once and for all.'

John nodded and with a steely look in his eyes he left the office. He looked around the general office and saw Alan hanging up his brown coat. His heart was pounding in his chest as he weaved between the desks towards him. 'Alan, I want you to go to Foyles Bookshop in Charing Cross Road in the morning to take some photographs inside and out. We want more than you usually take. Maybe take one or two of the staff working. We are going to write a feature on them because of their business model. We want quite a few, especially inside the shop because their shelves are stacked high with books. They also have a children's section where one of the staff will read to the little ones. I suggest you get there for when the shop opens because it's very popular and gets very busy.'

Alan nodded. 'I know where that is. I went in there once looking for a book on London and other places in England. If I recall a pretty young thing served me.' He lifted his bag on to his desk. The clasp sprang open.

John tried to hide his anger at Alan's laidback attitude. For a moment he wondered if he and Ellen had got it wrong, but they couldn't have done. All the evidence pointed to him. 'Well, don't be late and I'll let them know you are coming.'

Alan gave a wry smile. 'Who's going to write the piece? It would have been right up Irene's street, but it appears she's gone, which is a shame. I'll miss the glamour she brought to the office.'

John's lips tightened. 'Yes, well, we're not in the glamour business. Frank will be writing the article, not that we've told him yet.'

Alan chuckled. 'That's a bit beneath him, isn't it? I mean, I'm used to taking random photos to brighten up Irene's articles, but Frank doesn't need that.'

John shook his head. 'We don't know how much column space it will take up yet so it's always handy to have several photographs to use as fillers. I want you to spend some time there.'

Alan nodded. 'Of course. You're in charge so your word is my command. I will go first thing in the morning.'

* * *

Ellen gave a lopsided smile as she sat in the Foyles staff room with Alice, Victoria and Molly, each silently staring into their cups of tea. 'I hope we are right about Alan. Not that I want him to be a spy, but I just want anything that will prove it couldn't be Pa.' She sighed. 'This waiting is unbearable.'

Victoria stood up. 'I can't sit here waiting. Come on, we've all got jobs to do. At least out there we'll know what's going on and that's got to be better than not knowing in here.'

Alice and Molly nodded. They both scraped back their chairs and stood up.

Panic ran across Ellen's face. 'Please be careful.'

Molly reached out and squeezed Ellen's shoulder. 'Don't worry, we're on high alert. Even Mr Leadbetter is, although I'm not sure he knows what's really going on, but he trusts us.'

The girls began walking towards the door when Mr Leadbetter appeared in the doorway. 'He's here, or at least a man with a camera has just walked into the shop.'

Ellen pushed back her chair, ignoring the crashing as it hit the floor, and ran towards Mr Leadbetter. Her heart was pounding when she poked her head round the door frame. Her eyes scanned the shop. She stood on tiptoes, trying to see him. Suddenly, he was there, taking photographs of the many bookshelves. She gasped. 'That's him.' She began shaking as she turned back to Alice. 'Where are the police? I thought they were going to be here to arrest him.'

Alice moved Ellen away from the door and walked her back to the table. 'They will be here soon. Freddie said they'll search his property for evidence and once they have that they will come here to arrest him.' She paused for a moment. 'Anyway, he isn't going anywhere yet because Freddie told John to get him to take lots of photographs so the police could match the markings with some certainty.'

Mr Leadbetter nodded. 'Well, I had better go and talk to him and let him know what we would like photographs of, after all he's been here since just before nine this morning.' He peered over at the clocking-in clock as it ticked over to ten o'clock before glancing at the girls. 'Perhaps one or two of you could come out to assist this old man.'

Victoria and Molly stepped forward to follow him into the shop.

Victoria glanced over her shoulder. 'Alice, make sure she's all right.' She carried on following Molly and Mr Leadbetter.

Ellen sat in silence, clasping her hands together in her lap. She looked at the clock for what felt like the hundredth time. 'I'm sorry, Alice, but I've been sat here for over an hour now and I can't just sit here any longer.' She stood up and took a deep breath. A pulse throbbed at the side of her temple. 'I'm going to see what's going on. I can pretend I'm just here as a customer.'

Alice nodded. 'I know it's painful, but we have to stay out of the way.'

Ellen lifted her chin. 'I will.' She walked into the shop and looked around but couldn't see him. She walked slowly between the racks of books, whispering to herself, 'Please God let this all work out. Let my father be found innocent.'

Alan's voice carried towards Ellen. 'This is quite fascinating. I didn't realise how big the shop was. I've only been in here once and that was to get a book on London; that blonde lady from the children's section took me to find what I needed. She was helpful.'

Mr Leadbetter turned down the aisle and saw Ellen, who quickly reached up for a book to look at. He cleared his throat. 'We have very good staff here.'

Alan nodded as they walked past Ellen. 'I can't believe you've never been hit by any of the bombs that have been dropped on London either.'

Mr Leadbetter forced a smile. 'No, we've been very fortunate.' He paused. 'Maybe you could take some photographs of the outside of the shop.'

'I took a few before I came inside this morning. I also included the book racks under the awning.'

Mr Leadbetter nodded. 'That's good. Anyway, I'll leave you to finish off, but I'm in the shop should you need me. I shall look forward to seeing the photographs.' He held up his hand to Alan as he walked away.

Ellen placed the book back on the shelf and moved nearer to them. That was when she saw Freddie in his police uniform and a couple of constables come into the shop. They spread out to look down different aisles.

Alan paused and peered over his shoulder. 'Ellen, fancy seeing you here.'

Ellen tensed but forced herself to smile. 'Oh, hello, Alan, I come in here most days. It's my favourite shop.'

Alan walked towards her. 'Maybe I can get a photograph of you outside Foyles looking like a customer.'

Ellen frowned. 'I am a customer; I just haven't found the book I'm looking for yet.'

Alan noticed the police were walking their way. He didn't take his eyes off them. 'Ellen, I think you need to come with me and have your picture taken.' He reached out and grabbed her. He gave a beaming smile and slung his arm around her shoulders.

Ellen went to step away from him, but he pulled her in closer.

'I haven't seen you since you left the paper. Let's go and grab a cuppa and catch up with what you're doing now.'

Ellen shook her head. 'I'd love to, Alan, but I haven't got time.'

Alan gave her a threatening look. 'I need to get out of this shop and you're going to help me, do you understand?'

The colour drained from Ellen's face. She nodded.

Alan beamed at her. 'Then smile.'

Ellen couldn't see the police any more. 'Why can't you just see yourself out of the shop?'

Alan's lips tightened. 'Because I need insurance.'

'Why?'

Alan pulled Ellen closer before forcing himself on her. His kiss bruised her lips as she struggled to break free. He laughed. 'I've been wanting to do that since I first saw you. It's a shame I never had some time alone with you; we might have had some fun. Maybe it's not too late.'

Ellen snarled. 'In your dreams.'

Alan grabbed her arm and pulled her along the aisle next to him.

Ellen struggled to break free. She caught sight of Albert and Rosie behind them. She remembered Rosie had been helping Albert with all the returns in between being on the shop floor; both were carrying some large books, but where were the police?

Alan followed her gaze and laughed. 'That old-timer isn't going to save you.' He licked his dry lips as he looked up and down the aisle. 'You and I are getting out of here and we're going to have some fun. I obviously got ahead of myself. After all, the police could be here for you, what with your father being arrested.'

Ellen tried to yank her arm free of his grip, all to no avail. She lifted her leg and stomped on his foot.

Alan yelled out, 'Why you little—'

'The old-timer can't save 'er, ay.' Albert swung the books high and hit Alan hard, falling backwards as he did so.

Rosie dropped the books she was carrying and ran forward as Alan fell to the floor too. 'Are you all right, Albert?'

John ran down the aisle and wrapped his arms around Ellen. 'It's all right, I've got you.'

Ellen sobbed in his arms.

The police sped up both ends of the aisle and pulled Alan upright.

Albert laughed as Victoria came into view. 'I knew those 'eavy books would come in 'andy for somefink. I mean, who's going to read 'em.'

Victoria shook her head but couldn't help laughing.

Rosie frowned. 'I was frightened you were going to get hurt.'

'I'm fine, Rosie. Never underestimate the old man.' Albert shook his head and stared at Alan. 'I don't 'old wiv men frightening girls, especially not my family of girls 'ere.'

Ellen gave a watery smile. 'Thank you, Albert. You might have saved my life. I can't thank you enough.'

* * *

Ellen sat in the sitting room, deep in thought.

Phyllis eyed her. 'What's going on in that head of yours?'

Tears pricked at Ellen's eyes. 'I was so scared today. At one point I thought Alan was going to take me against my will or kill me.'

Phyllis leant forward and squeezed her hand. 'And yet you still tried to break free and stamped on his foot.'

Ellen smiled. 'But if it hadn't been for Albert and those heavy books, I hate to think what might have happened.'

Phyllis nodded. 'Don't think about it, because he was there, and so were John and the police.'

'I know, and I'm very grateful.' Ellen ran her hands over her face. 'It's getting late. I had hoped Pa would be home by now. Maybe they still think he's a spy.'

'He'll be home, you'll see.'

Ellen shook her head. 'You've been so confident all the way

through this, and yet I haven't been able to see the woods for the trees half the time.'

Phyllis smiled. 'That's because you were too close. That's where friends come into it; they help you to think and see straight.'

Ellen nodded. 'You were certainly right about that. The girls at Foyles showed tremendous faith in me, especially as they didn't really know me.'

Phyllis nodded. 'It's about trusting your instincts and believing what they're telling you.' She paused and tilted her head. 'You know what you should do after all this is over, write your own article about how this has affected you and your family. You know, put the record straight.'

Ellen laughed. 'I love the faith you have in me, but I could never write something like that.'

Phyllis shook her head. 'You need to have more faith in yourself. I know you've kept a diary for as long as I can remember. I also know you've been writing your memories down of your life before your ma died, so I think you should at least give it a go.'

Ellen was wide-eyed. 'All of that is just for me and Mary; no reporter or anyone else is going to see it. The thought of someone reading something I wrote scares me to death.'

Phyllis gave her a long look. 'You should write it for yourself then, but I do think it would be good to set the record straight; that will enable you all to get on with your lives as innocent people.'

Ellen listened to the knitting needles clicking together. 'I wonder how many pairs of socks and gloves you've knitted since this war began.'

Phyllis chuckled. 'I have no idea, but it's my way of doing my bit to help the men and boys on the front line. It's the least I can do.'

Ellen nodded. 'I should have been doing more. I'm quite ashamed I haven't.'

Phyllis smiled. 'Never mind, I'm sure I've knitted enough for all of us.' She glanced down as she pulled at her ball of grey wool. 'But you could make a difference with your article and it's no good you changing the subject, I'm not that senile yet.'

Ellen howled with laughter. 'Gran, I shouldn't think anyone would think you are senile. You don't always say much but when you do you let us know exactly what you think.'

'Does that mean you are going to write the article?'

Ellen shook her head. 'You're persistent, I'll give you that.'

'Then just say yes but don't lie to me.'

Ellen placed her hands in the prayer position. 'I can't promise but I'll give it a try.'

Phyllis nodded. 'That's good, but you mustn't be the judge of whether it's good or not. I want you to give it to John to read.' She paused for a moment and looked at her granddaughter from under her lashes. 'You do know he's smitten with you; in fact, I wouldn't be at all surprised if he asks you to marry him.'

Ellen blushed. 'What? Don't be daft, Gran; maybe you are going senile after all.'

Phyllis chuckled. 'He won't ask you yet, but I've seen the way he looks at you and he touches you every chance he gets. Remember, he's gone out of his way to help you when he didn't need to.'

Ellen laughed. 'He has gone out of his way to help but that doesn't mean he's in love with me. I think you're wanting to celebrate a bit of romance and you think I'm the nearest you're going to get.'

Phyllis rested her knitting on her lap. 'That is true but I'm right, you'll see.' She lifted her hand and pointed to the cabinet. 'There's a pen and pad in there so you can start writing tonight.'

Ellen stood up and ran her hands down her skirt. 'I will say one thing, you don't give up.'

The sound of crockery rattling announced Mary arriving with a tray of tea things.

Ellen smiled. 'You're always making tea; I've never known you to drink so much of it.'

Mary laughed. 'I need to keep busy when I'm anxious.'

The front door knocker fell hard against the door.

Mary gasped.

Ellen looked at the clock on the mantlepiece just as it began to chime nine o'clock. 'It must be the police; no one else has ever been here at this time of an evening.'

Mary frowned as she clasped her hands in front of her. 'Does that mean they haven't released him? Does that mean it was all for nothing?'

Ellen stood up and smoothed down her skirt. She cleared her throat. 'We need to answer the door to find out.' She walked out into the hallway. Standing in front of the door, she jumped as the knocker hit it again. Ellen glanced at Mary, who was biting her bottom lip. 'Don't do that, you'll make it bleed.' She reached up, twisted the lock and pulled it ajar. She beamed from ear to ear as she flung the door wide open. 'Pa! They let you go. So does that mean they are happy with the evidence?'

Harold stepped inside, closely followed by Freddie.

Harold grinned. 'I believe I'm a free man.'

Mary and Ellen rushed forward and flung their arms around him simultaneously.

Mary sobbed.

Harold lifted his hand and stroked her hair. 'It's all right, it's all over.' He stepped aside and Freddie patted Harold's back.

Ellen did a double take. 'I'm sorry, Freddie, I don't mean to be rude but how come you came back with Pa?'

Freddie smiled. 'I don't want to spoil the family reunion, but I thought after today you might want to know what happened after we took Alan Hutchins into custody.'

Ellen smiled. 'Of course, of course, please come in and sit down.'

Mary led the way into the front room while Ellen shut the front door before following them.

Freddie perched on the edge of the armchair.

Phyllis leant forward. 'Would you like a cuppa, Sergeant?'

Freddie glanced across at her. 'No, thank you, I won't keep you all long.' He peered up at Ellen's anxious face. 'You don't need to look so worried. We searched Mr Hutchins' house and found a lot of photographs of important London buildings and bridges, these have already been examined and have the same marks on them, but more than that we found drawings and maps of London, including the docks, a codebook for sending messages, along with books on London. We also found the brown coat with a tear in it, which matches the material that was found at the docks.'

Ellen breathed a sigh of relief.

'The codebook is a real find and is already being looked at by people higher than me.' Freddie smiled at Mary. 'You might be right about the man he met at Victoria station; we believe he could be his handler. We're hoping to catch him, but it's unlikely once he finds out about Alan's arrest.'

Ellen nodded as a tear rolled down her cheek. 'I can't believe we managed to do it. Thank you for believing in us.'

Freddie chuckled. 'When you get to know Alice and the girls better, you'll realise that not listening to them is not an option; they are caring but they are also very persistent. I've learnt to trust their judgement.'

Ellen nodded. 'Well, I... we can't thank you enough. What will happen to Alan?'

Freddie tightened his lips. 'He's been told if he admits his role and passes on any information he has he won't be shot as a spy, but he will be imprisoned. I don't know what he's going to do but at least he has a choice, so now it's up to him.'

Ellen shook her head. 'I still can't believe it was him all along.'

19

Ellen glanced around Monico's, soaking up the lavish decor. 'I can't believe I'm sitting here again.'

John grinned, reaching out he placed his hand over hers for a second. 'I think we deserve to be celebrating, don't you?'

Ellen beamed. Her slender fingers tucked a stray length of her brown hair behind her ears, which showed a glimpse of a pearl earring that had once belonged to her mother. 'I think you're spoiling me.' She pulled at the cuffs on the sleeves of her military style top, before picking up her cup to take a sip of her tea. The heat that touched her lips made her lower it again on to the saucer. The teaspoon chinked against the cup. 'Thank you for picking me up from home, although I was happy to meet you like last time.'

John nodded. 'I think it was only right your father met me properly, so he knows who you are stepping out with for the afternoon. He was telling me he'll be back working at the docks next week, so that's really good news for all of you.'

Ellen chuckled. 'Yes, I don't think he'll ever moan about his job ever again.' She paused for a moment. 'It's certainly been a strange experience, but my father has come to appreciate his family more and he now recognises that we are old enough to work and decide for ourselves what our own futures will be.'

John opened his napkin and placed it on his lap. 'That's good, because it means out of a bad situation some good has come.'

Ellen glanced down at the slice of Victoria sponge sitting in front of her. 'My grandmother has been nagging me, or perhaps I should say encouraging me, to write about how this whole business with my father has affected us as a family, and I suppose put the record straight.'

John nodded. 'That's a good idea. It would probably make for an interesting read.' He picked up his fork and prodded the end of his slice of cake.

Ellen laughed. 'Well, you could be about to find out. I didn't want to do it; after all, I'm not a writer, but she told me that I couldn't just accept my own opinion and that I had to give it to you to read.'

John laughed. 'High praise indeed, although, why she would think I know if something is any good is open to discussion.'

'Probably because you work at a newspaper; it won't have occurred to her you're not a reporter.'

John looked a little sheepish. 'I don't mind reading it, especially if it makes your gran happy. I can't make any promises though.'

Ellen frowned. 'Promises?'

John gave a wry smile. 'I don't have any sway in what goes into the newspaper.'

Ellen shook her head vigorously. 'Oh no, it's not to be published. My gran thinks I should write more, and I think she's just using what's happened to give me an extra push.'

John nodded. 'That's fine then. When you've written it, let me know and I'll read it.'

Ellen collected her small black handbag from her lap and placed it on the white tablecloth. She opened the silver-coloured clasp. She looked up and studied John for a moment. 'Are you sure? You can say no. I've only done it to keep my grandmother happy.'

John smiled. 'Stop worrying. I didn't realise you had already written it, not that it makes any difference to me.'

Ellen pulled out a few folded pages and passed them over to him. 'I thought it was best to write it while it's so fresh in my mind.'

John opened the pages and glanced down at them. He looked up again. 'You have beautiful handwriting.' He folded the pages again and opened his jacket to put them into his inside pocket. 'Forgive me, but I want to enjoy your company, so I'll read it when I'm on my own.'

Disappointment washed over Ellen. When had his opinion become so important? She couldn't wait. She forced a smile. 'Of course, I understand. I meant what I said about not wanting it to be published anywhere so please don't think I am using your position to do that.'

'I don't think that for one moment. Remember, I know you have more integrity than that.'

Ellen blushed.

'I just want to enjoy being here with you and nothing else.' John raised his eyebrows. 'I'm so glad your father is a free man again, even if it's only for very selfish reasons.'

Ellen tilted her head slightly. 'I don't understand what you mean about selfish reasons.'

John lowered his eyelashes for a moment.

Ellen sat quietly as she watched him studying his cup of tea. 'Have I said something wrong?'

John fiddled with his napkin.

'I've made you feel uncomfortable.' Ellen took a breath. 'I'm so sorry.'

John's eyes snapped open. 'No, no you haven't.' He shook his head. 'I started this conversation but now I don't know what to say.'

Ellen reached out and placed her hand over his. 'After what we have been through together, I would hope you could say anything to me.'

John shook his head. 'I don't want to frighten you off, but I want you to know I love spending time with you, and I hope one day we could be more than friends.'

Ellen raised her eyebrows. 'That's a kind thing to say but you don't really know me at all.'

John laughed. 'I know you better than you realise.'

Ellen smiled as she pulled her hand away. 'Really.' She picked up her cup and sipped the cooled tea.

John nodded. 'Of course.'

Ellen shook her head.

John chuckled. 'All right, let's see. I know you are honest with very high standards. That was very apparent when I asked you out for the first time in Foyles.' He smiled at her shaking her head. 'I've witnessed you being very good with lost children, so you are kind and patient as well. Family is clearly everything to you; the last few months are a testament to that. You're a hard worker—'

'All right, stop, you're embarrassing me.' Colour filled Ellen's cheeks. 'You've obviously given this some thought.' She giggled.

John lowered his head. 'Apart from trying to prove your father's innocence, I've thought of nothing else since I first saw you in Foyles.'

Ellen's colour deepened.

'When I picked up the books for you and stared into your beautiful eyes, that was it.'

Ellen reached over and rested her hand on top of his. 'I don't know what to say.'

John shook his head. 'You don't have to say anything. I hadn't planned to say anything about it but just being here with you... I don't know, it just felt right. I don't want to scare you off though. I'm happy to take it slow. I want you to be as sure as I am.'

Ellen smiled. 'I have feelings for you too, but I haven't stopped to think about what they are because I've been so focused on earning money to support my family and proving my father's innocence.'

John beamed. 'There's no rush. Believe me, I can wait for you to hopefully catch up with me.'

* * *

Ellen patted the back of her swept-up hair, then straightened and smoothed down her pale blue dress. She took a deep breath before entering the newspaper office and knocking on Mr Williams' office door. He beckoned her to come in. 'John said you wanted to see me.'

Mr Williams smiled. 'Indeed, I do.' He walked around his desk and perched on the edge. 'Please take a seat. Would you like a drink of some sort?'

Ellen frowned as she slowly lowered herself onto a wooden chair opposite him. 'No, thank you.'

Mr Williams shook his head. 'There's no need to look so worried. From what I hear, you could be an excellent investigative reporter, so well done.' He paused before taking a breath. 'You know I never wanted to get rid of you, but I have to say you had a few people fighting your corner.'

Confusion ran across her face. 'I'm sorry, I don't understand.'

'Well, let's take it from the beginning.' Mr Williams laughed.

'Frank came in and told me about Irene selling the story and how she had no proof about you or your father.'

Ellen glanced over her shoulder into the main office. 'Why would Frank do that? He never liked me, although I never understood what I had done.'

Mr Williams shook his head. 'I think you have Irene to thank for that. Thankfully Frank is a man of integrity, and he heard the conversation Irene had with the other reporter. To Irene's credit she only tried to deny it for a few minutes, but when Frank challenged her, she admitted she wanted you out and Alan helped by giving her some information about some photographs he had seen at your house.'

'Those pictures turned out to be the ones he had taken.' Ellen shook her head. 'I don't understand why Irene wanted me out. I never did anything to upset her, at least not knowingly.'

Mr Williams chuckled. 'Your innocence is a welcome change in this world we work in. She was worried about John wanting you and not her.'

Ellen gasped. 'I never knew they were stepping out together.'

'They weren't and never have been, except maybe in Irene's mind.'

The office door opened, and John walked in wearing a dark grey three-piece suit. 'Hello, Ellen, I'm glad you decided to come in.'

Ellen smiled. 'You look very handsome in your suit; I take it you won't be typesetting in that.'

John laughed. 'No, I'm learning management now.'

Mr Williams' gaze travelled between the two of them. 'Ellen, I take it John has never told you he's my son and that one day all of this will be his, if he wants it?'

Ellen's mouth dropped open a little. 'No... no, he didn't.'

John stepped forward. 'It wasn't deliberate. Well, actually, I suppose it was. I just didn't want you to be put off by my father owning a newspaper.'

Ellen's lips tightened. 'Or have me chasing you for your money.' She was quiet for a moment. 'Actually, it explains a lot.'

John's gaze flitted up to his father. He frowned as he looked back at Ellen. 'Does it?'

Ellen smiled. 'Yes, Irene warned me off, telling me you fancied yourself as a ladies' man and I'd just be another conquest to you.'

John shook his head. 'That's certainly not true.'

Mr Williams ran his fingers through his salt-and-pepper hair before clearing his throat. 'Perhaps you two could discuss this later, when I'm not around.'

Ellen blushed. 'Of course, sir, I'm sorry.'

Mr Williams nodded. 'I wanted to talk to you about the piece you wrote and gave to John.' He coughed. 'He naturally thought it was wonderful and passed it on to me.' Looking down at his desk, he picked up some papers. 'John, would you mind calling in Frank for me please.'

John nodded. Turning to open the door, he called out Frank's name.

'As you can see, John gave it to me to read, and I have to say it has everything going for it.' Mr Williams put the papers down again. 'I don't know if anyone has ever told you, but you have a real talent for the written word. It needs a little work but nothing that can't easily be done.'

'Thank you, that's very kind of you.'

Mr Williams glanced back down at the papers again. 'Does your father know you have written it?'

Ellen gave a wry smile. 'Yes, he does. He's read it and encouraged me to give it to John to read. Although I'm not sure any of us expected it to be in your hands.'

Frank sauntered into the office with his notepad and pen in

hand. 'Yes, Mr Williams...?' He stopped short when he saw Ellen. 'Hello, Miss Beckford, I'm glad you are here because I owe you an apology for not welcoming you to the newspaper and for being standoffish. I'm sorry and regret my attitude towards you.'

Ellen nodded. 'Thank you, Mr Harris. I must admit I never knew what I had done to upset you so much.'

Frank shook his head. 'It's important you know you didn't do anything. Unfortunately, I allowed someone to influence my opinion instead of forming my own, and that's a lesson for me to learn.'

Ellen watched him fidget from one foot to the other, while his fingers drummed on his pad. 'I assume that was Irene. It's strange because I always thought she and I were going to be friends but obviously when I left, I knew that wasn't the case.'

Mr Williams looked at Ellen. 'Irene no longer works here. She has told a lot of lies and Frank had rewritten more of her work than I'd realised under the guise of helping her, but alas, she took advantage of his good nature.' He picked up a pen and twirled it around his fingers. 'As I said I've read your article, and so has Frank, and we would like you to come back and work as a trainee reporter under Frank's guidance.'

Ellen was silent for a moment. She looked up at John standing next to her chair. He nodded his encouragement.

Mr Williams watched Ellen and could see the conflict on her face. 'You can be honest, Ellen; I can see you don't know what to say but whatever you say won't be repeated outside this office.'

Ellen licked her dry lips. 'I don't, except thank you, Mr Williams, and Mr Harris, for the opportunity.'

John cheered.

Ellen held up her hand to stop any further conversation.

John frowned. 'What is it, Ellen?'

Ellen sucked in her breath. 'I do truly appreciate the opportunity, but I don't think I belong in a newspaper office, and I don't think it would be good for John and I to work together, especially as I now know what that entails.'

John shook his head. 'It wouldn't be like that. Irene's gone.'

Ellen smiled up at John. 'Don't look so sad, John, there will always be other Irenes that want to cause trouble for you. Anyway, if we are meant to be stepping out together then we will.' She looked at Mr Williams. 'My first love is books, so I want to work in Foyles full time, if they'll have me; that's where I'm happiest.'

Frank smiled. 'You have great integrity and I admire you for that. What do you want to do about your article?'

Ellen beamed. 'You can have that and if you have to make changes to it so it can be published, please try not to change the meaning of what I was trying to say. I just wanted to put the record straight for my father and my family.'

Mr Williams nodded. 'We will pay you, of course, and please know you are welcome here anytime, whether it's for work or to visit.'

Ellen smiled. 'Thank you. Please make sure Mr Harris gets the credit for the work he does on it.'

Frank chuckled. 'Thank you, but please call me Frank.'

20

Ellen took a breath; a chill ran through her. She had been out walking for what felt like hours. Glancing at her wristwatch, she was stunned to find she had only left home just over an hour ago and it was just a little before nine in the morning. Their lives had been turned upside down in the last few months; yes, there had been disagreements, but they had coped.

Since she had ventured out, the London streets had gradually got busier and busier with sellers setting up their barrows ready to sell their wares. The strong smell of coffee mingled with the aroma of fresh bread and various soups. The fragrance from the flower seller's stall grew stronger as she got nearer. Shop doors were opening, and awnings were being pulled down in readiness for the day. The city was alive with activity and chatter. She pulled at the collar of her blue jacket; the sun hadn't ventured out through the low clouds yet. She put her hand to her mouth to stifle a yawn. Her disrupted sleep had ensured she was up and out early, trying to work out what she was going to do next. Had it been a brave or a stupid thing to do, turning down the job at the newspaper last week? The work would have been exciting, but her heart would always be with Foyles Bookshop. She smiled. The memory of her mother encouraging her to write about the boats and where everyone was going jumped to the forefront of her mind; maybe one day she'd attempt to write a book like some of the great ones she had read.

Ellen found herself outside Foyles. She sighed, she hadn't worked there for that long and yet it felt strange going in as a customer. It was time to ask Mr Leadbetter if there was any chance of her getting her job back. She took a deep breath and stepped inside the shop.

'It's lovely to see you, Miss Beckford, and so early in the morning, too. How have you been since that awful man tried to use you as a shield so he could get out of the shop?'

Ellen tightened her lips. 'It wasn't until later that I realised I could have been hurt.' She took a breath. 'Although, it was my own fault; after all, I had been told to stay out of the way in the back of the shop. I have to say, I'll always be grateful for Albert and his heavy books.'

Mr Leadbetter grinned. 'Who knew Albert had that much strength? It must be all the toing and froing he does and all the books he carries.'

Ellen laughed. 'Well, I'll always be grateful, wherever the strength came from.'

'I think we all will; it was quite frightening to watch it all going on.' Mr Leadbetter smiled. 'Anyway, I'm glad you've popped in—'

'I haven't just popped in; I've come to see if there was any chance of me getting my job back?'

Mr Leadbetter studied Ellen for a moment. 'I was giving you a couple of weeks to get over everything that has been going on and then I was going to come and see you at home.'

Ellen frowned as she swallowed hard. 'Really, I truly didn't mean to involve Foyles so much, or to put customers at risk.'

Mr Leadbetter held up his hand. 'I was going to ask if you wanted to come back but full time.'

Ellen beamed, and without thinking, she threw her arms around him. 'Oh, thank you, thank you.' She stepped back. 'Sorry, that wasn't appropriate at all, I just got carried away.'

Mr Leadbetter grinned. 'Is that a yes then?'

Alice, Victoria and Molly came rushing from the back of the shop.

Molly stepped forward and wrapped her arms around Ellen. 'I'm so pleased your father is free. I can't stop thinking about it, and now—'

'Ellen, thank goodness you're here.'

Ellen spun round at the sound of her father's voice. Frowning, she listened to his laboured breathing. 'What is it, Pa? Is everything all right?'

John, Mary and Phyllis rushed in behind her father.

Ellen's gaze travelled from one to the other. 'What's going on? Have the police been round again? Oh, my goodness, I thought it was all over with. Will this nightmare never end?'

Her father waved a newspaper in front of Ellen. 'I'm so proud of you, more than you'll ever know.' He reached out to pass the paper to her.

She looked at it but hesitated to take it.

Harold waved it back and forth again. 'Go on, take it. Unroll it before I do.'

Ellen bit down on her lip before she took the end of the paper and looked around at everyone.

Phyllis stepped forward. 'For goodness' sake just open it before we all have heart attacks. I don't think I can take any more.'

Ellen frowned as everyone around her laughed. She sucked in her breath and unrolled the newspaper. Her eyes widened and her mouth dropped open as she read the headline. *The Dock Spy Myth.*

Everyone around her started cheering and clapping, and arms were being thrown around her. The newspaper crumpled beneath them all.

John stood back and grinned at the scene in front of him. 'Isn't it brilliant, Ellen?'

Everyone stepped back and waited for Ellen to reply.

Ellen beamed and peered down at the front page of the newspaper. 'It's my article. I can't believe your father put it on the front page.'

John chuckled. 'And it's more or less as you wrote it.'

Without thinking, Ellen stepped forward and threw her arms around John and held him tight. She stepped back, colour flooding her cheeks. 'I'm sorry, I was—'

'Never be sorry.' John pulled her back into his arms.

Mary cleared her throat as she moved forward; her face lit up as she joined the hug. 'It's really over now.'

Ellen giggled as she turned and took in Mary's delight before peering back at the newspaper. 'I can't believe it.' She looked up at John. 'I must thank your father.' Her smile faded as she looked at her own father. 'I do have some news, Pa, and you might not be very happy, but I'm going to be working at Foyles full time.'

Ellen was surrounded by silence.

Harold wrapped her in his arms. 'Ellen, I am so proud of you, and I know why Foyles means so much to you and I'm happy about that.'

Everyone clapped and cheered. 'Welcome back, Ellen.'

ACKNOWLEDGEMENTS

I have had a lot of encouragement and support since I started writing, so I would like to thank everyone involved, you know who you are. I would also like to thank my wonderful children for their support when my mother passed away in May this year, which has made completing this novel very difficult.

A big thank you, and a lot of love, must go to the people I have never met, the virtual friends on social media and readers who have sent me messages, saying how much they have enjoyed my writing and are looking forward to the next book. I have had huge support from them, both in my writing and personal life, and that means the world to me.

I almost feel it goes without saying that I thank all the writing community and friends for their encouragement in the last year. I'd like to thank the Boldwood team, for their patience, understanding, and for giving me time and space in what has been a difficult year.

I truly hope everyone who reads this novel enjoys the fourth instalment of The Foyles Bookshop Girls.

Thank you.

Elaine xx

ABOUT THE AUTHOR

Elaine Roberts is the bestselling author of historical sagas set in London during the First World War. Previously published by Aria, she is bringing her successful Foyles Girls titles to Boldwood.

Sign up to Elaine Roberts' mailing list for news, competitions and updates on future books.

Visit Elaine's website: www.elaineroberts.co.uk

Follow Elaine on social media here:

 facebook.com/ElaineRobertsAuthor

Sixpence Stories

Introducing Sixpence Stories!

Discover page-turning historical novels from your favourite authors, meet new friends and be transported back in time.

Join our book club Facebook group

https://bit.ly/SixpenceGroup

Sign up to our newsletter

https://bit.ly/SixpenceNews

Boldwood

Boldwood Books is an award-winning fiction publishing company seeking out the best stories from around the world.

Find out more at www.boldwoodbooks.com

Join our reader community for brilliant books, competitions and offers!

Follow us
@BoldwoodBooks
@TheBoldBookClub

Sign up to our weekly
deals newsletter

https://bit.ly/BoldwoodBNewsletter

Printed in Great Britain
by Amazon